The Islanders

S. V. Leonard grew up in the little coastal town of Formby, a suburb of Liverpool. She studied Classics at Oxford University and has been lucky enough to live in Australia, Poland, and Malaysia. She is now based in London. When not writing, she can be found breaking out of escape rooms; doing historical walking tours of London; or drinking wine.

S.V. LEONARD
THE
ISLANDERS

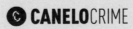

First published in the United Kingdom in 2021 by

Canelo
31 Helen Road
Oxford OX2 0DF
United Kingdom

A CIP catalogue record for this book is available from the British Library.

Print ISBN 978 1 80032 344 5
Ebook ISBN 978 1 80032 343 8

Look for more great books at www.canelo.co

Printed and bound in Great Britain by Clays Ltd, Elcograf S.p.A.

For my Gran, who loved whodunits but loved me more.

Prologue

Spyland.co.uk – News, Scandals and all the latest Gossip from your favourite celebrities

LoveWrecked to be axed from air after the horrific events that took place on their show

Posted on 1st August

It was less than one week ago when all of us at *SpyLand*, along with the entire nation, watched in horror at the gruesome scenes that unfolded live on our television screens. But despite the many eyes of the world, we still don't have answers for what the hell happened. This morning, the producers and management team of the hugely popular summertime show finally released a statement to the public after significant criticism for their silence over the past week.

A spokesperson said: 'I speak for everybody at the channel when I say that we are devastated at the events that took place on the show. We are working closely with the police to understand who committed these horrific crimes and will do everything in our power to ensure they face justice. It is with a heavy heart that we also announce that this season will be our last; we feel that it would be inappropriate for us to continue. We would like to thank the public for their continued support of us and our thoughts go to those affected.'

We at *SpyLand* aren't overly convinced this constitutes a sufficient response to what happened on the show, but we will reserve judgement until the perpetrator of these heinous crimes is caught. As always, stay tuned and *SpyLand* will bring you the latest news as we have it.

Chapter One

I wipe a bead of sweat from my forehead and let out a moan of frustration. This month is on-track with predictions to be the hottest since records began and my tiny apartment is like an oven.

'Where the hell are my keys?' I ask my bedroom, spinning around on my heels as I scan the surroundings. 'Please don't do this to me, I can't deal with this right now.' My head pounds, as if the beat of last night's club music got trapped in my brain and is replaying over and over again. My need for pain relief soon overpowers the search for my keys and I drag myself to the bathroom, my feet throbbing from the indignity of being forced into high heels all night. I wince, remembering how I walked barefoot along my street, my high heels clasped in my hands. I dread to think how much dirt I brought into bed with me. *Well*, I think to myself, *better than a stranger*.

In my bathroom, I deliberately avoid looking in the mirror. I don't need it to confirm what I already know: I am a mess. I open the cabinet beneath the sink and rummage for some painkillers; my new position causes blood to rush to my head and my brain gains its own heartbeat. Bile rises in my throat and I twirl around to hover over the toilet. Just in time. The orange-tinged liquid burns my throat as much on the way up as it did on the way down. Tequila.

I wipe my mouth with the back of my hand and retrieve a silver-foiled packet from the cabinet, depositing two powdery white pills into my hand. Popping the pills in my mouth, I dip my head, so my open mouth is under the running tap. I'm careful to swallow the tablets with small gulps of water as I can already feel my tender stomach threatening to erupt again.

Why did I go out last night?

I sigh and press my forehead against the mirror; the glass is cool against my sweaty brow. I know the answer to my question, but knowing the answer doesn't make me feel better about it right now. Catching sight of my reflection makes me cringe. Clearly, I didn't bother to wash my face when I stumbled through the door last night; remnants of make-up still cling to my skin like a thick layer of grease, and the layer of fuzz that has gathered on my teeth tells me I didn't bother to clean those either. The sound of my phone makes me jump as it screeches an alarm. The screen flashes an instruction: it is time for me leave.

Quickly, I pump hand wash into my palms, flick on the tap and scrub my face. The skin on my face tightens as the cheap hand wash strips it of moisture. I scrape my dark, curly hair into a low bun and give my teeth a quick once-over with the toothbrush. Overall, it's not a huge improvement but at least I no longer look like an extra in *Trainspotting*.

There's still the issue of finding my keys. Where would I, drunk Kimberley, have put my keys when I stumbled in at 3 a.m.? Then it hits me: they will be exactly where

I left them. I dash to the front door and a pile of bills sits on the table next to the front door, waiting patiently to be opened and paid. I wrench the door open in a move that sends the letters flying into the air.

'Ha!' My keys *are* exactly where I left them, in the lock of my front door. I whip them out, grab my handbag, shove my sockless feet into plimsolls, slam the door behind me, and charge down the stairs of my building, my stomach churning uncomfortably.

Outside, the air is almost as hot and sticky as it was inside. The tree-lined park opposite my apartment is alive with activity; the shouts of children shooting water guns at each other are enough to raise the intensity of my headache. I glance at the time on my phone – it's a twenty-minute walk to work and I have exactly that before my shift starts, so all being well, I should make it, no problem. I live to fight another day of employment. I wasn't always like this; I used to be reliable, on time, sober, but you can't help what life throws at you or how you react.

The sun blares down from high in the sky. Its rays scorch me as I march along the pavement, making me feel as if I'm on centre stage lit by a spotlight, as if all eyes are on me. The feeling of being watched makes me glance over my shoulder. The street behind me is empty apart from a man dressed in navy shorts and a polo shirt, and he wears a baseball cap pulled low, so his face is in shadow. This is nothing out of the ordinary – it is very sunny – but it isn't the hat that makes my muscles tense; it's the way he is holding his phone out in front of him, his stubbled chin lifting upwards as he looks at me and then retreats into the shadows as he looks back down at his phone.

'I'm going to get you for this!' A voice shouts from my left and my head whips round, searching for my assailant.

Another man stands at the edge of the park; his shoulders heave up and down, his fists are clenched. I take a step away from him, so I'm pressed up against the side of one of the houses, but before I can run, the man's face breaks into a wide smile and he whips round to chase a little girl, who squeals as he pursues her, an empty bucket swinging in her hand. A father and daughter playing and nothing more. Shaking myself, I continue onwards, commanding myself to get a grip. I'm not being followed, and I have no idea why I thought I was.

The road dips downwards as I hurry past the cathedral, tall and imposing, but its austerity seems somewhat out of place in the summer sunshine. Cars zoom past me as I walk alongside the main road, their speed creating a welcome breeze in the still air. It isn't long before I reach the crossing to get to the docks where the pub and my boss, Gary, await my arrival. I'm close and I should make it in time. The air is cooler as I enter the docks, a combination of a breeze coming off the Mersey and the shade of the covered colonnades. It's quieter, too; without the noise of the cars, all I can hear is the sound of my footsteps against the flagstones.

'Kimberley?' A voice calls to me, its echo reverberating off the brick. I whirl round to find the man wearing the baseball cap standing several metres behind me, my heart leaping at the sight of him. My instincts weren't wrong; he was following me. 'Kimberley King?'

A small bark of fear leaves my mouth involuntarily as the man strides towards me. Part of me wants to run but I'm rooted to the spot.

'Are you Kimberley King?' the man asks again.

'Yes,' I whisper.

'I'm so glad I found you.' The man is close now; he lifts his hand to his head and pulls the cap off his head, so I can see his face. He gives me a dazzling smile. 'And you're going to be glad I did too.'

Chapter Two

Spyland.co.uk – News, Scandals and all the latest Gossip from your favourite celebrities

BREAKING NEWS: LoveWrecked producer confirms its return after hiatus and announces massive twist

Posted on Sunday 13th July

One of the producers of the hugely popular show *LoveWrecked* has announced that it will return to our screens this summer after a five-year (and rather sudden) break from the air. Chill the champagne!

The show was a staple summer watch for the British public. Each year, millions of viewers in the UK would tune in to watch the contestants couple up before battling it out in survival-based challenges against the other couples. Their task was to win points and our hearts in order to be crowned King and Queen of the Island... and win a cash prize, of course! Before its break, *LoveWrecked* had a peak viewership of over 5 million and a revenue of over £80m.

'Many people were devastated when we decided to pause the show,' said Greg Barker, one of *LoveWrecked*'s producers. 'But many reality TV shows won't be remembered fondly because they didn't know when to quit. So, we took a hiatus to make sure that when we came back we were the best version we could be. It's been five years, so we think the time is ripe.'

But what will make this the biggest season yet?

For starters, the winners' prize will be a whopping £200,000 split 50/50, which is double past prizes.

And the twist?

For this season of *LoveWrecked*, there will be no application process. Yeah, you read it right, no application process. Our sources have told us that applicants will be chosen completely at random from none other than social media, which basically means they could have chosen anyone in the entire country. We could have politicians or plumbers or hardcore criminals in the villa. Talk about excitement!

Greg Barker said, 'Our scouts have spent months scouring social media for the twenty people that we think would make great television. We do, of course, have some back-up options if our chosen ones don't accept.'

Greg told *SpyLand* that the so-called chosen ones will be contacted by scouts today.

Cue us scrambling for our phones!

Comments section

@trashqueen2000: OMFG new LoveWrecked contestants will be chosen completely at random. What does this even mean?!

@Jackboxxx: @trashqueen2000 Hope it means a welcome change from the usual crackpots that go on this show

@islandlife: @Jackboxxx @trashqueen2000 Members of the British public chosen at random? There's gotta be AT LEAST one crackpot.

Chapter Three

I stand open-mouthed as the man in the baseball cap tells me who he is and how I've been *chosen*. I can't quite believe what I'm hearing, though maybe I shouldn't believe what I'm hearing. The phone in my pocket vibrates against my leg and jerks me back to reality, back to the docks and, when I see the time on the screen, back to the fact that I have a job to get to.

'Shit,' I curse. 'Look, Sam, did you say your name was Sam?' He nods. 'This is my boss calling me because I'm late for work so I have to go, but to be quite honest, I don't think I'm the person you're looking for.' Sam nods and produces a business card from his pocket. Sam Day, Talent Scout, Minerva Productions. I almost burst out laughing when I read what it says; surely this is a joke.

'Like I said, Kimberley, you along with nineteen others in the UK have been chosen. Take some time to think about it but this is going to be our most exciting year yet and we'd love for you to be a part of it. Plus, a £100,000 cash prize shouldn't be turned down without proper consideration.' I follow his gaze down to my plimsolls, scuffed and muddy, and there's an unspoken acknowledgement that we both know I could use the money.

'I've gotta go,' I say, shoving his business card into my handbag. Turning away from him, I swipe my finger across my phone to accept my boss's call. 'Two minutes away, Gary, promise.'

Glancing back, I see Sam raise a hand and wave as I retreat, his Hollywood smile firmly fixed in place.

I can't believe I let myself get distracted by what is very probably a scam, and Gary isn't going to be happy – ten minutes late would have been fine if this was the first time but it isn't, so it won't be. Pushing away the thoughts of Sam Day and the invitation to appear on *LoveWrecked*, I focus on getting to work. The pub is in sight now. It's built from the same red brick that built the docks with a tall round funnel that reaches high into the blue sky. I break into a sprint, or as much of a sprint is possible given that my feet keep slipping over the cobbles outside. The heat of the sun, the effort of my running and the stress associated with Sam's interruption all conspire to make sweat trickle down my back and my shirt stick to it. The doors of the Pumphouse pub nearly fly off their hinges as I push my way through them.

To my relief the pub is empty: the sturdy oak tables surrounded by leather-seated chairs that are dotted around the pub floor are free from people. Clearly everyone would rather be out enjoying the sunshine than sitting inside a dimly lit pub, and, far as I can see, Gary isn't even around, so I grab my apron, tie it around my waist and slip behind the bar. Hopefully, if Gary finds me here, ready to work, he'll look more kindly on my lateness. I place my elbows on the wooden bar and cradle my warm cheeks in my hands, as my heart rate and breathing return to normal. What a morning this has been.

'Well, hello, Kim. Nice of you to grace us with your presence.' Gary's voice hisses in my ear, making me jump. He must have slunk up behind me. I stand briskly to attention, accidentally knocking on one of the beer taps.

'Morning, Gary,' I reply, as I turn the tap off and give him my most winning smile. 'Sorry I'm a bit late.'

'Go on then,' he says, noticeably not returning my smile, 'what's your excuse today?'

Silence hangs between us for a second as I think what to say.

Well, Gary, despite being incredibly hungover I managed to drag my arse to work and was going to be on time until I was approached by a talent scout who offered me the chance to star in the returning series of LoveWrecked. I bite my lip; the truth won't cut it.

'I—'

'No, actually,' he says, holding out a hand to silence me. 'I don't want to hear it. Look, Kim, don't get me wrong, I like you but I'm running a business here and I can't keep making excuses for you. I think you're great and I know you've been through a lot over the past few years, I do, but you've got to get a grip of your life. You can't keep treating yourself like shit and I can't continue to employ someone who has given up.' I know where this is headed; I open my mouth to speak, desperately wracking my brains for an excuse, a reason Gary should keep me on but, before I can say anything, Gary cuts me off. 'I'm sorry, Kim, but I've got to let you go.'

My mouth falls open and I stare at him, momentarily unable to speak. Gary has been threatening to fire me for ages but I've always managed to keep this job, even if it is by the skin of my teeth. The pile of unpaid bills next to my front door is screaming at me to fight for this, to protest, to beg for forgiveness, to tell him how much I need this job.

'Gary, please, I need this—'

'What you need is to sort yourself out.'

Maybe I could say more to convince him but I don't; we've been here many times before and I doubt it will make a difference and I would do nothing more than embarrass myself. Instead, I nod my head, resigned to the fact that he must do this, unknot my apron and hand it back to him.

'You'll be OK, Kim, use this as an opportunity,' he says, taking a twenty-pound note out of the till and offering it to me.

'Yeah,' I say, my voice as cheery as I can make it. 'You're right, opportunity.' It feels a bit awkward taking the money but it's not as if I don't need it. So, numbly, I accept and place it into my handbag alongside the business card from the talent scout.

When I arrive home from work, I slot my key into the front door of my apartment and head straight down the hall to my bedroom, but not before I've had the chance to scoop up the latest notes that have been posted through my door. The longer the bills go unpaid, the redder the ink that is used on the letters and it seems no red ink was spared on my letters. There's also a handwritten note from Mrs Price, my landlord, reminding me for 'the third and final time' that my rent is overdue.

My bedroom is a safe place; there's not enough room to swing a cat in here but it feels like home. I flop down on my unmade bed with a sigh. I feel numb. What the hell am I going to do now? My phone pings, the screen lighting up at the arrival of a text. Lifting it to my face, I read:

Hi Kim, long time no speak but I couldn't NOT text. Can you believe it? LoveWrecked is coming back. This is SO GOOD. I can't wait to see the randomers that get chosen, it's going to be so exciting. Hope we can do our wine and watch sessions again, it's been too long and I miss you a lot. Love, Zoe.

My stomach squeezes in a way that for the first time today isn't linked to my hangover or being fired. It makes complete sense that Zoe, my former colleague and friend, chose to text me about it, although I take it from her message she doesn't know that I'm one of the randomers who have been chosen. She is right about one thing: it has been too long. It's been almost five years since the two of us curled up on the sofa with a glass of wine and the good humour needed to watch the cringe-worthy contestants of *LoveWrecked* compete for the cash prize.

We even joked how good it would be to spend the summer in a luxury villa in the sun. A summer free from work and responsibilities of the world, one filled with wine, fun, drama and survival challenges. Who could say no to that? If I remember correctly we even promised each other that we'd apply for that year's show. Although, I said to her at the time that even if we did apply we would never, ever get chosen; the producers wouldn't want us. I remember how Zoe looked at me, aghast.

'Why?' she asked, jumping to her feet. 'Am I not sexy enough?' She then proceeded to strut around my living room.

'Even if you were,' I said, 'nothing kills a vibe more than announcing you're a police officer.'

'They might think it's sexy. I could even turn up to my audition in my uniform, or the Halloween costume version of my uniform.'

I remember spitting my wine out at that. 'Do you want to get fired?' Police*women* costumes, along with naughty nurse and saucy schoolteacher costumes, sickened us both.

'Kim. It's all about priorities. Think of the money.' At that Zoe sashayed around the room pretending to arrest imaginary bad guys with so much sass and bum-wiggling that I erupted in laughter and said I would support her application wholeheartedly.

I pull myself back to the present. That was then; my life is very different now.

It's amazing how much life can change in such a short period of time and how much a person can lose. I'm a world away from the fame and fortune to be found on *LoveWrecked*. The type of person who is fired from work for constant lateness, who is behind on their rent and hasn't paid bills in months is surely not the type of contestant *LoveWrecked* typically goes for. And yet, this year people have been chosen at random and I was chosen. Me, the girl with dirty knickers strewn across her bedroom floor and half-drunk cups of coffee covering every surface; the girl whose home is a microcosm of her mess of a life. I can't deny that it would be nice to get away from it all and spend the summer in a gorgeous villa somewhere in the Mediterranean; it would be nice to meet some new people and maybe start afresh. I could leave my shitty, sad excuse for a life behind and, if I won, maybe I could start all over again, in a new place or even a new country, away from this city that is a constant reminder of my failings.

I reach my hand into my bag and pull out the business card. *Sam Day, Talent Scout, Minerva Productions* is typed across it, underneath which is a phone number and email address. It would be so simple: I've been chosen, they want me. The hand holding the business card shakes as my mind whirrs with worrying questions.

Do I want to do this, to go on television and allow myself to be scrutinised and judged by millions of people? Do I want people to know who I am? What I've done?

And then there's the unavoidable question: after everything that's happened today, do I have much of a choice? If I won £100,000 I could send some money to my mum, who I basically abandoned after the incident. A lump sum could make up for the loss of contact, and then I could disappear. It's a lot of money, far more than I could have ever made at the pub, even before I lost my job. My finger hovers over my phone screen and I punch in the eleven digits of Sam's mobile number. Before I allow my brain and better judgement to stop me, I press the green call button.

Sam answers after two rings. 'Sam Day.'

'Hi, Sam, it's Kimberley King.'

'Kim, so great to hear from—'

'I accept,' I say, cutting him off. 'I want to be on *LoveWrecked*.' And with that, I've done it and all I can do now is hope that I've made the right choice.

Chapter Four

Spyland.co.uk – News, Scandals and all the latest Gossip from your favourite celebrities

BREAKING NEWS: LoveWrecked line-up leaked: who's in the cast?

Posted on Friday 25th July

The identities of some of the *LoveWrecked* cast have been leaked ahead of the show returning to our screens tomorrow evening.

While the full and official line-up is yet to be released, an inside source (who *SpyLand* will be forever indebted to) has let slip the names of five Islanders that will enter the villa this summer. *SpyLand* are sharing their details, images and our thoughts.

The first on the list of names is Carly Chu. Carly is a twenty-eight-year old actress and model from Kent. This tall, slender, dark-haired beauty will definitely get hearts racing in the villa. Plus, rumour has it, she's a bit of bitch. Doesn't she sound fun?

Then there's Jack Peaks, a twenty-five-year old estate agent from Essex. We're hoping that this fake-tanned, white-toothed, hair-gelled chappie is as naughty as he looks.

Third on the list is Kimberley King, a thirty-two-year old barmaid from Liverpool. We hear she's a pretty wild party girl, so she should definitely keep things lively in the villa.

Mo Khan is a thirty-two-year old restaurateur from Birmingham. His gently stubbled chin makes him seem older and wiser than the others – let's hope not.

Valentina Novak is a twenty-six-year old DJ from Russia. She looks like a pint-sized pixie who packs a punch.

That's all we have for now, folks, but you can rely on *SpyLand* to keep you informed as everything progresses in the villa. And in true *LoveWrecked* style, I'm sure they'll all be harbouring some secrets. Tell us what you think in the comments section below.

Comments section

@M155ch1ef: Phwoar. Look at Jack. He is hot. Contestants are chosen at random? As if. LoveWrecked, share your algorithm with me… or failing that Jack's email? ;)

@Prinny_Jasmine: @M155ch1ef Getting an email isn't quite as exciting as finding a Golden Ticket in a chocolate bar though is it?

@trashqueen2000: @M155ch1ef Well if they weren't chosen at random, then how? #LoveWrecked

@M155ch1ef: @Prinny_Jasmine @trashqueen2000 Don't know how they were chosen, but I hope one of them is eliminated by turning into a giant blueberry. HAHA. #LoveWrecked #WillyWonka

Chapter Five

Fellow travellers throng around me and I doubt that any of them are the other Islanders as the crowd seems to consist almost exclusively of teenagers, all dressed in T-shirts with their nicknames emblazoned on the back. They shout enthusiastically to one another, buoyed by what is probably their first holiday without their parents, and the wheels of their suitcases click as they roll over the black and white tiled floor of the recently revamped Heraklion Airport. In unison, we head towards arrivals. I loop my fingers around the straps of my backpack and adjust it so it's sitting on a different part of my shoulders, hoping to relieve the pain that lugging it around is causing. Bag adjusted, I stride towards a short, slightly rotund man holding up a small placard emblazoned with my name.

'King?' says the man as I approach. He is dressed in a grey T-shirt that strains across his large belly and he wears dirty beige shorts that reveal very hairy legs. The man narrows his eyes at me, in a look that seems to tell me I don't quite meet his expectations, whatever those expectations were.

'Yeah, I'm Kim King. That's me,' I reply. And to avoid any confusion, I point at myself and then at the placard. The man nods, unsmiling.

'You late. Others at the boat already.' He glares at me and huffs as if the time it took for my plane to land and the airline to unload my luggage was entirely within my control. I want to tell him as much but before I can speak he turns away from me and heads towards the airport doors.

'Great to meet you too,' I mutter under my breath. I don't know what I was expecting but certainly not a welcome like this. It's already been a long morning so the prospect of further travel with a grumpy local isn't exactly in keeping with the paradise that was promised.

Well, I guess things can only get better and I follow him as he weaves around the other arrivals towards the airport's exit.

It feels unreal that I'm here, but already the feeling of not being in my flat or the pub is lifting my spirits. That and the fact that, for now, I'm off the hook for my rent – my landlady is such a fan of the show that she's generously let it go (although there is the strong possibility she will be able to make that and more by giving interviews to gossip mags about what I'm really like). My mind keeps returning, though, to the pile of other bills, Mum, and the small matter of what I am going to do after this is over. I'm unlike past contestants, winners or losers. I don't want big sponsorship deals or interviews in magazines; I just want the money, cash in hand. It is essential that I never lose sight of the fact that this is a competition and I need to win it, no matter what.

The airport doors whoosh open as I approach them and my skin is enveloped by the warmth of the late morning air. England, no matter how warm, could never match this. The air presses around me with all the intensity of the Mediterranean in summer, an intensity heightened by the craziness that is arrivals at Heraklion Airport; it's like rush hour on steroids. A sea of motorbikes and taxis crowding around the exit, riders honking their horns and shouting to the arrivals touting for business. I cough, waving a hand in front of my face as the fumes cloud from the many running engines.

I hover on my tiptoes, searching for my chaperone among it all and catch sight of him waving his placard in front of a battered, red minivan. I elbow my way through the mass of bodies, ignoring the many shouted offers of a taxi. I heave my backpack into the back of the minivan and clamber in after it. The engine sounds and I barely have time to slide the door closed before he jerks the car forward and whisks me away.

'How far is it to the boat?' I ask as we whizz along the narrow Cretan streets, my driver expertly dodging around the various street food stalls, numerous poorly parked cars, and even two old women shouting at each other in the middle of the road.

'Very close. Five minutes only.' The driver points a chubby finger in the distance. I grasp the back of the driver's chair and lean forward, squinting in an effort to make out whatever the man is pointing at.

'Wow,' I whisper as the azure-blue sea comes into focus, my view obstructed only by all sorts of boats, from monster yachts to miniscule rowing boats. I've not seen anything quite like this in a while.

The van slows as it edges closer to the port and approaches a group of people crowded around backpacks just like the one I was sent before departure. If these people have the *LoveWrecked* regulation backpack, then these people are my fellow Islanders, the people standing in between me and £100,000.

The minivan is within several metres of them now and they all turn to watch me arrive. Four of them: two men and two women. Sweat pricks in my armpits as I feel their eyes on me; there's something about the way they watch me, like I'm prey. I swallow, my mouth dry, and avert my gaze, choosing instead to fiddle with the straps of my backpack rather than enter into a staring contest. One of the men catches my attention as he waves and strides towards the advancing minivan. He wears a spray-on tight blue tank top which clings to every muscle on his six pack; his chest is pushed forward and his broad shoulders thrown back and there's a huge, white-toothed smile on his face. The man's eyes are bright with excitement and his smile is warm enough to melt away my initial nervousness. I can't help but smile back; it's nice to have a proper welcome. The moment the driver cuts the engine, the tank-topped man wrenches the door open.

'Hey,' he says, thrusting his hand forward to grab my bag. 'I'm Jack Peaks. Why don't you let me get that for you, darling?'

'That's very kind,' I say, slightly taken aback at his forwardness, 'but don't feel like you have to, I definitely overpacked.'

'Don't you worry. The boys can handle it,' he replies, flexing his muscles so his biceps bulge.

'Well, I wouldn't want to say no to the boys,' I say with a laugh, sliding my backpack towards him. The tilt of Jack's head makes me think he didn't think he was making a joke. 'I'm Kim,' I add, eager to move the conversation along. 'Kim King.'

'Nice to meet you,' says Jack, grunting as he tugs my bag onto his back. His grunt confirms my suspicion that I overpacked. It has been such a long time since I travelled anywhere and I seem to have lost the knack of how to pack appropriately. 'Come on then, Kim King,' he says with another wide grin and a wink. 'Come and meet the others.'

'Sir, yes, sir.' I give him a mock military salute but again, his expression tells me my playfulness is lost on him. Jack Peaks seems nice enough but maybe not the smartest tool in the box.

I slam the door behind me and turn to give the driver a wave of thanks, but the driver's seat is empty. I glance around for him and see that he's clambering onto a boat bobbing about on the waves at the end of a rickety wooden jetty. The boat, like the jetty, looks past its best. At one time, the boat was probably white but age, life on the water, and a distinct lack of care have dirtied the colour. The paintwork flakes in numerous places and the windows are clouded. I'm not convinced this little, aged boat is up to the job of carrying six of us plus backpacks across the water.

'Everyone,' says Jack, addressing the group at large, 'this is…' He trails off. I stare at him; please tell me he's not forgotten my name already?

'Kim,' I say, raising my hand in what can only be described as an awkward wave. I wasn't sure what else to do; it would seem a bit weird and formal to shake everyone's hand in turn, surely?

'Mo,' says the other man, reaching out a large hard. Maybe offering a handshake would have been the better option? Appearance-wise the two men couldn't be more different: Jack is muscular and all on display with his tight T-shirt, his hair is dyed blonde and teeth clinically whitened, whereas Mo's appearance is softer and less polished. He wears a salmon-pink linen shirt that hangs loosely, his hair is long, and it curls slightly on the top of his head; he's somewhat older than the others. For all Jack Peaks is a ball of nervous excited energy, Mo Khan seems calmer, more reserved.

'Valentina,' says one of the women. She doesn't offer her hand to shake but returns my awkward wave. Valentina has platinum-blonde hair cut in a pixie crop and a petite frame. A piercing protrudes from her bottom lip and she wears frayed denim jeans with military-style boots. She is like a punk version of Tinkerbell.

I turn to the final person in our small group. A woman. She is by far the most striking. She's about a head taller than me and her floral dress hangs loosely on her skinny frame. The dress is simple but distinctly expensive. Her hair is jet-black and scraped back into a low bun. Huge, round Dior sunglasses sit delicately on her head. Nobody looks that perfect after hours of travelling; it's like she's been airbrushed. What on earth is she doing here? She doesn't look anything like a woman who needs to win £100,000.

'Carly,' she says, staring at me through thick lashes. 'Carly Chu.' She doesn't offer her hand and she doesn't give a wave. Instead, she raises an eyebrow as if what she really wants to say to me is, *Seriously, you're my competition?* My stomach clenches and I give her a brief smile before quickly turning my attention back to the others.

'Well, it's, er, nice to meet you all,' I say, wracking my brains for what to say next. I open my mouth to ask how their journeys were but am mercifully saved by the boat driver.

'Boat ready to leave. Hurry, hurry,' he calls to us from the boat. He's waving his arm in the air in a desperate attempt to get our attention. 'Storm coming soon, boat no safe.'

'Right. Well, we'd better go,' says Jack with a laugh that doesn't quite match his eyes.

I'm with Jack on this one; the thought of getting into an unsafe boat doesn't fill me with excitement either. The feeling isn't helped by the fact the boat doesn't look like it could make any journey, let alone a crossing in a full-blown storm.

As a collective we grab the nearest bag to us and dash along the jetty. Jack steps onto the boat, followed by Mo. I go next, accepting Jack's hand as I do so. The boat's already rocking quite considerably against the force of the waves so better to accept his offer of help than allow face-planting to be one of the group's first memories of me.

Carly and Valentina pause for a moment. Their eyes shift from the swaying boat to the waves crashing against it.

'Come on,' I say gently. 'I'm sure the driver knows what he's doing.'

Valentina stretches her fingertips out and throws herself into Mo's arms in a way that I don't think was strictly linked to her uncertainty of stepping onto the boat. The moment Valentina's feet land on the deck the boat's engine revs and Carly's eyes widen.

'Come on, Carly. You don't want to be left behind, do you?' chimes up Jack, stepping forward and not-so-subtly elbowing Mo out the way. Mo narrows his eyes, clearly disliking the younger man's bravado.

'Urgh.' Carly chucks her backpack at me and wraps her delicate fingers around Jack's arm as she boards.

'Hurrah,' shouts Jack, punching the air. 'If we go down, we go down together.'

There's a pause for a second then Mo and Valentina both burst out laughing; even Carly manages a smile. I'm not sure if it's the delirium brought on by my tiredness or the fear that we might all soon be food for the fishes, but the laughter is infectious. I wipe away a tear and, as a group, we head into the boat's belly for the final stretch to the *LoveWrecked* island.

–

The shared comradery found through the terrifying request that we board a wave-battered boat is short-lived as the boat careens on the waves, up and down, left and right. Soon, my head is spinning, my palms pool with sweat and the humidity traps me in its prison. I close my eyes but this only exacerbates the feeling that I'm on a fairground carousel whirling out of control. The spinning threatens to consume me.

I open my eyes again; closed isn't helping the seasickness. Sweat glistens on Carly's forehead, her eyes have glazed over and the skin that was flawless barely minutes ago has taken on a green hue.

'I need some fresh air,' I say, jerking to my feet. I can't sit here and watch the others slowly transform into the colour of aliens. I stagger towards the small set of stairs and clamber outside onto the narrow rim that encircles the boat.

Air, cold and wet, slaps my cheeks and I exhale loudly. Freedom.

Pools of water collect on the decking and slosh from side to side as the boat pitches; the violence of the movement threatens to tip me over. I plonk myself down with a squelch, but I don't care – a wet bottom is nothing in comparison to the horror that faced me inside.

'Fuck, this is better.' Jack's head pops up and he takes a seat next to me. He's followed by the others. I guess none of them could stand it any longer either. The five of us sit in a line, our legs dangling over the edge.

'Where the hell is the island?' shouts Mo over the deafening crash of the waves. 'We need to get there before the storm gets us,' he continues, voicing what we're all surely thinking. I grip the salt-crusted steel bar behind me, the only barrier between us and the malevolent sea. Carly squeezes her eyes shut and a tear rolls down her cheek.

The land behind us is almost invisible now, faded into insignificance. The water surrounding us has changed; the crystal-clear, light blue water that lapped the shore and invited one in has turned evil. It's dark and cruel-looking, nature's equivalent of Dr Jekyll and Mr Hyde.

'Look,' I shout, daringly releasing an arm to point at a black speck in the distance. 'That must be it.' At least, I hope it is as it's the only piece of land on the horizon.

None of the documentation I was sent in advance of coming on the show gave me any indication of where the filming would take place and I only knew I was headed to Greece when I arrived at the airport. Although to be honest, knowing I'm in Greece isn't much help to me right now, given the remoteness of the island.

The dark speck looms larger as the boat chugs forward. On a good day, I imagine that the island would be beautiful. Gentle waves lapping against a thick strip of yellow sand; the clustering trees stretching their bottle-green leaves upwards to pierce the fluffy, white clouds. But the clouds aren't white nor are they fluffy now. They're a deep grey and they move slowly across the sky, swollen with the rain that I'm sure will come. Their darkness layers a filter over the landscape. If the island could speak, I swear it would tell us to turn the boat around and leave. But it can't speak, and we don't turn around.

When we're within ten metres of it, the sound of the engine dies and the boat's progress forward slows.

'Off,' shouts a voice and our captain pops his head up to the top deck to instruct us. I smirk; despite how harrowing this has all been, there is something quite satisfying about how little of a shit this man gives to pleasantries.

'We'll get wet,' says Carly, her eyes widening. 'Drive closer.'

'Cannot.' The captain's reply is short and sweet. I don't stick around to hear the rest of Carly's protestations. I get up and make my way towards the back of the boat. Water or no water, I want off this boat.

I totter on the boat's rim and jump, soaking my trousers as I plunge into the water. It isn't deep, only comes up to my knees. I hold my arms out for Jack to pass me my bag, waddle through the water to the shore and drop my bag and body to the sand. Running my fingers through the delicate grains, I allow myself to enjoy the moment of stillness. The others stagger towards me. Jack makes a joke of kissing the earth like a sailor returned from a long and dangerous voyage.

The humid air presses against my skin and beads of liquid cling to the hairs on my arm. I tip my head back as the first fat droplet of rain hits me. A clap of thunder rips through the air and the sky lights up with a flash of lightning. But in this display of nature's power, it's the wildlife that steals the show: the birds screech, the insects hum and buzz, and something much larger howls into the vast expanse of sky above us; together they perform a concert so wild it shoots through me like electricity. The storm darkens our surroundings and there's an intensity to it, due entirely to the lack of civilisation around. Now it feels real. I am one of the *LoveWrecked* Islanders.

The sound of the boat's engine re-starting grabs my attention and I watch as it moves away from the shore, tossed around violently on the increasingly large waves. The raindrop I felt is followed by one, two, three more and then the heavens open. The storm that has been threatening for the last hour has arrived.

I hope no one wants to go home tonight because there's no way anyone is getting off the island in this.

Chapter Six

'You're here. Thank goodness. I was so…' We all turn to see a woman running from a gap in the greenery; she holds her hand limply over her head as if that will stop the downpour. She hovers in front of us, hopping from foot to foot. The woman raises her finger and waggles it over us, muttering to herself. 'Five. Only five? Not a great start.'

'Hi,' I say, getting to my feet and brushing the wet sand off my hands before extending one out to her. 'I'm Kim.' The woman blinks at me and then smacks a hand to her head as if we have all the time in the world and aren't standing on a beach in the pouring rain.

'Goodness, where are my manners? Rosalind Jenkins, *LoveWrecked*'s producer. Well, one of the producers. Currently the only producer.' She smacks her hand against her forehead again. 'Stop babbling, Rosalind.'

I glance at Mo, who now stands at my side, and try my best to keep my expression straight. Mo raises his eyebrow ever so slightly. His first impression seems to be aligned with mine. The producer, the person who is meant to be in charge of things around here, seems a little frazzled. How long has she been stuck on this island for? Whatever the answer, it doesn't bode well for the rest of us.

Rosalind is short, plump and mousy and, if I had to guess, I'd say is in her mid-thirties but the baggy floaty shirt and skirt combination she's chosen to wear ages her.

'Five,' says Rosalind, counting us again. 'Right, well, you'd better follow me, so you can get yourselves dry and ready for dinner.' At that she turns and proceeds straight back into the forest from which she came.

'Rosalind doesn't look like she's best suited to life on a remote island, does she?' Mo mutters to me under his breath.

'No,' says Carly, coming up on Mo's other side and giving him a seductive smile. 'And looks even less like the producer of a dating show. Who the hell picked her outfit? She would never get a date wearing it.'

Jack steps behind Carly and gives her a nudge with his elbow. 'Good one, Carls,' he says with a snigger.

'Don't call me that,' she snaps back at him before I can tell them both to stop slagging off our producer before the show has even started. Rosalind might seem a bit odd now but I'm sure she has everything under control, so I shake my head at them and follow Rosalind deeper into the island.

The path that Rosalind leads us along is uneven and my feet slide on the wet leaves that litter it. Branches hang low and thick on either side and more than once I have to unhook my trousers and T-shirt from being caught in the thorns. I can't help wondering when this path was last used but I remind myself that *LoveWrecked* isn't all glamour; many of the past episodes have had challenges that require the Islanders to venture out into the wilderness to test their survival skills, so the location does make sense.

'Argh, get off me.' I turn around at the sound of Jack's shout and find him shaking his hands in the air.

'What? What is it?' I ask.

'Something slimy,' he replies with a shudder. I raise an eyebrow and make a mental note that Jack might not be the best person to partner with. If this is his reaction to something slimy, goodness knows what a night out here would do to him.

We press on and soon, the thick, green forest surrounding us dies away to reveal the place that will house us for the summer.

The villa isn't immediately visible, however, because the first thing that greets us is a huge stone wall, about five metres tall, the type of wall one would see around an embassy or an exclusive house. Or, perhaps, a high-end prison.

It's a weird set-up because surely the expansive body of water surrounding us is enough to stop people getting in. Certainly, enough to shield us from the prying eyes of the media or the public.

Unless, says a cruel voice inside my head, *the walls aren't to stop people getting in. The walls are to stop us from getting out.*

And that's even before I take in the solid metal gates as wide as two side-by-side vans. Rosalind, who has waited for us all to make it out of the forest, steps forward and punches in the door code on a keypad next to the gates. They swing open in unison and the villa stands before us. Like the island itself, I'm sure on a good day it would look impressive: two storeys of white-washed walls, with all sides of the bottom floor made entirely of glass. Through the glass I can see the villa's living room illuminated, the other side looking out onto the extensive garden, in the centre of which is a blue-tiled swimming pool. The rain bounces off the pool and the heavy clouds darken the villa's walls and it looks just as uninviting as the island on which it sits.

'Wow,' says Jack, lifting his hands in the air as if praising the heavens. 'This place is epic.'

I look at him, excitement written all over his face. Excitement that I can't match. I'm not entirely sure that epic is the word I would use. Immense? Certainly. Impressive? Maybe. But epic? No, epic isn't the word I would go for. Epic makes the villa complex seem warm and inviting and that it most certainly isn't.

Clunk, the gates seal shut behind us. I shiver; there's something about the high level of security that puts me on edge. My fears clearly aren't shared by the others; none of them give even the hint that they feel uncomfortable. I feel Jack's body practically vibrating next to me. He's like a horse in the starting gates – he is ready to go.

'Welcome to *LoveWrecked*,' says Rosalind with a tired smile. 'Please follow me.'

Rosalind leads us into the villa and down a long marble-floored corridor. We all walk slowly, our wet feet making it hard going. Streaks of muddy water trail behind us and the hair on my arms stands on end as my wet skin is cooled by the air conditioning. The interior is modern and sleek with minimal decor. Lights are built into the ceiling and dotted evenly along the corridor like cat's eyes staring down at us. Peering into the living room, I see an off-white L-shaped sofa, in front of which sits a coffee table made of a broad sheet of glass resting on a short, knotty tree trunk. In my mind's eye, I see someone knocking into that table by accident and the glass shattering everywhere. Everything is perfect in a way that doesn't feel real.

Rosalind stops and directs us into a room on the right-hand side of the corridor.

'This is the communal bedroom,' says Rosalind, gesturing around the room.

If I weren't inside a Greek villa, whose style is so typically white everywhere, I would be tempted to describe the bedroom like the inside of a fancy, private hospital or how Hollywood movies depict what a person sees when they die. The walls, the bedsheets, the floor, even the beams on the ceiling are white. Only a cluster of neon pillows laid out on the beds gives an indication that you haven't fallen into a cloud.

'You can all have first pick of the beds,' she continues. 'When the others arrive, you will end up sharing with the person you've chosen as your survival partner but until the others arrive you might as well enjoy the bed to yourselves. I realise that you're all still soaking wet from the rain, so I'll give you ten minutes to quickly dry off before I continue the tour.' Rosalind turns to leave but stops in the doorway. 'One more thing, could you all please hand me your mobile phones? From here on in, it's a no-phone zone.'

My mobile phone is nestled in a side pocket of my backpack; I slide it out. The home screen lights up to display the many messages and calls that have come my way since the *SpyLand* article leaked our identities. It's natural that people are surprised; many of them haven't heard from me for years so to find out I'm going to star on a reality television show probably came as a shock. It's also not surprising that my mum and old friend Zoe are using it as an excuse to get back in touch but I'm not ready to reply just yet. Once all this is over and I've done what I came here to do then maybe I will. Rosalind holds out her hand and I place my phone in it. With that she leaves us to change.

When Rosalind returns she points out the bathroom, which has a shower large enough to fit at least six people in one go. Which, come to think about it, is probably what the producers are hoping will happen at some point.

Rosalind leads us out of the bedroom to the villa's outdoor space. The rain has now stopped, and Rosalind points out the outdoor kitchen and dining area, the grassy area and swimming pool I saw before, and a BBQ area surrounded by two-tiered decking arranged in a semi-circle. I glance at others as Rosalind points things out: Mo nods at everything she says as if wanting to show her he is listening and soaking it all in; Carly has the expression of someone who seems impressed but doesn't want to come off as too eager and so keeps suppressing raised eyebrows; Valentina looks slightly bored and seems more interested in picking at her fingernails than listening to Rosalind; but it is Jack's reaction that steals the show – every word that comes out of Rosalind's mouth elicits some variation of 'wow'.

'Take a seat. Hello, everyone, let me formally introduce myself: my name is Rosalind Jenkins, I'm one of the producers for the show. My assistant producer, Sophia Dance, is currently setting up in the production room. You'll meet her later on tonight. Apologies for our slightly erratic start. As you probably noticed on your crossing over here, the weather has decided to not be our friend. I've just heard that, due to the storm, the rest of the crew and additional Islanders are stuck on the mainland but from tomorrow you'll be able to meet the others and I might be able to get some sleep.' Rosalind chuckles as if in an attempt to sound relaxed about this confusion but she fails to convince me. She looks ragged.

'So, it's just us five and you two on the island, alone?' asks Mo. Rosalind glances at her hands and for a split second a shadow of panic crosses her face. This clearly isn't the situation she was hoping for.

'Well, there are three of the crew here. Me, Sophia and our camera operator, Daniel. But yes, just the eight of us on the island tonight. That shouldn't be a problem, though – we'll be fine. Great, in fact. Anyway,' she says, evidently eager to change the subject, 'where we are now is the imaginatively named Fire Pit. We haven't lit the fire yet, but this area is one of the main communal spaces on *LoveWrecked*.'

I'm reminded of a Roman amphitheatre, a space to sit and watch gladiators sacrificed for entertainment. It's not a bad comparison really; *LoveWrecked* is the modern equivalent, I guess. It's survival of the fittest except the death, in this case, would be more of the social kind.

'As you may know, the aim of *LoveWrecked* is twofold: find your partner and beat the competition. During your time here, you are to find a partner of the opposite sex with whom you think you have the best chance of winning. Then as a couple you participate in the *Love-Wrecked* challenges. The better you do, the more points you get. Each week, the couple with the lowest score leaves us. Although I must say here that only half the points come from the challenges; the public vote on their favourite couples too. The final couple left standing will win £200,000 split 50/50. Here around the Fire Pit is where you get to connect with one another and scout out your partner-in-crime.'

I chance a glance at Valentina Novak and Carly Chu and I can't help but think they're looking at me differently. As if I've gone from campmate to competition in the blink of an eye and they're only now looking at me the way I've been looking at them from the very beginning. I look at Mo and Jack – which of them would make a better partner to beat the competition? Jack is probably stronger and certainly seems more energetic, but I get the impression he is skittish, and that quality doesn't appeal. I cannot deny that I'm a competitive person, or at least I used to be. At school, I excelled in almost everything, particularly sport. And at work, I always wanted to be the best; it was one of the reasons I was selected for the fast-track programme. Sadly, the competitive streak dulled in me over the years, beaten down by life, but as I appraise my 'enemy' there is a flutter inside me. Perhaps the Fire Pit isn't the only thing about to be lit.

'How does the filming work then?' asks Carly, jutting her chin out.

'Ha, of course you want to know that,' says Jack and, turning to Rosalind, adds, 'She wants to ensure that only her best angles are captured. Doesn't she realise that with a face like that she only has good angles?'

'Glad you asked,' says Rosalind, seemingly ignoring Jack and giving Carly a smile that says she's pleased to talk about something within her control. 'The villa complex is equipped with seventy-five cameras, recording everything that happens in the villa. Twenty-four hours a day, seven days a week. There is an army of people in London that work shifts and write down everything that is said and done. The "eavesdroppers", as we call them, highlight the best bits. The executive team and I review all of this and put the show together.

'On top of this, we have camera operators who carry handheld cameras around. It can be unusual at first but you'll get used to them and soon forget they're there. Daniel is here already, probably having a nap somewhere. The others should arrive tomorrow. Hopefully.'

I'd known we would be filmed but I hadn't expected there to be this many cameras and this many crew. Not that they're here yet but I can already feel their eyes on me, watching me.

'I should also say,' continues Rosalind, 'that the *Love-Wrecked* villa has been specifically designed to film a show of this kind. You may or may not have noticed that between all the rooms are doors with light bulbs next to them. Red for locked, green for unlocked.'

'What?' interrupts Mo, tensing. 'So, you could choose to lock us all in somewhere?'

'Yes. For example, when we want to set up one of the challenges, we might choose to lock you all in the bedroom or sitting room. The producers have control of the house but it's for your own protection more than anything else.'

So, my high-end prison thought upon arrival wasn't actually too far from the truth. It's a little unnerving. But I don't know anything about TV production, so maybe I'm being a bit sensitive. Rosalind glances at her watch.

'The CCTV is scheduled to go live in just over an hour and I'm sure you're all desperate for a shower and some food. So, I recommend you go and get yourselves ready and head to the outdoor dining area. Mo, I'd like you to be in charge of cooking tonight. Is that OK?'

'Sure,' says Mo, 'happy with that.'

'Brilliant. You should find everything you need in the kitchen. Aim to arrive at the table in one hour – you'll find your individual microphones there. It is a requirement that you wear them at all times.' We all nod. This doesn't come as a surprise; it was written into our contracts. 'Great, well, enjoy your evening. And you will see me and the other producers and Islanders in the morning.'

Rosalind turns away from us and walks back towards the villa.

'Oh, and remember, the competition will only really start when the others arrive. So, for this evening at least, play nice.' She gives us a wink and scurries away.

Chapter Seven

LoveWrecked @LoveWrecked
1.3m followers

Share your thoughts on this year's season of LoveWrecked. Use @LoveWrecked or #LoveWrecked for your chance to be read out on air and win some goodies courtesy of our sponsors.

@LoveWrecked: This year's LoveWrecked has begun. Are you one of those who can't wait for the first episode to be aired tomorrow? Head to our website to watch the live feeds from inside the villa. Streaming starts in one hour.

@adammcboy: I'm all about the unfiltered experience so I'll be watching live #Love-Wrecked

@safariprincess: Wonder what drama tonight will have in store…

Chapter Eight

When I exit the villa and arrive at the outdoor kitchen area, I find Mo leaning over the stove, stirring a wooden spoon in a pot the size of a cauldron. The smell of lemongrass wafts towards me and I breathe it in, welcoming its fresh fragrance. Mo moves fluidly around the worktop, sprinkling in a bit of this and that, tasting as he goes. This is evidently his domain. The kitchen is divided into two parts: the hob, sink and general food preparation area is laid out in a line against the wall of the villa and this is where Mo works with his back to me. The second part is its more dominant feature: a broad marble island sits in the middle of the kitchen and it is around this that Valentina and Jack sit perched on bar stools, each holding a glass of sparkling wine.

I tug at the bottom of my skin-tight Lycra dress. The cameras are now rolling, the show has begun, and it isn't my intention for the first thing they capture of me to be my bum. I had intended to be a bit more low-key on the island but this dress was left on my bed with a note saying, *A party dress for a party girl. Show the audience how the girls from Liverpool bring it*. So low-key wasn't an option.

Mo, Valentina and Jack were dressed and ready before I even got out of the shower but seeing them all now, I'm glad I followed the producer's instructions and made an effort as they most certainly have. Jack's hair is slicked back with copious amounts of hair gel and he's donned a ludicrously bright pink shirt that clashes quite terribly with his unnaturally tanned skin. Valentina wears a red, long-sleeved crop top and high-waisted denim shorts. The shorts are so short it's possible to see the curve of her bum from beneath them. Mo wears beige chinos and a navy-blue shirt on top of which he's wrapped an apron.

As I approach the group, two people nestled in the far corner of the kitchen catch my eye, making me jump and I wobble ever so slightly on my stilettos. One of them, her mop of red, curly hair tied in a scrunchie on the top of her head, must be Sophia Dance, Rosalind's assistant; the other I can't see because his face is hidden behind a large camera. It doesn't take a detective to realise he's probably the camera guy. All I can make out is his chestnut-brown hair which is cropped close to his scalp.

'And then there were four,' says Jack, giving me a smile that makes my insides squirm. He picks up one of the champagne glasses and holds it out to me. As I accept the glass from him, Jack gives me a little bow and says, 'For you, my lady.'

My lip curls slightly as I cringe at his cheesiness and I hastily rearrange my features to give him a smile of thanks. Jack might not be the man for me, but this is a personality contest after all. Mo, however, is doing a less good job at keeping his face straight. At Jack's bow, he bites his lip, clearly stifling a laugh, and when he turns away, I can see his shoulders shaking. The glass is cool as it touches my lips and the bubbles dance from the glass when I take a sip.

I've barely eaten anything all day, so I vow to take it slow tonight; champagne and an empty stomach isn't a good combination for anyone, let alone me. There's something about champagne that gets me particularly drunk – it's as if the bubbles have the ability to infiltrate my faculties faster than normal alcohol.

'Here she is,' cheers Jack, tilting his head to look past me. I'm already forgotten, it seems. 'Come on, Carly, we're all waiting for you.'

Carly Chu totters towards us, her dagger-like stilettos clipping on the tiled floor. Her hair remains scraped back in her characteristic low bun and her lips are painted an intense red, like blood splashed against a white wall. The straps of her thigh-skimming black dress are so thin and the material so soft-looking that every movement gives the impression it might slip from her body completely. Jack and Mo both stand for a moment, their mouths hanging slightly open.

'What?' says Carly, furrowing her brow and looking down at herself. I very nearly laugh out loud.

'Champagne?' I offer, giving the boys a moment to regain their power of speech.

'I'd love some,' says Carly provocatively.

'Nice dress,' I say, offering her a glass.

'You can borrow it from me some time. I try not to wear things more than once.'

My eyebrow raises involuntarily. The games, it seems, have well and truly begun.

'Dinner is ready,' calls Mo, heaving the pot from the stove and leading our procession the short distance from the kitchen around the corner to the dining table. The smell of it wafts behind him; it smells exactly like the type of meal I want to eat right now – warm, fragrant and comforting. Mo plonks the pot on the dining table and dashes back to grab a large bowl of rice and his champagne.

'Mo, seriously, this looks… incredible.' Carly lifts her glass and tips it towards him with another seductive smile; three guesses as to who she has set her sights on. 'Cheers to the chef.'

'Cheers,' I chime in unison with the others.

'Cheers to you all, here's to our first night.' Mo raises his glass and we all toast. The sound of clinking glasses makes me smile; to me it's the sound of promise and of hope. I can't remember the last time I clinked glasses with a genuine feeling that things might change for me.

'May the best team win,' says Carly, with a wink that somehow manages to make both the men, and probably the men in the audience, think it was directed at them.

Carly is good, I'll give her that. She will make stiff competition.

I drain my champagne glass and reach for one of the bottles of wine that are laid on the table. It is slightly worrying that I've barely been here a couple of hours and have almost forgotten about the cameras and the watchful eyes of the producers. I glance over at them and see that Daniel the cameraman pulls his head away from the camera and says something to Sophia. It's the first time I've seen him properly and I'm slightly taken aback to see his face. Daniel is a very attractive man: thick, arched eyebrows; deep soulful eyes; and a broad chest that I find myself fighting a strong desire to rest my head against. The humidity and the champagne must be getting to me, despite the fact I've only had one glass. I'm going to need to watch myself. I don't want to get too drunk; who knows what might happen. What I might do.

'What's this?' says Jack, pulling me from my Daniel daydream. He's waving a golden nugget of puffed tofu in the air.

'Tofu,' replies Mo.

'What the fuck is tofu?' Jack asks in a far more aggressive tone than I think is strictly necessary for such a question. The tone of light-hearted fun and conversation which had existed as we all happily drank our champagne and sat down to dinner is gone with his *what the fuck*. Carly lets out a huge sigh, clearly unimpressed with what she considers Jack's idiocy.

'Seriously?' says Mo. He chuckles and raises an eyebrow at Jack, who reddens and opens his mouth to retort.

'It's sort of like… vegetarian chicken,' cuts in Valentina, trying to come to Jack's rescue and get us back to where we were before his outburst.

Everyone giggles; it's a good-natured giggle but Jack's cheeks are glowing now, displaying his embarrassment and anger. He scowls and puts the tofu in his mouth, muttering that he doesn't think it tastes like chicken at all.

'Mo, this really is an incredible meal,' I say, changing the focus. 'Where did you learn to cook like this?'

Mo picks up his wine glass and leans against the back of his chair, his body arranged in a position of relaxed calm. 'I'm a trained chef,' he says, shrugging his shoulders as if it is no big deal but his expression betrays just how proud he is of himself right now. 'I'm really impressed with the kitchen here. So, there'll be lots more to come.'

'I can cook too,' interjects Jack, dropping his fork down on his plate with a clang. 'More than happy to share the burden.' Mo smiles at him condescendingly.

'Just watch yourself around those Japanese knives,' says Mo, his voice low and even. 'They can be very dangerous, especially in untrained hands.'

I take an extra-large gulp of my wine. Everyone is jostling for position, asserting their authority in this new environment. It isn't unexpected particularly given that this is a competition but that doesn't make it any less awkward from such obviously alpha males. It will die down once they get to know one another – at least I hope it will. I don't think I can handle sniping on a daily basis.

'Hey,' whispers a voice in my ear and I start. I didn't hear anyone approach me. I turn to see that the cameraman, Daniel, has crept up behind me, his camera pointed at the two men asserting their dominance. He turns away from the camera to give me a warm smile. The hairs on my arm stand on end as my body reacts to the proximity of our faces. The proximity of his beautiful face. 'We've not been formally introduced,' he says, releasing a hand from his camera and offering it to me. 'I'm Daniel, Daniel Oni. And as you may or may not have guessed, the camera operator.' His hand is rough against mine. I didn't realise camera operating would create such callouses. And shoulders. And biceps. His teeth shine between dark, full lips. God, he is so handsome.

I realise I've been holding onto his hand the whole time I've been taking in his handsome features, and I let my hand slip quickly. How is it that the first man I'm attracted to, properly attracted to, isn't even part of the competition?

'Everything OK?' he asks, his brow furrowed in concern. I give him a small nod. 'Don't worry,' he says, tipping his head in the direction of Jack and Mo, 'the dick-swinging will stop soon.' He smiles cheekily and gives me a wink that makes my insides quiver. I raise my eyebrows at him. Of everything he could have said, I wasn't expecting that.

'What makes you say that?'

'Once I show them what I'm packing, they'll back off.'

I snort with laughter. To my horror, red wine involuntarily sprays from my mouth, spattering all over the table in front of me.

Fuck.

I grab my napkin, assessing where I've done the most damage. My cheeks warm as the leftover liquid dribbles down my chin. Did Daniel do that on purpose to garner a reaction from me? He can't have known that I would react so… so… humiliatingly. Glancing at him, I find that he is helping to clear up the mess rather than filming.

Chair legs scrape over tiles and Carly stands, towering over me. She throws her napkin onto the table next to her uneaten plate of rice and curry.

'Ladylike,' she says to me with a sneer, standing up. 'I've already had a shower today, thanks.'

'Carly, I'm s—' I start to say but Jack Peaks interrupts me.

'Carly, let me—' he says.

'No,' replies Carly, cutting him off as she turns to leave the table. 'Both of you sit down. I'm going to the ladies' to dry off. I'll be back.' She storms off, without trying too hard to disguise her exasperated sighs.

I hide my face behind my hands, unable to look the others in the eyes. I'm such an embarrassment.

'Don't worry,' says Daniel, his breath hot in my ear. He wraps his fingers around my wrists and pulls them away from my face. 'She overreacted.'

'That was your fault,' I say to Daniel, not looking at him. Instead, I drain what is left in my wine glass and refill it.

So much for not overdoing the booze, says a nasty voice in my head. Although I haven't really been overdoing it, I don't think, but for some reason it is hitting me harder than I'm used to.

Daniel takes the bottle from me and fills himself a glass of his own.

'Guilty as charged, officer,' he says with a wink.

What did he just say? My hand wobbles. I strengthen my grip around the glass, so he doesn't notice the quiver that gripped me at his words. I will myself to relax. It is a turn of phrase and nothing more. He doesn't mean anything by it. There is no way he knows. He doesn't know. He couldn't know.

'But,' he says, carrying on in a way that convinces me he didn't mean anything by it, 'you can't say I'm not good at my job, that will make a good promo clip.' I try to disguise my moment of panic by nodding enthusiastically as if I understand what he's talking about. Obviously, I don't. I know nothing about TV production. But his enthusiasm for the clip convinces me his calling me an officer was nothing more than a turn of phrase.

'Yeah, promo clip,' I say lamely.

The clip-clop of heels on tiles saves me from having to say any more. Carly's returned. 'Carly, darling, don't worry. I've kept your seat warm for you,' says Jack. He winks at Carly in a way that he must presume to be cute and rubs his hand over the chair she was sitting on. Carly doesn't return his wink but instead gives him a tight smile and totters over towards him.

My lip curls; Carly Chu might be a bit of a bitch, but Jack Peaks is more than a bit of a creep.

'Did you miss me?' says Jack, in a failed attempt at a whisper. 'You even look different, since I last saw you,' he continues, brushing one of his fingers along her bare arm. Carly's head whips around to stare at him, the air of arrogance she was carrying gone in a flash.

'I'd better go catch this,' says Daniel, slipping away from me, his camera held in front of him.

'What are you talking about? Did I miss you?' Carly snaps. I shouldn't be watching them but there's something in their exchange that intrigues me; I can't look away.

'Yeah, darling,' drawls Jack. And I thought I was drunk? Jack is something else right now. 'Did you miss me when you were gone?'

'Gone where?' Carly, pale to begin with, is now white as a sheet as if Jack's words have drained the blood from her. Jack stares at her; a half-smile lingers on his lips, his eyes aren't quite in focus.

'Oh, Carly, darling, I'm sure there's more going up in that noggin than you give yourself credit for.' He taps a finger to her temple. I prod Mo's leg under the table and nod in their direction. I'm convinced a fight is about to break out.

'Jack, I…?' stutters Carly, her reaction more frightened than anything else. If Jack had tapped me on the head like that I'd have had him in a headlock seconds later.

'I was asking if you'd missed me when you were in the toilet,' says Jack, furrowing his brow. Carly's shoulders drop, and she exhales loudly. 'It was only my little joke,' he says, lamely.

'Well, I'd leave the jokes to someone else and stick to selling houses,' snaps Carly, twisting her body away from him and towards Valentina.

'Carly. Carly. Babe.' Jack is practically shouting now. 'Babe, don't turn sour on me. Here, a toast.'

Jack raises his glass in one hand and with the other grasps Carly's elbow, raising her glass. 'To the best-looking couple on this island.' Jack clinks his glass against hers and then downs it in one gulp. What he doesn't seem to notice is that Carly is looking at him as if she could kill him.

Chapter Nine

Saturday 26th July, 20:00

It must be well into the evening now and the alcohol has wrapped its way around my senses. The sun hasn't quite set but it's on its descent and the noises of the forest change and grow as if the dayshift creatures clock off and are replaced with the night shift. The garden is lit by lamps dotted haphazardly around it. In the semi-darkness the light from them does nothing to illuminate but instead draws monsters in the shadows and I can't help but think how easy it would be to hide in those shadows. The surface of the swimming pool is smooth now, absent of even a ripple, for this evening, unlike the day, is still and calm. The change in the weather is the complete inverse to the change in the Islanders and their behaviour.

'Wahey,' cheers Jack, raising his arms up in mock celebration. He dives forward, grabs one of the bottles of wine and replenishes his drained glass. 'Go on,' he shouts, stabbing a finger at us each in turn.

'What?' I ask, taken aback by suddenly being addressed by him. 'I missed that.'

'Finish it,' shouts Jack from across the table. 'I want to get the games started soon.' He laughs raucously as if he's just made a joke. 'Glass is still full, mate,' he says, raising his eyebrows at Mo and jabbing a finger towards him. Jack is too busy looking at Mo to notice that Sophia, Daniel and his camera have moved closer to him. Poor Jack, he seems to be having a fantastic time, but he is making a bit of an arse of himself.

Mo's lip curls. 'And by games, I presume you mean drinking games.' Disdain saturates every word, making my body tense. I don't know what it is with these two but they seem to have been at each other's throats all night. 'They're not really my thing, *mate*. Much prefer to just enjoy this delicious glass of Tempranillo.'

Jack's ears flush red and he plonks his elbows on the table, leaning in towards Mo.

'Mo, is it?' says Jack.

'Yeah, we were introduced about nine hours ago,' replies Mo. Our group is silent now, all watching the exchange between the two men. Daniel raises his hand slowly and twiddles with something on his camera, probably zooming in. Of course he wants to get this; I get the impression Jack is about to make quite the performance.

'Your face is so familiar, mate,' says Jack. Mo flinches in the way it is only possible to do when someone you don't know or greatly dislike calls you 'mate'. It's how I feel when men call me 'sweetheart'. 'Where d'you live?' Jack's words run together; he is slurring quite noticeably now.

'Birmingham,' replies Mo, turning to his right, towards me. I look from Mo to Jack, and Jack's expression tells me he isn't giving up that easily.

'Nah, can't be that, mate. Never been to Birmingham.' Jack's voice increases in volume every time he speaks. 'You didn't ever live in Essex, did you?'

'No.' Mo is practically snarling now, and I draw back from him, surprised at his vitriol. Good God, is Jack really so oblivious he can't recognise that this isn't something Mo wants to talk about?

'Do you work?'

'Of course I work, I've already told you I'm a chef.' Mo pauses and takes a deep breath. 'Look, man,' he continues. 'I'm pretty sure you're confusing me with someone else. It wouldn't be the first time. I have one of those faces.' Mo turns his body away, again towards me.

Come on, Jack, take a hint.

'What about—'

'Just leave it, for fuck's sake,' I interject, unable to take it any longer; it's excruciating to watch. 'Stop being so bloody nosy.'

Everyone turns to look at Jack, waiting for his reaction to being shut down like this. He flops back in his seat and stares at me for a moment. I stare back at him, holding my breath. Then he roars with laughter. 'Feisty one, you are,' he says, giving me a wink. I exhale.

Jack twizzles to his left and launches himself into conversation with Valentina. Valentina's eyes widen, clearly taken aback at this sudden change in focus. Mo's jaw relaxes, and he leans closer to me.

'Thank you,' he says. 'What is his problem?'

'He's just a bit drunk. Plus, he probably likes making you uncomfortable because it makes him look better.'

'Oh yeah, so he can impress the ladies,' scoffs Mo. 'He seems like such a creep.'

At Mo's words, Jack's head whips round so fast I can almost feel the movement of air.

'What did you call me?' he barks at Mo.

Valentina leans away, trying to get as far away from Jack as she can within the confines of her seat. Mo's mouth flaps lamely but no words come out; he clearly didn't expect

Jack's reaction to be this and it looks like he is regretting saying anything. Carly, sitting on Jack's other side, poorly suppresses a smirk; she seems to be enjoying all this drama.

'I am not a creep,' says Jack, banging his hand on the table, making the cutlery clang against our empty plates. 'And I won't have you accusing me of anything.'

Jack goes to rise from his seat but Sophia, the assistant producer, appears out of nowhere and places a hand on Jack's shoulder.

'Cool it, Jack,' she says and crouches forward to whisper something in his ear. I can only assume she got the shot she wanted if she is stopping the fight now.

Jack nods as she speaks and then says, 'Sorry, mate, took it the wrong way.' Mo gives him a pained smile and locks eyes with Sophia. I'm not sure if it is my imagination but I swear she gives him a tiny head bob and with it she turns around and leaves. Chatter resumes almost immediately but I don't join it instantly. Instead, I look from Mo to Jack and back again. Both men seemed to know the right buttons to push in one another and I can't help wondering what they're both hiding.

Chapter Ten

Saturday 26th July, 21:00

I've lost all track of time. My body warms and unwinds as the alcohol courses through it. I throw my head back and laugh at something Daniel says to me. I'm not even sure that what he said was funny. But I'm drunk now, so it was funny.

I place a hand on my belly; it has swollen slightly owing to the large quantity I've eaten but this food is so worth the food baby. Living alone, I rarely cook for myself and I can't afford takeaways regularly. My go-to dinner is usually a microwave meal or, if I'm in the mood to prepare it, pasta and a jar of sauce.

I stand up and, with a lot of clattering, collect everyone's plates. It's the least I can do given how much trouble Mo has gone to. Valentina rises to help and between us we manage to clear the table of a significant amount of the debris that has collected during our first meal. As the two of us walk to the kitchen, carrying a dangerous amount in our arms, I realise that I haven't had much interaction with Valentina so far. The petite blonde has a standoffish vibe but there's a softness to the woman's eyes that makes me think she is shy, not rude.

'What are you thinking so far?' I ask her as we load the dishwasher.

'About what?' she replies, slamming the dishwasher shut.

'About *LoveWrecked*, the villa, the others.' I say the last word in a whisper; I'm not really interested in hearing her bitch about our fellow Islanders at this stage, but I am intrigued about what she thinks. From what I've gathered of her up to now, she is different to your typical Islander.

'I'm thinking…' says Valentina, biting her lip, 'that I'm not the right fit for this show.'

'In what way?' Though I've sort of been thinking it too, I didn't expect her to say this nor did I expect the sad tone with which Valentina said it.

She shrugs. 'I'm shy, and while I know I'm not unattractive, my general look is quite different from the typical contestant they go for.' She looks me and my tiny dress up and down. 'No offence.'

'None taken.'

'And…' Valentina glances over her shoulder before leaning in closer to me. 'I actually hate this show. Always thought it was a pile of shit filled with vacuous individuals in search of fame.'

I chuckle. 'You're not entirely wrong about the last part.'

'But then, I'm not much better than them, not really. I'm trying to make it in the music industry. What about you? Why are you here?'

'I guess, I had nothing better to do,' I say, truthfully.

'I'll drink to that. Though I probably shouldn't, I haven't had too much tonight but I'm feeling really drunk.' Despite this, Valentina shrugs, strides to the fridge and collects a cold bottle of vodka. Filling two glass tumblers with enough vodka to strip a wall of its paint, she holds one out to me. 'Cheers,' she says, raising her glass then downing it in one.

I'm impressed; Valentina manages to make shooting vodka look classy. I follow suit, gasping as the clear liquid slips down my throat.

Valentina giggles. 'Stick with me, you'll get used to it.' It might be the effects of the alcohol but I'm warming to Valentina in a way I haven't to any of the others.

'Hey, beautiful ladies,' shouts an obnoxious male voice. I don't need to turn around to figure out who it is. Jack Peaks has been drinking so aggressively for the last couple of hours that the smell of alcohol coming from him stings my nostrils.

All the progress I've made helping Valentina relax shatters as he staggers towards us. Valentina's body visibly tightens and her arms fold across her body. I don't blame her; there is something in the way he says 'ladies' that makes me clench. If we were in a bar and not being screened on national television, I probably would have told him to fuck off, but I hold my tongue. Jack flops onto one of the bar stools positioned around the kitchen worktop. He folds his bottom lip down in the way a child about to have a tantrum would.

'You're doing shots without me?' He grabs the vodka bottle and swigs directly from it. I narrow my eyes at him; he is repulsive. 'So,' says Jack, somehow managing to stumble over the two-letter word. 'Tell me about you. What d'ya do?' He points his finger at Valentina.

'I'm a DJ,' she replies curtly. Jack's mouth falls open.

'Teacher? Better behave myself, then, shouldn't I? Don't want to get spanked. Or do I?' Jack erupts into laughter. I stare at him, pulling my face into an expression that I hope allows me to convey as much contempt as I feel. This man is a pig.

'No,' replies Valentina. 'I am a DJ.' She places particular emphasis on the final letters, ironically like a schoolteacher trying to explain something to a particularly dense teenager.

'Nice,' says Jack, elongating the vowel so the word drags on. He leans into her, licking his lips like a hungry wolf. I take a step closer to Valentina, feeling a sudden urge to protect her. 'You're a DJ? You're a DJ.'

'Yes,' I snap at him. 'She literally just said that.'

Jack slides off the bar stool and stumbles to our side of the worktop. With every movement he makes, the smell of alcohol and sweat wafts in our direction. Jack comes right up to our faces and prods Valentina in the arm.

'Stop that.' I slap his hand away.

'Need more… *you know*. Something to really kick this party into gear. A higher gear.' Jack gives Valentina a slow wink.

'I don't do that,' she snarls at him and storms off.

'Ooooooh, touched a nerve, have I? Hey, DJ. Where are you going?' Jack shouts. Valentina ignores him. 'DJ. Come back, babe, we're chatting.'

My nostrils flare.

'Jack,' I say softly. 'I think it might be wise if you slowed down a bit. And, maybe, you should have a big glass of water.' I grasp Jack by the shoulders to steady him.

'Oh, fuck off,' he roars, swaying with every word. 'I know your game. Need me out of the picture. So Mo can get to Carly.' I frown. What is he talking about?

'Leave me out of this,' calls Carly, who is still sitting at the dining table with Mo. 'And for the record, I'm not an object you can just get. Prick.'

'Come on, leave him to it,' I say to Daniel, realising now through the haze of my own drunkenness that he's been standing nearby this whole time, filming everything. 'I'm going for a swim. Do you fancy coming with me?' I ask, beckoning him away from the kitchen and towards the pool. He gives me a wry smile and unclips the camera from his body.

'I'm sure a quick dip won't hurt me. Just don't anything too interesting because Sophia and Rosalind would kill me for not filming it,' he says, and I giggle.

Daniel unclips his belt and once it's free he pulls it through trouser loop after trouser loop. As his belt reaches the final loop, he flicks his wrist, pulling out his belt with a flourish. The leather cracks as it rips through the air. I throw my head back and laugh, applauding him as I do so. He is so funny.

'Whit woot,' I shout after failing an attempt to wolf whistle. The other Islanders turn to see what I'm whistling at. He smiles at me and gives me a cheeky wink. Despite being behind the camera, Daniel clearly loves the attention and as he stands there shirtless, I don't hate giving it to him.

'Well, ladies and gentlemen, seems we've got ourselves a fucking show-off.' Jack's shout reverberates through the still evening air.

Daniel's trousers, now unbuttoned and unzipped, fall to the floor and gather around his ankles but he doesn't step out of them. Under different circumstances this would be funny, but Daniel's jaw tightens, and he narrows his eyes at Jack. My stomach clenches; here is a man who doesn't wear embarrassment well. I want to say something funny, to get us back to the relaxed vibe we had moments before, but the alcohol clouds my mind and I can't think of anything. I'm frozen.

Come on, Daniel, say something. Everyone is watching now. Their eyes moving from Daniel to Jack and back again. The silence that hangs in the air pains me. I want to scream at him to speak, reply, save face.

'Nice to see you're impressed, mate,' says Daniel, flexing his arms in an imitation of Hercules.

My shoulders drop, and I want to applaud him; he played it well. Daniel steps out his trousers and swings them around his head. I whoop, giving him all the encouragement I can, wanting Jack to know that he didn't win this round. The hilarity of the situation is amplified by the awkwardness that came before. Daniel lobs his trousers in the direction of Jack, who is advancing towards us. The trousers hit Jack square in the face and hang there for a moment. My breath catches in my throat and then I roar with laughter. We all do. Well, all of us except Jack.

Jack rips the trousers from his face, throws them to the floor and charges towards Daniel. 'Two can play this game, mate.'

'Hey, come on, Jack. It was a joke,' I say, stepping in Jack's path. I'm getting a bit sick of him ruining everyone's fun. Jack's sweaty palms wrap around my arms and I stumble as he pushes me out of the way. I regain my balance quickly and whirl round just in time to see Jack press two hands against Daniel's chest and push.

The sound of Daniel's skin hitting the water makes me wince. Jack stands at the pool's edge and a Joker-like grin spreads over his face. I stand, transfixed, watching as Daniel's head emerges from the water, gasping for breath. A vein in Daniel's neck throbs violently. It beats almost in time with the laughter that is coming from the others, but

I don't laugh. Daniel's eyes bore into Jack's and he looks as if he's about to jump from the pool and throttle Jack. I can't let that happen and I can't let this humiliation hang in the air any more.

There's only one thing to be done. I kick off my shoes and take a running jump. In the air, I pull my knees into my chest and fall into the water like a cannonball. The water roars around my ears as I fall to the bottom. My skin, warmed by the wine and vodka, practically hisses against the cool water. I paddle towards Daniel and wrap my arms around his thick neck. I sense that this is an intimate gesture but the alcohol coursing through my blood convinces me it is the right move.

'Don't stress about him. Jack Peaks is a knob.'

Daniel laughs at my words, but I know with great certainty that if Jack continues to behave like this, his days in this villa are numbered.

Chapter Eleven

LoveWrecked @LoveWrecked
1.3m followers

Share your thoughts on this year's season of LoveWrecked.

@trashqueen2000: Who else is watching the LoveWrecked live feed? How did they all get so drunk so quickly?

@dannidoes: @trashqueen2000 Jack is the drunkest. Kim is pretty bad too. But the others? Nah, I think they're just playing to the camera.

@LoveWrecked4eva: @dannidoes @trashqueen2000 OMG did you see what Jack just did? He is wasted.

@trashqueen2000: @dannidoes @LoveWrecked4eva At 18:00 Jack Peak-ed. At 22:00 Jack fell. LOL

@M155Ch1ef: Real zero to hero story this one #LoveWrecked #jackhaspeaked

@Chriscomments: Jack Peaks is the type of guy that's going to piss people off. Fact. If the public don't get rid of him, one of the others will #jackhaspeaked #LoveWrecked

Chapter Twelve

Kimberley
Sunday 27th July, 9:01

I roll over onto my side and pat the palm of my hand across the surface of my bedside table. I'm sure I put my water bottle here before I fell asleep. My mouth is so dry that my tongue is practically sticking to the side of my mouth.

The beds that surround me are occupied and the sound of not-so-gentle snoring fills the air, overpowering the noise of the air conditioner. Its cool breeze runs over the top of my head and I'm grateful for it; there are too many bodies in one room to be without it, and yet, even with the air conditioning, my skin is sticky with sweat and I can feel it gathering in the nape of my neck. I glance upwards towards the hidden cameras, the cameras that are catching me in all my morning glory. Oh God, I really hope Daniel isn't waiting for me outside, camera at the ready.

I peel back the covers and swing my legs out of bed and onto the floor. My sweaty feet make contact with the marble floor and I relish the coolness of it. Pushing myself into a standing position, I creep out of the bedroom and head down the corridor towards the kitchen in search of water. Debris of clothes and underwear from the previous night litters the floor. We'd really better sort it before the newcomers arrive; what will they think of us if they see this mess?

There's a pair of men's sunglasses lying discarded by the door. I pick them up and inspect them. They'll do for now. I place them over my eyes before pulling aside the curtain covering the wide glass door that leads to the garden. Light streams into the hallway and I'm thankful for the shades, whoever they belong to.

I open the patio door and step straight into the outside kitchen. It seems the kitchen too has taken a hit from the festivities of our first night in the villa. Glasses, stained with red wine or filled with half-drunk gin and tonics, are clustered together in a group and plates laden with the crusts of late-night toasties cover the kitchen counter.

I will deal with this, but later. First water and coffee.

Less than ten minutes later, I'm sitting at the breakfast bar, my legs dangling from a bar stool, my fingers wrapped around a steaming cup of strong, black coffee. Its smell alone is enough to convince me that it will do the trick. It's the elixir of life.

From my position, I can see part of the table at which we sat last night and the outer edge of the decking that surrounds the pool. I hear the water lapping gently against the sides of the pool moved by the gentle morning breeze and I imagine it splashing little flecks of water over the side, darkening the light-coloured wooden decking. The soft breeze brushes against my skin, warm and kind. Its caress makes me feel slightly more human. I'm still fragile but I feel much better.

Blowing on my coffee, I try to piece together the night before.

I remember dinner; I sat next to Mo. That is clear at least. I can picture his dark, thick hair and strong chin.

He is a chef – I'm sure we discussed his work. I even remember noting that he spent most of the evening glancing towards the actress. Well, both the men did.

What is her name again? I shake my head; my brain throbs – best not to put too much pressure on myself right now, the name will come. Although I can't remember the actress's name, I can vividly recall that she didn't seem to be enjoying the company of Jack. Jack Peaks, well, he certainly made an impression last night. I smile, comforted with the notion that if I feel like shit this morning, Jack is probably dead in a ditch somewhere.

Then, after dinner, there was music and dancing and…

A scream rips apart the peace of the morning, wrenching me from my remembering. My body jolts forward, unprepared to hear such a noise and my fingers loosen around the coffee mug. The mug hits the worktop and shatters into several pieces. Brown liquid stains the white marble.

'Shit,' I say aloud, twisting my legs away to avoid them getting burned as the coffee flows towards me. The dark brown liquid splashes onto the floor.

The scream comes again. So piercing, I feel like it's stabbed my brain. This time, reacting in the way it was trained to all those years ago, my body springs into action. Instinct punches out any lingering remnants of my hangover.

Chapter Thirteen

Sunday 27th July, 9:17

The bar stool clatters behind me as I push myself off it but I don't stop to pick it up. There was something in the scream that I've heard before. It wasn't a scream of someone who's seen a spider, it was the scream of someone who's seen a ghost.

My feet pound against the tiled patio floor as I whip past the dinner table. I jump down the steps to the grassy area of the garden and step onto the wooden decking.

It takes me barely any time to reach the pool and the screamer, but it's far from enough time to prepare myself.

I freeze, my moment of action stopped dead.

Valentina Novak, dressed in a hot pink bikini, is sunk into a low crouch at the side of the pool, tears streaming down her cheeks. She whimpers as she looks down at it.

A fresh wave of nausea crashes over me.

A body.

Jack Peaks floats in the pool, face down in the water.

'Well, don't just stand there,' I say, my voice coming out as a rasp. Valentina turns her eyes up towards me and I see they're rimmed with red.

I stalk closer to her and to him, past the sun loungers and down one more step to the pool's edge. The wood of the decking is sharp against my recently pumiced soles but I ignore the pain.

Without waiting another second, I slide into the pool. The water isn't cold, but I gasp as my body, warm from the sun, hits the water. Waist deep in the pool, my pyjamas flap around me as I stride towards Jack, my feet bouncing off the pool's bottom.

I get myself behind Jack and push him; his body moves in response to my push like a lifeless buoy bobbing in a rough sea.

'What is going—' A soft voice comes from the side of the pool. It's Carly, Carly Chu. The actress – her name comes back to me in a rush.

'Help me! Help me get him out of the pool,' I say, exasperation clinging to my words. She dashes to the poolside and drops to her knees and Valentina, already on her knees, crawls towards us. I push Jack's body close to the pool edge and the two women plunge their hands into the water, hooking their arms under his limp ones.

'One, two, three,' I say and in unison we push and pull.

The muscles in my arm scream as we haul him from the water. He's heavy, a full-grown, muscular, water-clogged man. A strangled voice shouts from behind us.

'We're calling the medics. Is he alive? Please tell me he's alive.'

It's Rosalind; she flies towards us at breakneck speed, the baggy shirt of her dotted pyjamas billowing out behind her. I turn back and heave Jack flat onto his back. The sound of his wet skin slapping against the poolside tiles makes my muscles tighten; there's something grotesque and undignified about the noise.

Valentina gags beside me. It's an understandable reaction and I'd have probably had the same one had I not been here before. Jack's face is pale and swollen from waterlogging, his skin is wrinkled, and his features are distorted out of proportion.

It's been a long time since I've seen a body. I try to stop the thoughts that come to my mind, to push away the vacant stare of the last dead body I saw. My ghost, my demon, my fault. No, I can't think about that, not now. Nothing about this is similar to then.

I press my hands against the rough surface surrounding the pool and heave myself out, spraying water everywhere like a wet dog shaking itself.

'Jack,' I call, diving towards him and shaking his shoulder. His arm flops limply at my movement but his mouth, puffy and wrinkled, remains firmly shut. 'Jack, can you hear me?' He's completely unresponsive. I press my fingers against the soft hollow beside Jack's windpipe; there's nothing.

Placing my hands against his chest, I pump.

One, two, three, my heart hammers in my chest.

Fifteen, sixteen, seventeen, my breath shortens as I tire from the effort.

Twenty-eight, twenty-nine, thirty. Pinching Jack's nose and tilting his head back, I blow into his mouth. Then again.

But Jack doesn't rouse. Not that I expected him to.

'Here,' says Carly. 'Let me.' I clear out of the way and watch as Carly mimics my actions but despite all Carly's efforts, it's pointless. Jack Peaks is dead.

'Leave it, Carly,' I say, placing a hand on Carly's shoulder. 'He's gone.' Carly stops and twists to look up at me. The actress's face is pink with the effort of pumping his chest. She nods at me, a mutual understanding. We both know that there is no saving him.

'Gone? No. He can't be. Oh my God. Oh my God.' Rosalind's voice is strangled and she slumps to her knees; her breathing becomes so fast and ragged that she's in danger of hyperventilating.

'But I only chatted to him yesterday,' mutters Valentina, her lip trembling. 'He was drunk. So, so drunk.'

I glance at her; I never understand why people say that – *I only saw them yesterday* – as if those who are about to fall victim to an accident would have the aura of tragedy about them.

I don't point this out, of course. It isn't the time; it's never the time. People say these things for a reason – it's a way of coping with their shock. The very fact that I have the presence of mind to point out the illogicity of said statement puts me in the minority, not the other way around.

Slow footsteps pad across the grass behind our huddled group. We all turn to see two men. The two men that survived the night. Mo walks towards us accompanied by Daniel. The former is dressed in black linen pyjamas, the latter fully dressed with his camera strapped around his waist. The red 'on' light flickers from the top of the camera.

'Good morning, ladies,' says Mo, his mouth breaking into a smile, clearly missing the true horror of the scene. 'How are we—' His smile drops as quickly as it came. Both men stop short, metres away from the group of women clustering around the body of Jack Peaks. 'What the fuck is going on?' Mo says instead.

'He's dead,' whispers Valentina, not taking her eyes off Jack's body.

'Dead?' asks Mo, his face slackening. 'Jack's dead? What the fuck happened?'

'We don't know,' replies Rosalind, getting to her feet and running shaking hands through her hair. 'I should call an ambulance. Yes, I'll do that, I'll call an ambulance. Oh God, I can't remember the emergency numbers. Where's Sophia? She'll know.'

'A doctor isn't going to help Jack now. We need the police, Rosalind.' I speak in a calm but assertive voice, the one I've used so many times before. Jack is dead so unless the nearest hospital employs Dr Frankenstein, Jack will remain dead.

'Can you turn the camera off?' I snap at Daniel; I can't allow him to film this.

Despite my tone, he shakes his head, pulling me an apologetic look as if to say, *I'm sorry but I have to*. I scowl at him; maybe he isn't the nice guy I thought he was.

'He was so drunk last night. He must have fallen in the pool and drowned,' says Carly.

I stare at Carly, perplexed. Carly's voice lacks any real empathy and her face isn't contorted in horror or shock like the others. And, despite being the one who attempted to resuscitate him, Carly Chu clearly isn't rattled, upset or, apparently, even surprised by the death of Jack Peaks.

My first reaction is to protest Carly's assertion, but I stop myself. It doesn't feel right to disagree and something tells me that I should keep my suspicions close to my chest for now. At least until the police arrive. Whenever that might be, given how far we are from the mainland.

Keeping my face as neutral as possible, I drop to my knees, feigning a need to be closer to Jack. I press my fingers against his neck to check for a pulse I know I won't find. Nothing. I reach out my hand and grasp his, giving it a squeeze. His hand is cold to the touch. None of the others question my motives; they assume I want to hold his hand, to provide him some comfort, but I don't want to hold Jack's cold hand, I want to look for proof that my suspicions are right.

Dead bodies found floating on the surface of the water are unlikely to have drowned, especially if they're face down. As someone drowns their lungs fill with water and they sink, at least in the short term. Bodies that float are usually dead when they hit the water. It was one of the first lessons I learned in my old job. My old life. If Jack didn't drown, then something else killed him but I'm not sure what.

My stomach knots as I draw my eyes closer to Jack. The first body I ever saw was of a child who'd drowned; since then, I've always been repulsed by the puckering and wrinkling of water-exposed skin. It's other-worldly, like a creature out of a sci-fi film.

My eyes continue to scan Jack's body. There's no blood or obvious markings so he wasn't strangled or beaten, plus if he had been I'm sure we would have heard it. Sure, Jack was drunk last night but he's a big man and is unlikely to have gone down without a fight. So if not that, then what? I check the pockets of his sodden trousers but they're empty. I don't know what I'm looking for, though I'm sure I will when I find it.

There's nothing suspicious around Jack's body or within my current sightline but there must be something, some clue as to what killed him. The eyes of the others are on me as I crawl on my hands and knees around the pool. The sun loungers are bare of cushions, allowing the sunlight to shine through the slits and illuminate that there is nothing beneath them, and neither is there anything hidden behind or wedged underneath the umbrellas.

The decking is clear. I get to my feet, step onto the grass and return to my crouching position. It's hard to see objects that might be hidden because of the grass's length so I comb my hand through it like I'm petting a dog. My fingers collide with something solid and I grab whatever it is, holding it in my outstretched palm.

A double-sized shot glass, like the ones Valentina and I drank vodka out of last night. Except this glass didn't serve vodka, for clinging to the bottom of it are remnants of a lurid coloured liquid, a bright blue like the sky above us. Bringing the shot glass to my nose, I sniff: the smell is sweet and sickly. If it is what I think it is then this is what killed Jack, and if it is what I think it is then someone must have given it to him. Jack might have been a bit stupid and was very drunk but shooting anti-freeze doesn't seem like something he would do.

'Who gave him this shot?' I ask, holding it out to the others, who all still stand around Jack's body.

'Not me,' says Mo. 'Last night, I was doing whatever I could to avoid that bastard.' We all gaze at him in disbelief; his face screws up and his cheeks flush when he realises what he has said. 'I mean, avoid that guy. Shit, sorry. I didn't mean anything by it.'

'It wasn't me,' says Rosalind, turning back to look at me. 'I didn't even know you were all doing shots.'

'I only did one shot last night and that was with you, Kim,' says Valentina.

'Do you think that's what did it?' says Carly and I twist around to look at her; she nods towards the glass. I feel my eyebrows furrow. Carly's face is impassive so it's impossible to tell if it's a genuine question asked with the complete absence of any emotion or a pointed question that hopes to pass Jack's death off as one shot of alcohol too many.

The others are all now looking at me, waiting for me to reply to Carly's question. As I return their look, they all change subtly beneath my gaze as the reality of what this is sinks in.

'Hard to say,' I lie because instinct tells me that there's no point upsetting anyone with accusations of murder. But that's what this is, isn't it? Murder. 'But,' I say, continuing, 'I assume until a proper investigation has been done we can't be sure.' I stand up, my hands on my hips. Again, I appraise the group. Every movement of their faces, every glance of their eyes, every twitch of their hands could be a sign of guilt. Everyone has a tic, a tell that gives them away.

Someone gave this shot to Jack, probably passing it off as some sort of sweet liquor, and given our current location, that can mean only one thing: someone here is responsible for his death. And like that, they're no longer my companions in the villa, they're no longer my competition for the *LoveWrecked* prize, they're not even Islanders any more. They're suspects.

One of them killed Jack Peaks, but who? And why?

Chapter Fourteen

'Rosalind, have you called the police?' I demand. It's frustrating to not be able to call them myself but Rosalind took our phones off us when we arrived yesterday, a part of the contract that is hugely problematic right now.

Jack Peaks is dead and if I'm judging the evidence correctly, dead at the hands of one of the others. The police need to get here as soon as possible because the longer it takes the police to arrive, the more contaminated their crime scene will become. Crime scenes are delicate things that need to be protected, though I fear this particular crime scene is already a lost cause. All of us, me more than most, have interfered in some way: stepping on the grass, touching the body, leaving our DNA all over the place.

I rub my temples, trying not to dwell on how alive my brain is. It feels like it's gleefully kicking off the dust that has settled on it over the last five years. I decide it's best not to think too deeply about how the death of this young man makes me feel more excited than I have in a long time.

'I'm trying my best,' says Rosalind, punching trembling fingers against the screen of her phone. 'But I can't seem to get a signal.' Her voice increases in pitch the longer she tries.

The rest of the group seem to vibrate with fear and anticipation as they watch Rosalind. They glance at one another, their faces blank and confused and I realise that they need me, they need to be guided through the next steps.

'What will happen now? To us?' asks Valentina to no one in particular. She crosses her arms across the top of her pink bikini; her short-cropped hair sticks out at all angles.

'Once we've spoken with the police and answered their questions,' I reply, 'we'll probably be sent home.'

'Why do we have to speak with the police?' asks Mo, his voice sounding more on edge than I suspect he wanted it to. 'I don't really want to speak with them. Especially not foreign police.'

'No, I don't particularly want to speak to the police, either,' says Carly, placing her hands on her hips. My nostrils flare.

'Given that a man is dead, and we were the last people to see him alive, it does seem like the logical next step that the police would want to speak with us,' I reply, hearing the sarcasm hanging on my words. My words come out ruder than I intended but I don't care.

Out of nowhere, Valentina takes a step towards Rosalind and starts shouting, flailing her arms about her. 'Why aren't you calling the police? Why aren't they on their way? We need them to come. Jack is dead and we might be in danger.' Her eyes dart about in all directions but, I notice, never landing on Jack's body. With every movement she makes, she inches further from it, desperate to get away.

'I can't get a signal,' cries Rosalind, jabbing the mobile frantically into the air. 'I'm trying, but I can't, I can't...' Her voice trails off as she dissolves into tears. The woman is ill-equipped to handle this situation. All of them are.

Valentina's cool I'm-a-DJ mask slithers to the floor and Mo is sweating in a way that seems to have nothing to do with the heat of the day.

But Carly is calm, eerily calm; her arms are folded across her chest now and her hip juts out to the side in a relaxed stance. She looks as if she is waiting for a bus and she has none of the intensity or jitteriness that's consuming the others.

'Rosalind,' I say, my voice low in an attempt to soothe, 'we all brought mobile phones with us when we arrived, didn't we?'

Rosalind nods and wipes her sodden cheeks with the material of her pyjama top. I doubt she will look back on this moment as her finest hour.

'Great,' I say instead. 'Where are they?'

'In the safe,' murmurs Rosalind.

'Perfect, could you take me there?'

I speak in the way one would speak to a particularly shy child; it's a voice I've used in many distressing situations before. Often people gripped in the throes of panic just need clear direction, gently delivered, and it seems that Rosalind is no different. She whispers in assent and shakes herself as if attempting to shake off her current state of being.

'I'm coming too,' says Valentina, starting forward to follow us. I sigh; as much as I find interfering annoying I don't have the energy to tell Valentina she can't come with us. Nobody put me in charge and I need to be careful about putting myself at the front and centre of all of this. I don't want people asking questions.

'OK, we three will go. Carly, Mo and Daniel, stay here. Whatever you do, do *not* touch anything. The police are going to need this area as undisturbed as possible.'

Carly, Mo and, to my relief, Daniel nod. I smile, relieved they didn't protest. But why would they? They are all in shock. Well, Mo is at least. I don't know what Carly and Daniel are. I turn my back on them and follow behind Rosalind and Valentina, in search of some way to escape this place.

We walk past the table where we congregated last night. When we first arrived. When all five of us Islanders were alive. I shiver and pull my eyes away from it. We enter the main body of the villa and walk down the corridor. We walk in silence. I have nothing to say. Neither, it seems, do the other two.

Someone killed Jack. One of our group killed Jack.

We are on an uninhabited island sealed in a walled complex. It has to have been one of them; who else could it be? *This isn't your problem*, I tell myself.

And it's true, it isn't my problem. I will do what I can to get the police to the scene and keep everyone calm but once the police arrive it is their problem, their investigation. I'll answer their questions and do my best to help them catch the killer and then I'll disappear.

Rosalind stops in the corridor facing a part of the wall that I wouldn't have noticed had my attention not been drawn directly to it. There are small slits cut into the wall and Rosalind pushes; the part of the wall she touches swings inwards. It's a door revealing another corridor behind. Though part of the villa complex, the producer's room would have been impossible to find without Rosalind's guidance. A secret corridor for a secret world. The world of off-camera.

'Wow,' says Valentina as we enter what I can only assume is the production room Rosalind mentioned last night. The room isn't small but the number of screens and vastness of the IT system dwarfs it; the sheer complexity of everything boggles my mind. There's a wide, black desk laden with keypads and buttons, above which two rows of screens run the full length of the wall, about twenty screens all representing different cameras dotted around the villa. It looks like most of them are outside: two overlook the gym; two more the kitchen; about six show various shots of the garden and seating areas; and another two of the screens seem to be placed inside the pool itself. This homage to Big Brother will surely make the police's life easier as Jack's demise will probably have been caught on camera.

Not your problem, I remind myself for the second time.

Rosalind heads straight for the far corner of the room and punches in the code. The safe's buttons light up at her touch and she presses the green arrow. I hold my breath; Rosalind's stress seems to radiate from her. It infects me, wrapping itself around my heart and squeezing until I feel it beat faster. I lean forward, ready to grab my phone as soon as the safe door swings open, I'm desperate to make a call to the police and then remove myself from the nervous energy that's in danger of consuming me. The safe makes a noise that says, *Wrong answer, try again*. I blow out air through my lips. This is painful.

'For fuck's sake, hurry up,' curses Valentina. The DJ's body vibrates as she too leans over Rosalind.

'Sorry, I must have— Let me— Sorry.' Rosalind trips over her words, her cheeks pink with fluster. She tries again but this time the safe beeps at her aggressively; she didn't wait the allotted time after a wrong attempt.

'Why this is so fucking hard for you?' spits Valentina through gritted teeth. The temperature in the room is rising rapidly.

'Valentina, this attitude isn't helping anyone,' I snap. 'Why don't you stand outside and wait for us? We will bring you your phone as soon as possible.'

Valentina scowls and rolls her eyes. 'I want my phone. Soon as I have my phone I can start arranging tickets out of this place. And I want to leave as quick as fucking possible,' she replies, placing emphasis on every word; it makes me want to slap her. Doesn't she realise that's what we all want to do? To get away from this moment and escape the horror of Jack's death.

Of course she doesn't. I narrow my eyes at Valentina but hold back my retort. I take a slow breath in through my nose and out through my mouth; I learned this once in a meditation class. The meditation classes that I'd reluctantly agreed to on my mum's instance, the meditation classes that failed to help ease my dreams and relax my days.

I don't want to snap at Valentina; the short-tempered DJ is stressed, that much is obvious.

Ding.

The safe clicks open and Valentina springs forward, pushing Rosalind aside to snatch her phone.

The scream that follows forces me to stuff my fingers in my ears.

'Who did this?' shouts Valentina. 'Was this you? Why would you do this?'

Valentina whirls round to face us; the DJ's cheeks are flushed with anger and her chest heaves up and down with heavy breaths. My stomach squeezes at what she presents. Valentina holds in her hand her mobile, or at least what was once a mobile phone. The screen is shattered, and the back hangs off it.

I lunge forward to reach my own hand into the safe. A sharp prick stabs my finger and I pull back with a yelp. What the hell was that? Droplets of fresh, red blood appear on the tip of my finger; a small shard of glass is wedged in my skin. Gritting my teeth, I pull out the glass. Shit. Valentina's phone isn't the only one destroyed: every phone in the safe has been smashed to pieces.

Dread slides down my throat like an ice cube. The instinct that I cultivated during my years in the police force awakens from its slumber and rings the alarm of danger. A dead body and five smashed mobile phones? This is no coincidence.

'Rosalind,' I bark. 'Give me your phone.' She hands it to me without question. I pull off the cover and unclip the back. 'Shit.'

'What? What is it?'

'There's no signal because there's no SIM card. Who apart from you has access to this safe?'

Rosalind pulls herself up into the producer's chair and tilts her gaze to meet mine. Her lips quiver and her cheeks have drained of colour.

'Err…' She sniffs, picking at a loose piece of skin around her fingernail. 'Me, I have access.'

'Apart from you.' This is important; doesn't she understand how important this is? I work to keep my voice calm now – I can't lose my cool.

'In my team, Sophia is the only person who'd have access.' Rosalind's brow furrows. 'But it can't have been

Sophia. Why would she do this? Why would she smash our phones? Unless, unless...'

The dread travelling through my body hits my stomach with a clunk.

'Unless she gave Jack the shot that killed him and has smashed our phones and taken all our SIM cards to stop us contacting anyone,' I say, finishing her sentence.

Chapter Fifteen

I rub my forehead, as if trying to rub out the furrow of confusion that knots my brow.

One of the first rules of being a good detective is to never let your own emotions be visible and I'm teetering on the edge of breaking that rule; thoughts swirl in my head.

Did Sophia really kill Jack and smash our phones to allow herself more time to get away? That's what the evidence is loosely pointing to right now. But no, I can't think that; there's still so much that's unknown.

Why would Sophia poison Jack? Why would she do it here at the villa? Surely that would put herself too much at risk. I do wish I knew where she was; her absence certainly looks suspicious, but maybe she isn't absent. Maybe she is still here on the island, with us.

I feel as if someone is hugging me so tightly that I can't breathe, like they've wrapped their arms around my chest and are squeezing tighter and tighter. My chest rises and falls raggedly as I try to fight against the imaginary grip. My body grows hot; I need to get out of this villa, I need to get away from whatever the hell is going on here.

'We need to get back to the others,' I bark.

Valentina, who is staring wide-eyed at her smashed phone, jumps backwards at the sharpness of my words. I don't have time for this. I storm out of the producer's room and gesture for them to follow me. The villa's corridors are as empty as they were before so if Sophia is hiding somewhere in here she's doing an excellent job.

Outside, Mo, Carly and Daniel sit on the tiered decking that encircles the unlit Fire Pit. The sun blazes down from the clear blue sky, fiery and merciless but, despite the sun's cruel heat, the three of them seem to have barely moved a muscle since we left them. They sit stock still, all staring in different directions with glazed expressions; they're like waxworks of their former selves. They're as calm as the water in the swimming pool now that it no longer houses a dead body. And until I know for certain what's going on, I'm not about to disturb that. Quickly, I decide to make up some excuse for the phones, maybe say that Rosalind couldn't remember the code.

I slow my approach as I near them. 'Everyone, I think we should—'

'Look,' screeches Valentina, holding forward the pieces of her broken mobile. I nearly kick her, then myself. Why didn't I brief Rosalind and Valentina first?

Mo and Carly turn their heads towards Valentina. Their eyebrows raise as if united in a single question. Daniel's face slips behind his camera, clearly deciding this is something he should capture. I can't allow her to announce this, not yet. Telling Mo, Carly and Daniel that someone has smashed our phones will cause pandemonium. I step in front of Valentina and mutter under my breath for her to keep quiet. Valentina ought to understand that we need more information before sending the others into a frenzy.

I don't think they can handle Jack's death coupled with this very evident sabotage.

'Look at this,' screeches Valentina again, wrenching her arm from my grip. I clench my fist, bracing myself for the reveal. 'They're smashed. Someone has smashed our phones. Sophia has smashed our phones.'

Mo jumps to his feet and peers into Valentina's hands. 'What are you talking about?'

'In the safe. Someone opened the safe, smashed our phones, and then locked them in there.'

'I don't understand,' says Mo.

'Sophia, the assistant, she has smashed our fucking phones,' screams Valentina, shoving the phone in Mo's face.

'But why?' Mo's face crumples into confusion. Valentina's response is to throw her phone across the garden; it separates into several pieces as it flies through the air. 'But why?' repeats Mo, directing his question towards me.

What am I meant to tell him? Telling him what I think would not only worry him but expose me as knowing more about death and murder than I want the Islanders to know. They'd ask me questions that I don't want to answer.

'Surely that's obvious,' says a curt voice. I turn to Carly as she speaks. 'Our phones have been smashed because someone doesn't want us to contact anyone.'

'But why?' repeats Mo. I grit my teeth; his idiocy threatens to turn him into somewhat of a broken record.

'Because,' I sigh, cutting in before Carly can deliver the blow more brutally than I would like, 'because I think that Jack's death wasn't an accident. I think he was murdered with poison disguised as a shot. I think there's a strong possibility that whoever gave him the shot pushed him in the pool to cover up what they did and make it look like he drowned. And I also suspect that whoever did this to Jack wants to delay us contacting the police.'

As I speak, I can almost see my words whistling like a grenade; they shoot from my mouth and settle slowly on the grass. I can almost hear the explosion as the grenade blasts us all with the weight of the truth.

Silence follows my pronouncement. The type of silence that film and television directors use seconds after a bomb is detonated. When the scene keeps on moving but the sound is cut as the characters react to what has just happened to them.

It is no different here, in the *LoveWrecked* villa.

'What?' screeches Valentina, the first to break the oppressive quiet. 'What the hell are you talking about?'

'No,' says Mo, shaking his head at me as though I'm completely mad. 'That's not possible.' He paces back and forth as he lets my words sink in. 'He was murdered? So, someone killed him? On purpose?'

'Yes, Mo. Someone killing someone else on purpose is the usual definition of "murdered",' snipes Carly. Mo turns to face her, his jaw set, his anger at her sarcasm oozing from him. 'Oh my God, stop being so dramatic,' she adds. The hand I've looped around Rosalind's shoulders is shaken free as Rosalind drops her head into her hands and sobs. I replant my hand on this wreck of a woman, more tightly now for fear she might collapse. The air in the space between us all seems to tighten, their tempers rising in line with their fear. They need me to keep the peace, though I don't relish the role of nanny.

'Carly, please,' I urge. 'Mo is in shock.'

'In shock? Of course I'm in fucking shock.' Mo directs his attack at me but I don't even flinch; there's no real anger in his tone, just fear. 'You've just told me Jack was murdered and whoever did it wants to stop us from getting help.'

'I want to get out of here,' wails Valentina. 'Now!'

'Everyone, please calm down and listen to me.' I release Rosalind and step up onto the seating, raising my head above the others. I try to sound commanding, but it doesn't matter; they all ignore me.

'I'm with Valentina. Where are the exits?' growls Mo. 'Rosalind, how do we get out of here?'

'Show us,' snaps Valentina. Rosalind nods and looks at me with tear-filled eyes as if seeking my approval for her next move.

'OK, everyone,' I say, deciding it is best to follow the will of the many on this. 'If we are going, I think we should go there together.' Something tells me that it would be a mistake to leave anyone alone right now.

I lead the way accompanied by the direction of Rosalind. The others – Carly, Valentina, Mo and Daniel – follow behind. My insides fizz as adrenaline courses through me and my skin tingles as if the nervous energy from the rest of the group bounces off their skin and converges to enclose me in a bubble of anxiety.

Keep calm. They need you to keep calm.

Right now, I'm the glue keeping everyone together. If I expose my concerns that exiting may not be as easy as we hope then everything will descend into chaos. Though I know if we reach the gates and my concerns are real, it's going to descend into chaos regardless.

With Rosalind's direction, I lead the group through the villa, past the door to the producer's corridor, and along the white corridor through which we came on our first day.

Yesterday. Our first day on this island, in this villa, was yesterday. Only yesterday and yet a lifetime seems to have passed me by. Even back then, despite the luxurious and modern feel, the white walls with their clean lines and minimalist style have felt hospital-like but now the feeling twists and intensifies and it's like I'm walking down the hall of an asylum, one from which it is impossible to escape. Our group proceeds down the corridor in silence, the only sound coming from the hum of the air conditioner and our bare feet connecting softly with the smooth marble tiles.

At the end of the corridor, there is a sliding door made entirely of glass; I remember it from when we arrived. I wrap my fingers around the handle and heave. Some of the tension in my shoulders releases as the door slides open without a problem; it rolls smoothly on its tracks, unleashing the heat of the Mediterranean air as it does so.

I step out of the villa and onto the flagstones that make up the perimeter of the complex.

The air is thick with the honeyed scent given off by the trees which surround us. This sweet smell reminds me of holidays I've taken in the past, of relaxing summers long gone. A smell that signalled warmer climes and a week in the sun, but that was before our nostrils were stuffed with the whiff of death.

Directly ahead of me are the solid gates. The gates, like the walls, give no view of the world outside. My heart picks up its pace and the nausea I felt this morning following our long evening of merriment and heavy drink washes over me. What I wouldn't give to just go back to bed and hope that when I wake this will all be over.

On the left side of the main gates there is a square hut and I think that if this hut mimics a security hut, then not only will it be possible to exit through it but also the switches needed to swing open the electric gates will be accessible here. I proceed towards it; this is our best hope of escape. The immediate door of the hut poses no problem and a quiet giggle escapes my lips. Perhaps this isn't going to be as bad as my gut first thought. I jerk open the door and step inside.

The sight that greets me makes my legs wobble and I press my back against the wall to stop myself from crumbling. This cannot be real.

The switchboard which controls the movement of the electric gates from inside the villa complex is a mess of wire and plastic. Buttons litter both the wooden table and the floor, ripped from their position and tossed carelessly aside.

This is sabotage.

My life experience has made me hypersensitive to danger and right now, my senses are screaming their alarms.

'What? What is it?' calls Rosalind, her head floating from outside the hut, the bevelled glass distorting her face.

'Stay outside,' I say, raising a hand to stop them entering. I can't let them see this. I try to control my breathing; they're all watching me, watching my reaction. I stride towards the other door of the hut, the door that would allow me to exit the complex. *Please let me be wrong, please let the door open.*

But I shouldn't have doubted my instincts. I don't even need to try the door handle because the door handle isn't there; the door has been locked and the handle ripped off. With no handle and no switchboard, there's no way we're getting out from this part of the villa. I lick my dry lips and swallow. How the hell am I going to break this news to the Islanders? I can't predict how they're going to react to this but whatever their reaction, it won't be pretty.

'What's going on in there?' Mo shouts, his voice conveying anger I haven't seen in him before. I close my eyes and take a deep breath. Minimally more centred, I exit. Four sets of eyes and the lens of a camera stare at me as I walk towards them. How should I tell them? What words can I use to explain this?

'We're...' I start but my voice trails off. I can't bring myself to say that we're trapped, that someone has trapped us. We are, in fact, being held hostage. Probably by the same someone who killed Jack. Up until this moment, I've remained calm for the most part. My previous experience means I've been in danger before. A dead body and smashed phones weren't enough to scare me. But this? This incarceration in a villa that has borne witness to a murder is entirely new and the fear that has engulfed most of the others since discovering Jack catches me. All the signs of panic are there: my breathing is quick and jagged; sweat gathers in my palms; and my heart drums against my chest. I want to speak but I'm frozen.

'We're what?' snaps Valentina, her eyes wide. I shake my head; my lips tremble. I can't answer. I don't want to tell them, I don't want to have to say it out loud. Mo pushes past me, bumping my shoulder as he marches into the hut.

'Oh my fucking God,' he roars.

'What? What, Mo? What's in there?' cries Valentina but Mo doesn't answer her. All that can be heard is the banging and I peer in to see Mo throwing his body against the door.

'Mo, don't do that, you might hurt yourself,' I say, knowing he isn't strong enough to fix this. There is nothing he can do but he doesn't listen to me.

'I have to do something, I have to get us out,' says Mo as he storms out of the security hut, past the group, and back towards the villa. We watch him go, open-mouthed but unable or unwilling to stop him.

He returns moments later, a bar stool raised high over his head.

I stand motionless watching him as he hurls the stool at the outside door. Again. And again. And again. It's like he is in a trance as he tries and fails to make any impact on the outer door.

'What about the walls?' asks Valentina as if deciding to ignore Mo and let him wear himself out with thrashing. I know why she's asking. It is our last hope but it's nothing short of hopeless. The walls are too high and covered in hedges that would only hinder our ability to clamber over.

'No, I think it's impossible. I think we're—' I pause, composing myself for the announcement. 'We're trapped.'

Chapter Sixteen

LoveWrecked @LoveWrecked
1.35m followers

Share your thoughts on this year's season of
LoveWrecked.

@Scandalina: Hey @LoveWrecked, where
have all the Islanders gone? The live feeds are
just showing an empty garden and that isn't
exactly entertainment.

@trashqueen2000: @Scandalina Err…
shouldn't we be more concerned that one of
them is dead?

@Scandalina: Oh, come on @trashqueen-
2000. Jack Peaks isn't dead.

@Judgeinthevilla: I'd stay tuned if I were you,
things are about to get MUCH more enter-
taining.

Chapter Seventeen

Kimberley

Sunday 27th July, 11:21

'We're trapped?' asks Rosalind. 'No, we can't be trapped.'

Mo emerges from the security hut, his brow slick with sweat, his chest heaving as he gasps for breath. The bar stool hangs limply at his side.

'I can't do it. The bloody door won't budge an inch. You saw how long I was trying for, no amount of force will make it move.' Mo wipes his forehead with his sleeve. 'Look, Daniel, I know you have a job to do but, seriously, Jack is dead, and we're trapped here meaning we can't get any help so would it be much trouble for me to ask you not to point that camera in my face? In fact, I think it would be best for everyone if you just turned it off.' Daniel swivels the camera away from Mo but doesn't immediately turn it off. 'What is wrong with you?' asks Mo, charging past Daniel and back towards the villa.

There's silence for a moment and then Valentina launches herself at Rosalind, grabbing handfuls of her pyjamas.

'Sort this out,' she screams, 'this is your villa, your show. I want to go home.' Rosalind tries and fails to bat Valentina off with cries that she didn't have anything to do with this.

I reach to catch Valentina's arm in my hand, but it swings round and collides with the side of my jaw.

'Help me,' I say, turning to Daniel. He swivels his camera away from his face, leaving it suspended to the side, and steps forward. His strong arm wraps fully around Valentina's tiny waist and he pulls her from Rosalind.

'Easy now,' he whispers to her as if trying to calm a startled horse. She looks up at him, her eyes glistening with tears, and turns away, readjusting her bikini and smoothing down her hair. Carly stares at her with a look of complete horror, seemingly unable to contemplate how one could lose their cool quite so dramatically.

'Sorry,' mutters Valentina, her back still to Rosalind. The producer goes to reply but I decide to step in; I don't want Rosalind to say anything that might set Valentina off again.

'Look, everyone. Let's go back inside and calm down. Can we do that?' I ask. They nod. 'Despite what it looks like, I'm sure that everything will be OK.' I give them all a tight smile. 'People know where the villa is. So even though we can't reach the outside world, the outside world knows we're here.'

If, as I suspect, Jack's death has been broadcast to the entire nation, surely someone will be on their way to rescue us? Plus, there are many more Islanders and a handful of crew arriving on the island today. Although the dark voice inside of me isn't convinced that the other Islanders are real.

Luckily, the reminder that people know where we are and that there are others on their way, combined with the tiredness that often accompanies intense emotion, seems to placate the group and, eventually, Valentina, Carly, Rosalind and Daniel retreat, defeated but resigned, to the

Fire Pit area where we find Mo already sitting, his head wedged between his knees.

So exhausted is the mood by this point that neither Daniel nor Mo protest when I ask them to move Jack's body. I'm grateful they don't argue and I'm equally grateful that the villa has a commercial-sized walk-in freezer. The intense heat wouldn't be good for it and whilst the cold temperature of the freezer won't stop his decomposition, it will certainly delay it.

Once this is done, we sit. Together. In silence. A sombre group whose feelings are completely incongruous with the gloriousness of the day.

How can the sun continue to shine even over this?

But I can't settle, so instead I pace around the garden trying lift some of the thick fog clouding my brain.

Pop.

I whirl around as the sound cracks through the air, disturbing the silence that has hung over us for hours.

'Help us,' someone shouts. 'Send help. Please.'

The five of them, Mo, Carly, Rosalind, Daniel and Valentina, are now on their feet, chattering as a single body towards the giant outdoor television screen. My jaw drops when I see what has roused them.

The screen has, somehow, switched itself on and is displaying a single image.

Facing directly into the camera is a person. A person that seems to be dressed in dark, flowing robes with thick shoulders and a white wig that rises high on their head, its curls draping over their shoulder. It looks to me as if they're dressed as a court judge, though it's been a long time since I've been in a courtroom. My eyes widen as I take it all in; there's something both cartoonish and extremely disturbing about the image. But worst of all is

97

the judge's face, or more appropriately their lack of face. It's impossible to tell who this person is because they're lit entirely from behind, meaning their face is in complete darkness.

'Who are you?' asks Mo, approaching the screen.

My shoulders tighten and my hands ball into fists; whoever this judge is, something tells me they are not a friend.

'Who are you?' asks Rosalind, as if Mo hasn't spoken. 'Where are you?' She too takes a step towards the television.

'Hey,' chimes in Valentina, clearly feeling the need to say her piece. 'Whoever you are please, help us. We're trapped here. Send the police. Send anyone! Jack's dead.' Her voice breaks when she mentions Jack and she stretches out her arms as she pleads.

I can't figure out if the person on the screen can hear us for they show no sign that they can. Their body doesn't move in reaction to the words directed towards them and, as it's impossible to see their face, there's no way other way of knowing. From their words and body language, all of the other Islanders seem convinced that this person is here to save us but I get the overwhelming sense that they'll be disappointed. My gut tells me that whoever this person is they are most definitely not our saviour. My skin prickles as the hair on my arms stands on end.

'Please sit down,' says the judge person, without acknowledging the entreaties coming from within the villa. I narrow my eyes at the menace in the voice. It's a male voice and now not only am I certain he isn't our knight in shining armour, something tells me he is quite the opposite. The others take their seats in a semi-circle around the Fire Pit, immediately obedient, but I ignore his request, I don't like where this is headed.

'Please sit down, I'm going to tell you what will happen next,' says the judge, a bit more forcefully this time. But I again don't listen, I refuse to be compliant like the others. I'm not taking orders from him. So instead of sitting down, I take a step forward closer to the screen.

'Oi, can you hear us?' I ask him, waving at the screen. The judge's head tilts downwards at his lap.

'Please sit down, I'm going to tell you what will happen next,' he repeats. He has either chosen to ignore me or he can't hear me.

'Can you hear us? Can you see us?' I ask. I'm right next to the screen now.

'I said, sit down,' growls the judge; his tone is sharp. So, he can hear me. My lip curls; why is he ignoring us? Fingers tug at my wrist.

'Sit down,' hisses Mo. Mo's face is drawn, the desperation for me to obey writ large in the fear in his eyes. I don't want to be ordered around by this faceless man, but I also don't want to upset the others. So, I oblige.

'Thank you,' says the judge figure. He clears his throat and continues, 'Islanders, as you may have already gathered, the villa has been locked down.' My fellow Islanders nod at his words. Next to me, Mo's fists unclench as the words boom around the garden; Valentina exhales loudly and leans back against the seating; and Carly's lips push outward into a pout. They're all letting their guard down; they don't think this is real; they think this is nothing more than a *LoveWrecked* challenge.

I don't unclench. I'm still on high alert and Rosalind, the person who would know if this was a challenge, mirrors my tension. I hold my breath as the judge holds his pause. An imaginary drumroll sounds in my head.

'The cameras are rolling, and this is being watched live by over half a million people.' The judge's voice quavers just a fraction at this as if he too is nervous. 'But before I continue, Daniel Oni – switch your camera on, I want to make sure we catch this all in the best possible way.'

Daniel turns to look at Rosalind; he raises a questioning eyebrow to her. Rosalind's expression is blank, and she shrugs. Maybe the others were right, and I was wrong. Maybe this is a challenge. But if it is, Rosalind and Daniel don't seem to know anything about it.

Daniel flicks a switch and the red light of his camera comes on.

'Thank you, Daniel, and thank you, Islanders, for joining me in the Fire Pit. I am the Judge and I'm pleased to make your acquaintance. You, on the other hand, may be less pleased to make mine.' The Judge clears his throat. 'Jack Peaks is dead. Jack Peaks was murdered.'

The gasps of the Islanders come in unison. Valentina's fingers squeeze around my arm, and I exhale slowly as the shock ripples around the group. Even though I knew this to be the truth, to hear it spoken aloud is like a slap in the face; heat flares in my cheeks.

'What the hell is going on?' I whisper, but my question remains unanswered as the Judge ploughs on with his statement, speaking over the cries of fear and sadness that surround me.

'Kimberley King,' says the Judge, his pixelated face pointing vaguely in my direction. I snap upright as my name reverberates around the garden.

Oh my God, is he going to pin this on me? Is he going to announce that I killed Jack?

All the other Islanders seem to think the same. Valentina slides a couple of centimetres away from me. My heart pounds against my chest. The Judge said my name.

Why did he say my name? I don't have anything to do with this. Do I?

Before I can question him, the Judge continues.

'Kimberley King, did you know that, in the UK, only 8 per cent of crimes are solved?' I look up at him. Of everything he could have said, I didn't expect that. '92 per cent of reported crimes go unsolved and, therefore, unpunished. We cannot let Jack Peaks be among that statistic; I refuse to let that happen. So, Kimberley, as the former police officer among us, I need your help. Everyone in this villa has secrets but one of them is keeping it secret that they killed Jack. It is your task to find out who murdered Jack Peaks. And you must do it live. On television.'

Chapter Eighteen

Spyland.co.uk — News, Scandals and all the latest Gossip from your favourite celebrities

BREAKING NEWS: Islanders held hostage in REAL nightmare scenario

Posted on Sunday 27th July at 11:39 a.m.

Footage, streamed live from *LoveWrecked* villa, seems to show that Islanders are being held hostage following the death of Jack Peaks. An unknown person dressed as a court judge took control of the video feed to announce that Jack Peaks was murdered, and that Kimberley King is tasked with solving the crime.

It is unclear why Kimberley King has been chosen to complete the challenge, but rumour is that before becoming a barmaid, she served for a number of years as a police officer, though her reasons for leaving the force remain unknown. We'll keep digging, don't worry.

ChannelUK, the broadcasting channel of *LoveWrecked*, have blocked the video stream but channels such as Channel Z continue to broadcast this despite the show's producers urging them to take it down. It is unclear how Channel Z have been able to access the footage but we're sure it won't be long until they too are forced to remove it.

All major news channels are now reporting the story as a crisis and just minutes ago the Minister for Foreign Affairs announced that both the British and Greek governments are involved.

Greek police were sent to the address that *LoveWrecked*'s management team had as the villa's location, but the police were greeted with a rustic-style farmhouse, nothing like the villa shown on our screens and, according to reports, empty. Furthermore, sources have told us that the company who rented the villa to *LoveWrecked* have been questioned by police but they vowed that they had no idea that the villa was not being used due to the no-greet check-in facility. Even the livestream is providing no clues to their whereabouts; the high hedge and specific focus of the camera makes it impossible to pick up features which may distinguish the island.

Though we know the Islanders flew into Heraklion Airport, Greece is made up of thousands of islands (depending on which estimates you look to, anything between 1,200 and 6,000) and there is nothing to say if they are on an island near Crete or whether they've ventured further afield.

The Islanders are, therefore, being held captive in an unknown location.

Fans remain unconvinced that this is reality and continue to share their excitement at this new and immersive challenge. #Love-Wrecked is the top trending hashtag on social media. Plan or not, the producers got their wish: this is the most talked-about show in the world right now.

SpyLand will keep you informed as the situation progresses.

Comments section

@Scandalina: THIS IS THE BEST SEASON EVER!!! #LoveWrecked #realitytv

@dangerousgrl: WTAF?!?! Is this real or not?

Chapter Nineteen

Kimberley
Sunday 27th July, 11:40

The words blare out from the television screen and seem to smash against my body like a freight train. My body throbs from the impact.

What did he just say?

Silence hangs in the air like a noxious gas. In unison, my fellow Islanders' heads spin around so fast they're at risk of whiplash; all of their eyes are on me and somehow, through the lens of Daniel's blinking camera, I feel the eyes of the half-a-million-strong audience burn into me. It's as if the audience are transported from their homes to sit among the other Islanders and stare at me. My cheeks warm under their piercing gaze and the movement of my chest rising and falling quickens as I breathe short, shallow breaths. The sound of the Judge's voice rings in my ears and seems to ping off every corner of my brain.

The Judge said Jack was murdered.

The Judge said my name.

He knows I used to be a police officer and he wants me to solve the crime live on television. What the fuck is going on?

'This doesn't make any sense,' I whisper. I shake my head, my body involuntarily rejecting him and his horrific instruction. My thoughts go from asking myself, *What is going on, what is happening?* to denouncing what I've heard, telling myself that no, this simply cannot be happening.

I get to my feet. I spin from left to right. I need to get away, away from the television screen, the cameras and the prying eyes of the Islanders.

I stumble as I career on trembling legs towards the kitchen. Step by step, I move away from the screen and the Judge's demands and from the stares of my fellow Islanders.

'What the hell is going on, Kim? Why does he want you to do this? What have you done?' asks Mo, standing by my side. When did he approach me? Despite his proximity, he sounds miles away.

My heart beats so loudly it pounds in my ears. It roars in my head, threatening to consume me. I reach out for the back of a nearby bar stool; the metal of it is cool against my sweating palm.

The analytical part of my brain, the part that singled me out for the fast track to detective, kicks into gear. I need to review the options.

Could this be a dream? I've had many vivid dreams in my life, particularly after I left the police force all those years ago. But those dreams were different to this. Dreams and nightmares are all-consuming, an experience that is somehow deeper than real life. No, this isn't a dream. I'm awake and experiencing this in the flesh.

Could this be a joke? A prank thought up by the producers? My brain changes tack. *LoveWrecked* challenges are infamous in their complexity, something which gets the British nation excited like nothing else. And if it is a challenge, then none of this is real. Jack's murder, the Judge, the request for me to investigate is all fake. Nothing more than a set-up.

They said this would be a series to remember, nothing like anything that had gone before. My breathing momentarily eases and the heartbeat I feel in my throat slows.

But the moment of respite is short-lived because the idea that this is made up doesn't fit either. Reality television producers will sink to deep depths to attract audiences; the plethora of horrendous reality shows available to the public testifies to that. But fake the death of one of the contestants – is that really something they would do?

I glance over at Rosalind. The seemingly sweet but out-of-her-depth producer of this year's *LoveWrecked* has broken into a fit of violent shivers completely incongruous to the ever-rising temperature of the Greek island. If this *is* a set-up, the *LoveWrecked* management team have neglected to bring Rosalind in on the deceit.

And then there's Jack. It might have been possible to fake a dead body for the other Islanders. There are some convincing dummies out there, or the producers could even have gone so far as to stick a golf ball under Jack's armpit, giving the illusion of his pulse stopping, falsifying his death for the uninitiated. Plus, for the inexperienced, even checking for a pulse is riddled with complications. When I found my first dead body, my heart raced so fast my fingers had their own heartbeat, so it was impossible to tell where my own pulse began and the girl's ended. I'm not 'the uninitiated'; I know a dead body when I see one and the body of Jack Peaks was real and very, very dead.

I came on this show for the chance to escape my past and the death it saw. I'm not going to relive it; I don't have the strength. Jack is dead and there's nothing I can do that will bring him back. There is no way in hell I will indulge the Judge in this game of his.

And even, even if I agreed to do it, could I do it? I must consider that my investigative skills are extremely out of practice.

No, I shouldn't even be thinking like this. I won't give into his demands. I won't.

The eyes of the Islanders bore into me; their stares sear my skin. No one says a word and I don't intend to be the one to break the silence first. I'm going to make myself a drink, a stiff one.

My fingers tremble as I unscrew the cap from the gin bottle and lift it to my lips. My stomach protests at the smell of it; I'm not even properly over last night's hangover.

'Hey, hey, easy now,' says Daniel in a gentle voice; he's pushed his camera away, so it isn't facing me. He tugs the bottle away from my lips and attempts to prise it from my fingers. Reluctantly, I give in.

My family might be watching and despite all I have done to them, I don't really want them to see me like this. My chest squeezes when I think about my family. When did I last speak to them? When did I last see them? It's funny that they should come to my mind now; I'm well practised at pushing them from my mind.

'Why is he asking this?' I whisper to him. 'This is fucking crazy. Why has he done this? Doing this?'

Daniel shakes his head, his eyes bloodshot and raw. 'I'm sorry. I don't know. I wish I knew.'

'I'm not doing it. He can't make me.' I welcome the squeeze that Daniel gives my hand. It's a show of solidarity and I'm grateful for it but he can't possibly understand.

I've been singled out for reasons I don't understand and as much as he wants to stand by me, I am completely alone.

'Come on, let's get back to the others,' says Daniel, pulling my hand and leading me back towards them.

Clammy hand in clammy hand, we walk across the grass. I focus on my feet, unable to meet the gazes of the others. I can't stand their watchful, questioning eyes.

Pop.

I jolt, stopping short as the screen turns itself on for a second time. My breath catches in my throat and my hand slips from Daniel's. I fold my arms across my chest; the only thing I can do to protect myself. It is the Judge, again.

A sheen of sweat gathers on my forehead but I resist the urge to wipe it away. I won't show the Judge how nervous he is making me.

'Hello, Islanders,' he says in a voice that may have been an attempt at mock cheeriness but instead sounds deranged. 'This is your presenter; you are live on most UK and international channels – please do not swear.' He chuckles humourlessly at the line made famous by one of the previous presenters of *LoveWrecked*. My face twists in disgust; the man is a monster.

'Let us out of here. You're fucking insane, let us go,' shouts Mo.

'Mo, Mo, Mo. You'd better watch that temper of yours. What will the viewers think? Talking of viewers, do you want to hear what the public have been saying about our little challenge, Kimberley?' The Judge pauses.

I ball my hands into fists and direct all my energy there; it's the only thing I can do to stop myself erupting into angry shouts. What do the public think of the challenge?

A man has been murdered. This isn't a challenge, this is torture.

'Great,' says the Judge, taking my silence as assent. 'Let me see.' The screen changes and the Judge's image is relegated to a small square at the bottom corner of the screen while the rest fills with comments from social media. My heart sinks as I read; half of the comments don't even make sense. The Judge's stunt has blown open the gate for the trolls and conspiracy theorists.

> @Givesacrap42: why's everything always hidden? bravo #LoveWrecked for exposing the abuse and corruption of the police

> @Thisis1984: @LoveWrecked is turning the tables. Instead of the police spying on us like they always do, we're spying on them. Taste of your own medicine #werewatching #georgeorwell #justice4Jack

> @Eyeofthetigger: Judge Justice slamming that gavel #thejudge #LoveWrecked

> @Scandalina: THIS IS ALL FAKE. It's a ploy to hook viewers. @LoveWrecked it's a rather desperate attempt but not gonna lie… lovin it

> @trashqueen2000: @Scandalina if this is staged, the Islanders are convincing actors

'It seems,' says the Judge, his image re-filling the screen, 'that #policetransparency seems to be the most popular hashtag at present and, despite the fact it doesn't really make sense, I'm also pleased to see that #judgejustice is doing respectfully well in the UK and America. All in all, the general public are pretty pleased that the realities of a police investigation will be streamed live, and they don't like all the secrecy. Oh, and for added fun, people have been sending in all of the examples where the police didn't serve them well and all the mistakes the police have made over the years. But we don't have all day to review those now, do we?'

Blood surges through me, warming my cheeks and ears and my whole body seems to vibrate with the fury of it. I can't stand here. I can't watch this. Listen to this.

I storm to the kitchen, grab an empty gin bottle and hurl it at the screen. The bottle shatters upon impact and the Islanders shield themselves from the shards of glass that fly through the air. I ignore their protestations and anger at my actions.

Me? They're annoyed at me? I've only thrown a bottle; I haven't killed anyone. As the hubbub quietens and the glass settles into the grass, I see the Judge's image wobble. The screen has cracked ever so slightly, but his image doesn't die. I've barely scratched him. I groan; my inability to hurt him riles me.

'My colleagues put their lives on the line every day. Every single bloody day to protect the public.' I'm shouting at the screen now. I don't care how I look. Deranged, probably. But the judge's outrageous accusations override everything else. 'They're only human. And they work all manner of hours, for barely any money. Why? Because they care.'

I shake off the hand that tries to pull me away from the shards of glass. So what if I'm in danger of standing on them? All I see is the Judge and my anger. 'They're not superheroes, they're people protecting people. Yeah, mistakes are made. But who are you to talk? You don't seem to be risking your own safety for anyone. You've even hidden your face to protect yourself. And do you know what? If the danger, the hours, the pay weren't bad enough, we must live with those mistakes. Carry them with us for the rest of our lives.'

My chest heaves as much from the emotion as from the effort of shouting. The Judge keeps his face neutral; his lips don't even twitch. As if he's just waiting for me to burn myself out.

'Thank you for that, Kimberley. You've hit the nail on the head when you said we live with our mistakes. Will you be able to live with the mistake of not accepting this challenge?'

'What do you mean?' I ask, my breathing still heavy. 'I don't see it as a mistake to not accept your horrid, distasteful challenge. I don't want to play your game.'

'That's where you're wrong,' he says with all the glee of a magician pulling a rabbit out of a hat. 'Drumroll please. The longer it takes Kimberley here to solve the crime… the more people will die. It is 12 p.m. Kimberley King, you have one hour to find out who killed Jack Peaks or you'll find another of your number dead. Start the clock.'

Chapter Twenty

The villa changes before my eyes. The sun is too hot, the grass too perfect and too green. It's as though a monster has been unleashed. This villa, the place that was meant to be an escape, a last-ditch attempt to move forward with my life, a potential place of comfort and hope, has turned on me. Any final feeling that this might still be a joke evaporates. The Judge is out for blood and I'm the only person that stands in his way.

My head swims as the Judge's words swirl around inside me, ricocheting through me. It's as if I've been shot. I want to scream, to yell at the top of my lungs that I won't do this. The Judge can go to hell. But hell, it seems, has come to me.

Around me, all is chaos.

Rosalind clamps her hand over her mouth and falls to the ground, as if finally giving in to the emotions that have threatened to overwhelm her all morning. Tears stream down our producer's cheeks.

Valentina screams at the television screen, banging her tiny fists against it and begging the Judge to reconsider.

Carly's previously calm demeanour snaps and she stands by Valentina, their shouts mingling into one mighty roar.

A vein throbs so violently in Mo's neck that it threatens to explode.

And even Daniel, who dutifully followed the Judge's request to film, pulls his head away from the camera and swears loudly.

I want to curl into a ball and block out the sounds of their panic. Their screams of *why me, what have I done to deserve this*, make me want to jump in the pool, sink to the bottom and never resurface.

Space. I need space to think. But how can I do it when all around me is chaos? And what the hell am I meant to think about? The Judge, whoever the hell he is, wants me to solve a murder, live on television, and the longer it takes me to, the more people will die.

Rosalind told us when we first arrived that the villa was controlled by the producers, which means it is possible for someone else to take control. Plus, we've already discovered that we're trapped. Locked gates, high walls. There's no way out.

The air seems to press against my body making it hard to breathe. But it's the former police officer in me that stops me from flying off the handle, from reacting instantly to accept the Judge's demands.

I remember the acronym. The steps I must go through before responding. SARA: shock, anger, reflection, acceptance. Like the stages of grief, it isn't wise to respond when still gripped by the effects of shock and anger.

The garden, the source of the horror, isn't a place that will allow me to think clearly. I need quiet. I turn my back on the group and head in the direction of the bedroom. Fingers squeezes around my arm. I inhale sharply as Mo's strong fingers dig into my flesh. He's going to break my arm in two.

'Where are you going?' he says in a voice so full of nerves it pitches with every word. Grabbing my other arm, he pulls my face up close to his. The red wine he drank last night still lingers on his breath. I yank my arm, trying to twist away from him, but he grips tighter. He is too powerful.

'Let go of my arm, Mo,' I say, forcing my voice to remain calm. I don't owe him any explanation of where I'm going. This is my challenge, my lot, and I will handle it as I deem appropriate. It's nothing to do with him.

'Not until you agree to do this.' His fingers dig in deeper. I wince; his fingers are like hot brands burning my skin, his eyes are wild.

'Mo, let her go, you're hurting her,' says Daniel, appearing beside us. The camera pointed directly at Mo, like a weapon.

'Get that camera away from me. I've told you before,' he snarls at Daniel. I'm taken aback by the change in Mo. My first impression was of an even-tempered man but that is not what I see right now; now he is a man who has let fear control him. 'She has to agree to do this. We'll all be dead if she doesn't. You know that, right?'

'She will, Mo. Let her go,' says Daniel, taking a step backwards, one hand raised conciliatorily. His voice is soft as if talking to someone threatening to jump off a ledge.

'Will you?' hisses Mo, pulling me in tighter.

'Let me go. I won't talk to you until you let me go,' I reply.

I'm no coward and I won't be intimidated by his brawn. Does he think he is the first man to try and push me around? Mo surveys my face as if trying to assess how much of a flight risk I am. Not that it matters; we're trapped in here – doesn't he remember that?

Clearly deciding that I'm not a risk, Mo's fingers loosen, and I'm released from his bind. My shoulders sag a fraction and I rub my arm; that is going to bruise.

'Sit down, Mo,' I snap. 'And you, Carly.' Carly is hovering near us, watching our interaction. Both nod, responding to my authoritative tone. 'Rosalind, get up off the floor and go and sit down. I'll be with you in five minutes; I need to think. Then, we all need to talk.'

'And me?' asks Daniel.

'You just do what you've got to do,' I say to him as I walk away from them.

I pace around the pool. The rough decking, subjected to the intense rays of the sun, scorches the soles of my feet but I continue to walk. The sharp pain grounds me somehow and keeps my mind on track.

The game has changed. No longer is this about winning; this is about surviving. Something I'm well practised at, particularly recently. I also now realise that this isn't about me accepting the challenge. This isn't a case of *Do I want to do this or not*; that would never have been a choice. There are bigger things at play here. This is a plot, part of someone's masterplan. I glance over at the five people locked in the villa with me; they look back, waiting patiently for my instruction.

What more do they know? Who else is involved?

There is more than one crime and more than one culprit here. There is a murderer and there is a games master. Maybe they are one and the same, maybe they aren't, but I'm determined to find out. But I can't figure out whether finding Jack's killer will lead me to the real culprit. Or culprits.

'Kim?' Rosalind calls out from the other side of the pool. I raise my index finger at her.

One minute.

I'm not ready to face them yet. There is still one thing I need to accept. One important thing. I can't do this as the Kim I came into the villa as. The person I became as I tried to cope with the mistake I had made, the person who eventually turned her back on the police force. I changed then. I turned my back on the serious, driven, responsible officer and became Kim, the scatter-brained, reckless party girl. But I can't be her any more. She isn't someone who can deal with this sort of crisis. I need to try to emulate the woman I once was, and that woman wouldn't conduct a police investigation in wet pyjamas.

'Right,' I say, clapping my hands together and striding towards the Islanders. 'I need everyone to stay here and stay calm, I'll be back in five minutes.'

I ignore the blank looks on their faces and head to the bedroom. Grabbing my face wash from my pink, monogrammed make-up bag, I lean over the sink and remove the remnants of last night's make-up and scrub as if physically washing away my new self, allowing my old self to be revealed like the layers of wallpaper hidden for years unseen. I never have been one for make-up, really.

I stare at myself in the light-studded mirror under the golden lettering scrawled across it that proclaims the viewer as gorgeous. I can't believe I ever agreed to come here in the first place. The old Kimberley would be ashamed of what I've become. Who am I kidding? I'm ashamed of what I've become. It wasn't a quick transition to where I am now; it sort of happened in peaks and troughs. After the incident it became impossible for me not to think about, I stopped sleeping and my constant tiredness made me irritable and unable to concentrate at work. Colleagues noticed and tried to help; they meant well but they didn't understand. Leaving work somehow made things better and worse at the same time: I felt better because I knew I deserved to no longer do a job I loved, but I no longer had the stability of loyal colleagues or the routine of my shifts. Thread by thread, everything started to unwind.

I tear through my suitcase, cursing myself for not packing anything appropriate. Although what is appropriate in these circumstances? I settle on a pair of khaki cargo pants, pairing it with a black Lycra top. In an outfit that makes me feel more equipped to deal with the situation presented to me, I re-join the group. Carly is the only one who outwardly reacts to my mini transformation, giving me a half-raised eyebrow as I approach.

There's more where that came from. If my new attire surprises her, they're about to be even more surprised by the shift in my tone, my new seriousness. But then what else am I meant to do?

I walk towards them. Daniel's camera follows me as I walk; eventually he gets up and stands behind me. So the camera, like me, can take in the four people sitting before me.

The four others sit, their expressions running the gamut of human emotions. Anger, fear, suspicion, disbelief and, worst of all, hope. They're silent now, their wide eyes looking up at me. Silent, waiting for me to speak. As if what I'm about to say will solve the problem, calm their fears. But it won't, of course. I place my hands behind my back, so the others can't see me wringing them.

'This is a situation unlike one I have ever, ever been in. Even after being in the police force for almost seven years. As you may, or may not, have gathered, I used to be a police officer.' I clear my throat quietly. 'I left the police five years ago and have since been working as a barmaid.'

'Why did you le—' Mo tries to interrupt but I raise my hand to silence him. I'm not answering that question right now.

'If I'm completely honest with you all, I don't have a fucking clue what is going on, why it's happening or who is behind it. But if the Judge is to be believed, one of you committed this crime, one of you is capable of murder.'

Rosalind whimpers, Mo averts his eyes, Valentina fiddles with her necklace, Carly scoffs, and, most suspiciously of all, Sophia is still nowhere to be seen.

'*And* if the Judge is to be believed, the death of Jack Peaks wasn't an anomaly. There will be more. Whoever is doing this murdered someone and is threatening to murder again.'

'Will you do it?' asks Mo, his chestnut eyes wide. 'Will you try to solve it?'

'I will do what is asked of me because I have no choice.' The group lets out a collective sigh of relief like they've just received particularly important medical test results. 'But I'm going to lay down a couple of ground rules.' They look up at me with blank expressions. 'From now on I want complete transparency. From everyone. Anything you think you might know, anything you might have seen. Anything, no matter how small it might seem, I want you to tell me. Information is the most important asset we have at our disposal.' Sometimes asking for all information doesn't always yield the best results; it can be a real mixed bag. It often means wading through heaps of shit like finding a needle in a haystack. A haystack that is the boring, mundane details of people's lives. But sometimes, it is the smallest pieces of information that make the difference. The eureka moment. I allow this to percolate with them before continuing.

'I want you to all stay together from now on. At the very least in pairs. No one must go anywhere alone, understand?' They nod.

'OK, Kim,' says Mo, giving me a half smile, a kind one that shows willingness, not mal-intent, as if trying to make up for his past aggression. 'Whatever you need from me, I'm at your service.'

I nod at him in thanks and give him a tight-lipped smile. A smile that tries to hide the fact I have less than one hour to solve a murder with an audience of by now probably millions and absolutely no idea where to start.

Chapter Twenty-One

LoveWrecked @LoveWrecked
1.5m followers

Share your thoughts on this year's season of LoveWrecked.

@adammcboy: Does Kim seriously think she can change her hair and we'll suddenly believe she's a policewoman? What logic is that?

@safariprincess: Kim be like, I don't wear make-up now and that makes me a police officer.

Chapter Twenty-Two

I hold the shot glass in front of the group for the second time today. I realise that the best way forward is to keep things simple, be logical. I need to start at the beginning, at the thing that started this off.

'I am convinced that this is what killed Jack. The bright colour, the sweet smell could easily be mistaken for a sour shot, but I think it is something more dangerous, anti-freeze for example.'

Carly laughs. 'Anti-freeze. You do realise where we are?' She gestures her arms around us. 'It's Greece; where would we get anti-freeze from? I doubt it is something the villa just has.' Carly twists her body to look at Rosalind, who cowers under Carly's condescending gaze.

'Carly is right,' says Rosalind. 'Temperature is one thing but there isn't a garage here because cars can't come to the island so there'd be no need for it.'

I place my hands on my hips and pace up and down in front of the group; both arguments are compelling.

'So you're saying someone brought it with them?' asks Valentina, her voice coming out in a squeak. 'Because they wanted to kill Jack.'

'Or,' I reply, 'it is another substance entirely.'

I'm not an expert in the matter but if memory serves there are a whole host of household items that if administered would have exactly the same effect, that of poisoning. I rule out bleach, nail polish, cleaning fluids because the shot smelled sweet and alcoholic, not clinical.

'I didn't kill him,' says Mo, getting to his feet, 'but I know what it could have been.' Everyone turns to look at him and he clears his throat, obviously disliking the scrutiny. He takes a step closer to the Fire Pit and bends down to inspect its base. The Fire Pit comprises a square slab of stone upon which a smaller square, filled with charcoal, is cut out in the centre.

Mo stops and slides back a section of the stone base to reveal a cupboard which I assume was designed to house the things necessary to start the Fire Pit and keep it going.

'Is this what you're looking for?' asks Mo. In his hand is clasped a ribbed plastic bottle, three quarters of the way filled with bright blue liquid. Mo is holding fire starter gel. Colour-wise, it fits the bill. I take it from him and sniff; it smells sweet. If this is what killed Jack, which the evidence strongly points towards, then it means I can't rule out anyone yet. The Fire Pit is easily accessible to all of us and though it was Mo who pointed it out, that doesn't mean that one of the others doesn't secretly know the lethal qualities it has.

I also don't yet know where the Judge fits in; did he incite someone to murder in order to prepare the game for me or is an accomplice of the Judge among us who had their own reasons for killing Jack? Either way, I need to learn more about my suspects. I don't know anything about these people; not yet anyway. I head away from the group and beckon Rosalind over to me.

'How much information do you have on us, on the Islanders?' I ask, keeping my back to the group and my voice low. The microphones hidden around the garden might pick up my words, but I don't want the Islanders to know where I'm starting.

'I have files on everyone; they contain mostly background information,' says Rosalind, following my lead and turning away from the group. 'I don't know how much use they will be, but shows like this usually have files to help the producers to create...' Rosalind swallows. '...drama.' She finishes her sentence awkwardly and blushes as though ashamed of what she had planned to do.

'Great, please could you collect them for me?'

'Of course, whatever you need.'

'Bring them to the living room, that's where I will be. Oh, and some pens and sticky tape, if you have them.'

I enter the living room for the first time since arriving at the villa. Unlike the other areas, it remains in pristine condition, unsullied by us. The glass coffee table stands where I saw it yesterday. I almost laugh at how I was worried about one of us smashing it by accident; I realise now that the dangers were far less obvious than shards of glass. The linen couch stretches out for almost the length of the room and has the distinct advantage of looking out into the garden, the view unobstructed thanks to the broad glass doors.

I look out into the garden and towards the outdoor television screen. Carly catches sight of me and, for a moment, watches me before returning to her conversation with Mo. I sit down and run my hand over the fabric, its texture rough and thick like a wire-haired dog. Cool air flows from slits in the ceiling, drying the sweat that has formed on my brow, in my armpits and on my back.

The dread rises again; will the Judge have already thwarted my attempts to gather information? Will he have removed it all to make things even more difficult?

'Kim,' says a voice from behind me and I turn to find Rosalind standing in the doorway, her arms laden with a pile of documents. My shoulders drop in relief at the information she has been able to source. Daniel and his camera stand behind Rosalind, its lens trained on me.

'I need to find Sophia,' says Rosalind as she hands me the documents. Her bottom lip quivers and her breathing is short and shallow.

'Yes, you do. But please don't go alone. Take the others with you and search the villa together.'

She nods and turns away, slipping past Daniel, who hovers in the doorway silent as a ghost.

'Need any help?' he asks, tilting his head away from the camera. His voice is soft, and he gives me a gentle smile. I don't answer his question immediately; I should really do this alone. Suddenly, my body tightens as I get a stab of embarrassment about how I behaved around him last night. Talk about trying to keep things professional after that! And *LoveWrecked* crew or not, as far as I'm concerned, Daniel is a suspect.

But the pile of papers weighs heavy in my hands; there are more documents than I expected and, given the time limit, it will be impossible for me to wade through these alone. I have less than one hour until the next murder and no idea where to start. Daniel waits patiently for my answer, but I can see from the way his teeth tear into his bottom lip, he is in desperate need of distraction. I sigh; it's not as if anything else about this is going to follow procedure.

'Help would be welcome.'

Daniel gives me a tight smile. He detaches the camera from its holster and sets it down on the coffee table, its lens still pointing it at me. He unclips the straps from around his broad chest and sits down on the couch a little along from me. I hand him half of the documents.

'Divide these into person-specific piles. Once we've done that we'll go through them.'

He nods and sets to work. I try to ignore the fact that what we're about to discuss is a clear violation of the privacy of the Islanders but I don't really have much of a choice and as far as I see it, it isn't the worst crime committed in this villa. I rub my forehead; I'm about as ready as I'm ever going to be.

'I think the best place for us to start would be try to establish any links between the Islanders and Jack Peaks,' I say, in a voice louder than I would normally use. This isn't the time for conspiratorial whispers; my words need to be captured. I'm not just speaking to Daniel, I'm speaking to the Judge and whoever else is involved in this horrid scheme. I need them to see that I'm complying with their request.

I get to my feet and, collecting the photographs of the Islanders from the files, gather them up and carry them so I'm facing the wall of glass. I flick through the pile and pull out Jack's photo, hold it against the wall with one hand and say over my shoulder, 'Sticky tape, please.'

Daniel hands me the roll and, using my teeth, I break off a small piece. I stick Jack's photo on the wall. His face hangs there smiling out at me, his bright white teeth and gelled hair the same as it was last night.

What happened to you, Jack?

I do the same with the other photographs until all five of the Islanders stare at me from the wall.

'Even yourself?' says Daniel, his head tilted to one side.

'Even myself,' I reply and, returning to the sofa, I rip off three pieces of paper over which I scrawl: *Daniel Oni*, *Rosalind Jenkins* and *Sophia Dance*.

'The crew need to be investigated too?' he asks as I stick the three names on the wall next to the photographs.

'Yes, someone has a motive to kill Jack either because they're working with the Judge or because the Judge knew this person wouldn't be able to resist. I just don't know which of those options is correct or who did it.'

'In that case,' he says, lowering his voice slightly, 'Sophia Dance might be a good place to start.' I raise my eyebrow at his words and sit back down on the couch.

'What makes you say so?' I encourage.

'The producers and assistant producers of shows like these know lots of secrets about the contestants and they use those secrets to make good TV. Good producers know how to run their Islanders. And Sophia, she was a good producer. From what I saw, she was running Jack all night.'

'Woah, wind back,' I say, shaking my head. 'Run them? Sophia was running Jack, what does that even mean?'

'Yeah, how do I explain this?' He scratches his head and looks, if anything, a bit awkward. 'Now, I don't like this part of the show but *LoveWrecked* is good TV. Right?'

'Right,' I confirm.

'But it's good TV because of the drama, the scandal, the secrets. Nobody's perfect, we all have pasts. Well, the producers use that information to create conflict between you all. Do you know who Sophia Dance is?'

'Aside from the assistant producer, you mean?'

'Yeah. Sophia Dance is relatively well known in the social media world. She fancies herself as the UK's answer to Gossip Girl. She has thousands of followers and each week she spills the tea, as they say.'

I roll my eyes; the Internet and world of social media never cease to amaze me, the way people can have careers, friendships, relationships, almost complete lives online and yet sitting in front of a computer they look no different to anyone else.

'So what is she doing on *LoveWrecked*?' I ask. 'If the girl has thousands of followers on social media, what need does she have of a reality TV show?'

'She told me she wanted to get serious. Don't get me wrong, her online presence is huge, so it can't be for the money. The prestige perhaps? I did think it was strange that she made the move very quickly. But then like I said, she is a secret-spiller and producers of reality TV love secrets.'

I get to my feet and pad towards the wall of suspects, stopping in front of Sophia Dance's name written in my messy handwriting. Black ink on white paper; if only the truth was as black and white as this sticker. I stare at her name, pausing for a moment to take in what Daniel has just said. Sophia Dance arrived on *LoveWrecked* quickly and unexpectedly and she is well practised at airing people's dirty laundry. The speed of her arrival on the show is strange and her proclivity to expose people's secrets doesn't exactly lump her in with the great and the good but does that make her the perfect candidate to play the role of Judge?

There are certainly things that arouse my suspicion but equally there are some unanswered questions. If Sophia is involved and working with the Judge, why go missing? Surely all it does is implicate her. If she's a social media star, then she must be recognisable at least to some people, meaning there would be no easy way she could escape this. She'd be hunted down by the authorities wherever she went. Hounded by the public who, even if they didn't turn her into the police, would want a picture with her or something ridiculous like that. No, something about this doesn't smell right.

'Fine,' I say, turning around to face him, my back to wall. 'So, what about her *running* Jack?'

Daniel crosses one leg over the other and lifts his head towards the white-washed ceiling. Whether he's remembering or deciding how much to tell me, I'm not sure. 'Last night,' he says, turning his chocolate-brown eyes to me, 'off-camera, I saw Sophia whispering to Jack on numerous occasions. And after their chats, Sophia would signal to me and I'd follow Jack to whoever he went to speak to. The drama ensued.'

'And what did Jack say? What secrets had he been told?'

Daniel's brow furrows. 'Telling Mo he recognised him was one and I'm sure Sophia told Mo to call Jack a creep. But that's all I really remember; I sort of stop listening after a while. I just film and Sophia and Rosalind direct me. Oh, I do remember that Valentina slapped Jack, though. It was pretty heated.'

'She slapped him?' I ask, surprised. From what I know of Valentina, that seems rather out of character for her but then, I remind myself, I don't know these people at all, not really. 'And you don't remember what it was about?'

'No, I'm sorry. Rosalind will probably know, though. And Sophia definitely will, if we can find her.'

If we can find her. Unwelcome, an image of her comes to my mind; she is crouched somewhere out of sight, smiling as she watches us squirm at the threat of having our secrets revealed. I rub my eyes. The night before is hazy for me but now I think about it I do remember Jack being particularly antagonistic.

'Jack pushed you in the pool last night,' I say, remembering.

A flash of anger crosses Daniel's face but he composes himself quickly and fixes his smile back into place. 'Yeah, he did. He didn't like me showing off my muscles; I think he'd decided he was the strong man in the villa. Come to think about it, Jack was quite the shit last night. No wonder he...' Daniel trails off.

'Ended up dead?' I finish his sentence.

'Sorry, I shouldn't think like that.' Daniel looks sheepish.

'No, you shouldn't,' I say, but maybe Daniel isn't wrong; someone killed Jack because of what he said to them last night. 'Tell me about you,' I say, changing the subject. 'How did you end up here?'

Daniel looks at me with his warm eyes and gives me a weak smile. 'Honestly, I can't really believe that I'm here, that I was picked for this. Whatever the fuck this is. The media doesn't know it yet or at least they didn't yesterday but I was scouted just like everyone else.'

'What did the scout say?' I ask, picking up a pen and some paper.

Daniel shrugs. 'Probably the same as what was said to you: the opportunity to spend the summer in the sun in a luxury villa, being part of the hottest show on UK television.'

'Why would *LoveWrecked* randomly choose their crew? Isn't that a massive gamble?'

'Greg Barker, our executive producer, loves a gimmick. But to say this was random is a bit far. For me, it wasn't completely unexpected. I've worked on similar shows several times before.'

'Do you know who came up with the idea to find Islanders at random?' I ask.

Daniel bites his lip. 'I don't really think it was random. As I'm not a producer, I don't know heaps about it, but I suspect that the process was similar to the way the show found the Islanders in the past. In previous years, the Islanders who participated in the show came from two different pools: applicants and "chosen ones". Applicants had applied and survived a rigorous interview process. The chosen ones were different in that they were approached by *LoveWrecked*'s talent scouts usually because they had large social media followings. The talent scouts would scour the various social media channels to find young, beautiful people with lots of followers. In short, the more you stood out, the more likely you were to be chosen "at random". Sort of like writing "pick me" on your forehead for a police line-up. The executives wanted people with a good media presence; if they already had followers, they'd have people watching the show. It was all about the numbers.'

'What are you saying?'

'I'm not saying anything, I'm assuming that the talent scouts would have scoured the Internet and chosen people that would make the best TV and these people would have been invited.'

This makes me pause. Somewhere along the way a person was chosen to kill Jack Peaks; I wonder if they know that was why they were chosen. Did they enter the villa with the intention to kill him or did it happen by accident?

'And the other crew members, it was the same for them too?' I ask.

'They told me it was. But I don't know. I'm not really paid to think, I'm paid to film. And no disrespect, I'm going to keep doing that.'

I stare at him, the calmness with which he talks as if untouched by the horror. 'Daniel, you seem pretty nonchalant about all of this. What are you not telling me?'

He licks his dry lips and stares deep into my eyes. 'Look, I told you I've worked on similar shows several times before. And there's one rule for the camera operators. Well, one rule if you ever want to get a job again.'

'What?' I say, leaning into him.

'Never stop filming: contestants might beg, cry, scream; they might be completely naked, or wasted, or both; they might be injured. Whatever. Other people deal with the problems, I just film. You do a couple of years of that and you forget how to react. Being here, on this show, it doesn't feel like I'm filming real life. Contestants on shows like these are as unreal to me as characters on a TV show. Well, they felt unreal to me before I met you.' He pauses and looks down at his hands; his eyes are hidden under his thick eyelashes. Then he looks me square in the eyes. 'I'm so impressed with how you're handling everything.'

My cheeks warm and I avert my gaze. There's something about him, his handsomeness coupled with his calm, logical demeanour, that makes my stomach flutter but whatever I'm feeling has to stop. Immediately.

A chime sounds, and we jolt as the Judge's voice comes over the tannoy.

'There are only forty minutes remaining. Tick, tock, tick, tock.'

I swallow; my throat is dry. Shit, how is time slipping away from me like this? My investigation needs ramping up and fast. Everything is a muddled mess in my mind.

The beginning, start at the beginning. I pick up one of the thick felt-tip pens that Rosalind dropped off with the documents and head towards the wall. I write Jack's name underneath his picture. The black pen scars the clear glass wall and despite the violations this villa has seen I still feel uneasy graffitiing. I guess it's the police officer in me: no crime is acceptable. I tell myself, *This isn't a crime, this is a necessity.*

'Right,' I say, clearing my throat and attempting to shake off the blush that rose when Daniel said he was impressed by me. 'What do we know about Jack Peaks? There's his file there.' I bring the end of the pen to my lips and bite it.

'He is— was,' says Daniel correcting himself, 'a twenty-five-year-old estate agent from Essex.' I write these things down.

'What else?' I ask. Daniel's brow furrows as his eyes scan the page. He really does have such a nice face, a kind face.

'He's applied for the show before. Got pretty far as well but then pulled out, personal reasons.'

I raise my eyebrow. 'What personal reasons?'

'It doesn't say,' says Daniel with a shrug. 'Do you think it could be relevant?' I don't answer but write *personal reasons* followed by a question mark on the wall. 'Don't forget the slap and the argument with Mo,' he adds.

I write down 'Mo and Jack argument' and 'Valentina and Jack argument'. I wonder about Valentina. She was the one who discovered the body; she was standing over

Jack's body when I arrived and I don't remember hearing her leave the bedroom.

'Is there anything else we know about Jack?' I ask, re-focusing on Daniel. He flicks through Jack's file once more.

'The only thing that might be relevant here is that it says he's a self-professed ladies' man,' he says and I hear the scorn in his voice when and it reminds of the tone Mo used when he called Jack creepy. I felt that too, when I met Jack yesterday; there was a certain intensity to his 'charm' that made me uncomfortable. I write it down – it might be relevant. Could that have been the reason for his argument with Valentina? Carly certainly wasn't overly impressed with his behaviour from what I can remember and Jack ramped up his advances with Carly particularly hard.

'OK, that's enough on Jack for now. Let's move onto the other files.'

We pore over the documents, writing down the basic facts of the lives of the Islanders. When we're finished, I grimace at the wall; it isn't enough. It isn't nearly enough information to build a case.

Names, ages, places of birth, occupations, the airports the Islanders flew from and their arrival times, their likes, their dislikes, their favourite music, their celebrity crushes, dating history. Information that on the show might provide a good basis to create drama but when trying to solve a murder, completely pointless.

I struggle to see how any of this will help me. Under normal circumstances, information about a person's back-ground can be vital, but these aren't normal circumstances and the information provides a mere snapshot of the people that they are. The words on the page mingle into one another, making it impossible for me to focus.

What am I missing?

My head is aching, and my body is gripped by the unnatural chill of the air conditioning. My eyes are raw and one of them has developed a twitch. I feel awful but then how am I expected to feel when I've been asked to solve a murder live on television? My stomach squirms; this, all of this, is being screened into people's homes.

'Thirty minutes remaining,' shouts the Judge over the tannoy. It's time I started interviewing.

Chapter Twenty-Three

My eyes move from my makeshift suspects wall to the glass window and out into the villa's garden. Daniel stands next to me, his camera on and pointed at me. I try to ignore how the camera's on light blinks with every second that falls from the killing clock. Instead, I focus my efforts on scrutinising the group of people who over the course of a couple of hours have gone from competitors in a reality show to murder suspects in a horror show.

Rosalind, still dressed in her pyjamas, sits alone on the wooden seating around the Fire Pit, staring blankly into the distance. I follow her eyeline and find that Rosalind is staring at the spot in the pool where Jack was found. Only Rosalind's dazed expression and attire suggest that anything is wrong, for nothing else in the garden looks out of place: the decking has dried in the midday sun, erasing any trace that we fished a body out earlier today and the hedges are as tall and perfectly manicured as they were when we first arrived.

Carly has changed into swimwear and lies on a sun lounger on the far side of the pool. Her dark hair, black bikini and black linen kimono make her look like the holiday version of a widow in mourning. And if this were a TV murder mystery, she would probably have inherited the money. I shake my head; it seems rather strange that she has chosen this moment to do a spot of sun-tanning.

It takes me a moment to find Mo and Valentina because they've moved to the kitchen area, which isn't visible from the pool although it is from the living room. When I catch sight of them through the corner window of the room, I find they are sitting next to each other propped up on stools around the bar. The very place I was sitting when I first heard Valentina scream. Neither of them has bothered to clear away my dropped mug.

Valentina has her pale fingers wrapped around a large mug and Mo's legs are spread wide on the stool; his hands cling to the fabric of the chair in between them. They are leaning in close to one another. Mo glances over his shoulder as if checking he isn't being watched, and then leans forward and brushes his hand against Valentina's cheek.

Their closeness intrigues me; is it normal for people to connect as quickly as they have or is there more to their relationship? I intend to ask them this when I question them.

I try for a moment to assess who looks the guiltiest but it is, of course, impossible. If guilt were simply a badge that someone wears, my life as a police officer would have been a hell of a lot easier.

I reassess the facts at hand. Mo, Valentina, Carly and Daniel all had a run-in with Jack Peaks in some way.

There were Jack's advances on Carly. He had singled her out as the one he wanted, and he pursued her relentlessly for the entirety of the evening. And, I remember, regardless of how much she appeared to resist his charms, he persisted. Did Jack overstep the mark with her? Did he say something to her that pushed her over the edge? Add to that Carly's reaction to the discovery of the body. Where everyone else reacted in ways typical of those suffering from a shock, Carly didn't even make the effort to look surprised and she certainly didn't seem affected by his death. No, Carly couldn't give less of a shit that Jack was dead. But not caring that someone is dead – heck, even wanting someone dead – is a far cry from actually murdering them.

There's potential here but I need more to fill in the gaps.

Valentina's evening was somewhat ruined as Jack basically accused her of doing drugs. From what I remember, Valentina didn't respond well to his accusations and Daniel said she slapped Jack.

And then there's Mo. When Jack insisted that he knew Mo, pushed him for information about his past, refused to give in to Mo's obvious divergence tactics, the exchange was so heated that I intervened.

I wonder what I would have found out if I hadn't intervened. If Jack did recognise Mo and it wasn't a case of mistaken identity, does that mean Jack knew something about Mo that got him killed?

And then there's the crew: Rosalind, Daniel and Sophia. It doesn't seem likely that they would risk their jobs, their careers, their freedom to kill Jack and I don't have any obvious motive for any of them.

And who is the Judge?

'Urgh,' I say aloud. None of it makes sense; I have more questions than I have answers, more gaps than I have plugs. I massage my forehead. My hangover, driven away by the adrenaline, has returned with a vengeance, making my head throb, but time is ticking. I must proceed on.

There is only one place that seems logical for me to go next so I slide the door of the living room a fraction and call through it.

'Rosalind, please can I speak with you?' Rosalind glances around, unsure for a moment where my voice is coming from. 'Inside, please.'

Her red, watery eyes meet mine and she nods, pushing herself to her feet as if she has the weight of the world on her shoulders. I look quickly towards Mo and Valentina and notice that they have moved slightly further apart.

Stepping aside, I allow Rosalind to enter the living room. I push aside the folders and files Rosalind gave me and sit down. She doesn't follow my lead but instead steps towards the wall of photographs and my messy scrawls. Even from my sitting position, I can see that her lips tremble as her eyes hover over the suspect wall. In that moment, I see it all through her eyes and I cringe. My makeshift operations room is amateurish and the lack of information laughable.

'You know I usually set up a wall just like this,' she says, turning to face me. 'Me and the other producers would, I mean. We use it to map out the Islanders' stories and secrets. And mark a big red cross over your faces when you're eliminated.' Rosalind reaches a hand out and presses it against the wall for support. 'How awful that seems now.' Her voice catches in her throat and she stares down at her bare feet.

Map out the Islanders' stories and secrets. So, Daniel was right and it confirms that Sophia probably knew things about us all.

'Please sit down, Rosalind,' I say, waving my hand to the sofa. I don't have time for her tears. Rosalind wipes her cheek with the back of her hand and pads across the marble-tiled floor towards the sofa. She sits facing me, her back straight and hands clasped in her lap in a pose that seems to say she understands the seriousness of this all and she is here to help.

'Last night, Daniel said that Sophia was whispering to Jack at regular intervals, that Sophia was using him and the secrets you've just mentioned to create drama. But it does appear that this drama got Jack killed. What did Sophia know?'

'Producers are in charge of their own contestants and they use the weeks leading up to the show to dig into their past,' says Rosalind, her voice coming out in a rush. 'I don't get told the secrets unless the producers want my advice on how best to use them.'

I close my eyes; she can't be serious. 'So you're telling me you don't know?'

'I don't but it should all be in the files I gave you.'

'Well, it's not,' I snap. I feel my temperature rising; I'm not getting anywhere. 'Tell me what you know about Sophia. How long has she worked for you? Do you think she has anything to do with this?' Rosalind picks at the leg of her pyjamas and avoids my gaze. 'Look at me, Rosalind; I need you to tell me the truth.'

Rosalind clears her throat and shakes her head as if trying to get a grip. 'Sophia is new, she only started about six months ago. She's new to production too but her *experience* lends itself well to this. She knows…' Rosalind looks at Daniel as if unsure what to say or how much. 'She knows how to make good television.'

'And…' I prompt. I can see in Rosalind's eyes there is more that she wants to say.

'And – please don't take this the wrong way. But as awful and horrible as all of this is, this is good TV.'

I draw back from her. 'Sorry, are you suggesting Sophia did all of this for TV? She murdered someone for ratings?' It's hard to keep the incredulity out of my voice.

'No, no, that's not what I'm suggesting at all. I just think, if anyone was going to come up with something like this, it would be a producer. Or someone who works in the business.'

Almost imperceptibly Rosalind glances at the suspect wall and I wonder if she's glancing at Carly, the actress, but I don't follow her gaze.

'So,' I say instead, 'Sophia Dance knows how to make good TV, Sophia Dance knows our secrets, and Sophia Dance is missing while all of this rages on.' I jump up from the bed and storm to the suspect wall, grab my pen and draw a big circle around Sophia's name. I turn back to Rosalind. 'So how do I know that you're not behind all of this? You're a producer.'

She picks at the leg of her pyjamas again. 'I guess you don't.' Her voice trembles. 'I can only tell you what I know and hope that you believe me.'

'Did you notice anything unusual last night?'

Rosalind squeezes her eyes shut. I wait while she thinks, trying not to notice every beat of my heart and how it corresponds to every passing second.

'Before I went to bed,' says Rosalind, opening her eyes. 'I was in the producer's room watching some of the live footage. There was so much happening. I remember radioing for Daniel to capture interactions multiple times. If Sophia was filling Jack's head with secrets, he was a busy bee revealing them all last night.'

'Can you remember anything specific?' Daniel has already told me about Valentina, but it seems as if there's more.

Rosalind scratches her head. 'Jack and Carly got into a bit of a tiff at some point, but she was also angry at you, wasn't she? For spilling wine down her.'

Frustration builds inside me; this isn't getting me anywhere. I stand up.

'I want to see the tapes,' I say. Time might be tight, but it's more tangible than this. Rosalind bobs her head and jumps to her feet.

'Of course. Good idea!'

When we enter the production room, we find the safe still hanging open and the debris of broken phones scattered on the floor. Rosalind plonks herself down, drags her chair towards her switchboard and begins to fiddle with the knobs.

Suddenly, every screen is filled with the image of Jack's body as he floats face down and lifeless in the water. The lights at the bottom of the pool give his body an eerie quality, like a spectre in the night. Oh God, it's so horrible. My stomach drops; if this was being screened on live TV last night then the public might already know what has happened to Jack. Maybe they're sitting at home screaming at their television screens. *It's obvious, Kim, you idiot.* I push the image from my mind; my priority is solving this.

Rosalind turns a dial on the switchboard. The image of Jack wobbles and the timestamp in the corner reverses. Seven in the morning, six in the morning, five in the morning, then like a scene from a horror movie at just before 5 a.m., Jack's body starts moving. As the image rewinds, his body is lifted out of the water as if by some invisible force and dropped onto the poolside where he sits in a slump. Then he stands, walks backwards around the pool several times and then stops a couple of metres away from the pool's edge on the grassy verge where I found the shot glass. His position is off far to the side of the camera, but he is just in shot. The image shows Jack holding the glass, it re-filling as he takes it from his lips and him handing it over.

'Stop,' I say, and Rosalind obeys. Jack stands frozen on the screen in front of us, the timestamp reads 12 a.m. 'Right, now, roll it forward, slower than normal if possible.'

Jack sways unsteadily on his feet but the way he is holding out his hand and the fact that someone handed him that shot suggests that there's someone off camera that he's talking to. 'Who is he talking to? Can I see it from another angle?'

'Yes, hang on.' Rosalind clicks a couple more buttons. 'It should come up here.' She points at a monitor, but the screen is blank.

'What's going on?' I ask. Rosalind turns her chair to face me, her forehead knotted in concern.

'I'm not sure, it isn't working. Either it's faulty or...'

'Or?'

'Or someone cut its wires.'

'Of course they have,' I say through gritted teeth. 'OK, keep playing the one with Jack. Slow the speed of it.' Rosalind nods.

In slow motion, Jack reaches out his hand and accepts the shot glass and its bright blue contents. He lifts it up to his face; a distant smile spreads across it. The speed makes for even more uncomfortable viewing. His head jolts back and he downs the shot in one go, then drops the glass onto the floor to be found in the grass by me many hours later. He stretches out his arms to the person out of shot, giving a wobbly thumbs up in what I can only assume is thanks.

And then, nothing happens; Jack just turns away from the camera and blunders around on the grass for a while.

'Move it forward, faster this time.' Jack continues to move around; he starts circling the pool, his hand clutched against his stomach and his face twisted in pain. An hour passes on the timestamp. I grip the back of Rosalind's chair as I watch Jack's legs no longer able to hold him in a standing position and he plonks himself down on the side of the pool, his feet dangling in the water. Then his body twists and he tips sideways hitting the water where he bobs, face up, for forty-five minutes before flipping over and the water around him grows still.

This confirms for me that it was whatever was in the shot glass that killed him, and timing-wise it fits. I think of the shot Valentina and I did together when Jack interrupted us; he was annoyed we didn't offer him one. He was drinking so excessively last night, it would hardly have been a chore for someone to get him to drink the shot, and the video confirms that Jack took the shot eagerly and without question. Whoever gave it to him wanted him dead.

'Oh God,' says Rosalind, pitching forward, her head in her hands.

'What? Rosalind, what is it?' I look down at her and my heart starts hammering against my chest.

'This is all my—' She breaks off and turns to face me. Her eyes glisten over and she bites her lip as if pulling herself back from the brink of tears. My breathing slows; she is fine, just upset.

'All of this is what?' I ask but she struggles to catch her breath. 'Tell me,' I say, softly but firmly, reaching out to place a hand on her arm.

'Yeah, sorry. Being silly. I just—' Rosalind pauses, biting her lip again. She averts her eyes from me and picks at the fray in the pyjamas. If she keeps on like this she won't have any pyjamas left.

'What?' I prompt. 'Whatever it is you can tell me.' Rosalind's shoulders hunch and she begins to cry.

'This is all my fault,' she sobs. I lean into her; is she about to tell me she was involved? Might this explain why she has been so upset?

'What is all your fault?' I'm firmer now. She doesn't answer immediately; her crying stops her ability to speak. 'Look at me,' I say, hoping to get her to focus. 'What is all your fault?'

'This. Jack. The Judge. Sophia. I've—' Rosalind's lips quiver. I hold my breath. 'Someone I was meant to be caring for is dead. I've allowed everyone to be put in danger. This villa. It's meant to be in my control and it's not.'

'Oh,' I say, releasing the breath I was holding and trying my best not to sound too disappointed. It was obviously too much to ask for, a shotgun confession.

'And do you know the worst part?' says Rosalind, leaning in closer to me, her voice in a low whisper. 'When we found him. Jack. When we found Jack dead, do you know what the first thing I thought was?' Rosalind sniffs loudly. 'The first thing I thought was, *I hope this is caught on camera because this will be good ratings.* Then I realised how awful that was. Someone is dead. But then I thought, *If it's my fault he's dead my career is over.* All I could think of were ratings and my career. I'm an awful, awful person.' At this, she howls a cry of anguish and starts up a fresh set of sobs. I can't help myself, but I pity her; guilt is a horrible thing. I know that more than anyone. 'Don't you think that makes me a terrible person?' Rosalind asks, her eyes boring into mine as if desperate for some relief from the pain. I place my hands on her shoulders and look her square in the eyes.

'No, it doesn't make you a terrible person. It makes you human. Our natural state is survival. But do you know what you can do to make up for it?' I ask. Rosalind shakes her head. 'Help me catch his killer. Give me everything you can on the people here and make sure no one else dies at his hands.'

Rosalind sniffs again, a pathetic, gurgling sound. She wipes away her tears and nods.

'Chin up,' I say, with as much wartime spirit as I can muster. 'I need you to focus.' Rosalind lifts her head back up and looks at me. Her expression is tighter than it was before.

'Do you think we can do this?' she asks.

'I know we can,' I reply, giving Rosalind a thumbs up, to better hide my lie. This game was rigged from the start but I'm not about to let someone else carry that worry.

Beep. Beep. Beep. Beep. Beep. Beep.

'What the—' shouts Daniel, his words barely audible over the noise. Rosalind and I clamp our hands over our ears. The blaring seems to bore into my brain.

'Islanders, report to the Fire Pit,' says the voice over the tannoy. It's as if a dead weight has been dropped into my stomach. The Judge is back.

Chapter Twenty-Four

I tear from the production room, my bare feet slapping against the marble floor. Daniel and Rosalind run behind me. The clink of Daniel's camera equipment adds to the noise as the alarm blares on.

Beep. Beep. Beep. 'Islanders, report to the Fire Pit.' *Beep. Beep. Beep.*

I sprint through the garden. Up ahead, Valentina, Carly and Mo sit on the wooden seating, pressed together like penguins huddling against the cold. They turn their faces towards me, desperation written all over them.

The outdoor television screen is switched on and the Judge faces directly into the camera. His robes are as dark and billowy as before. His wig as white and coiffed. The only difference now is what he holds in his hand. A shiver takes hold of me when I see it. He's holding a gavel. There are only four minutes left on his killing clock and this evil man is holding a gavel.

'Sit down, Rosalind. Kimberley, you remain standing. And Daniel, you should be filming this.'

Rosalind shuffles towards the others and gently lowers herself into the space on Valentina's side. She hooks her arm through Valentina's and squeezes her hand tightly.

147

Daniel, on the other hand, climbs to the top of the tiered seating and sits at the top, his camera seemingly able to take us all in from this angle.

'Thank you,' says the Judge. 'Kimberley King, there are three minutes until the next murder. This should be just enough time for you to explain who killed Jack Peaks and save one of the group from elimination.'

'Oh my God,' whimpers Rosalind, pulling herself closer to Valentina, who sobs silently. Fat, mascara-filled tears roll down Valentina's face, streaking her cheeks with inky smudges.

I stand before them, tensing my muscles to stop them from shaking. This cannot be happening. They're all sitting here. How can one of them die right in front of me? It's impossible. But I don't want to take any chances. I clear my throat, hoping it will stop my voice from quivering.

'Are you telling me you don't have any ideas?' says the Judge before I have the chance to speak. I can almost feel the lens of Daniel's camera zooming in on my face and I fight to keep it steady. But my heart is beating so violently I feel as if I'm being shaken from the inside.

'I... I...' My voice fails me; I don't know who killed Jack but I'm not about to announce that to the Judge. I need to give him something, I need to make some attempt at solving this. And the easiest person to point the blame at is the person who isn't here to defend themselves, so instead I say, 'Last night, Sophia Dance was filling Jack Peaks' head with secrets. Secrets about all of you.' I'm looking at the Islanders now. 'I know that from what I saw at dinner and from gaining a better understanding of how producers on shows like *LoveWrecked* work. All of you have secrets and it seems one of you was willing to kill for that secret. Did Sophia know that you'd be willing to kill to keep Jack quiet? Because if she did Sophia is either working with the Judge, or is the Judge, and she set Jack up to be murdered. When Jack came to you and teased you about the secret you knew you had no choice but to kill him. And by doing that you played into her hands.'

'No,' shouts Mo, his dark eyes blazing. 'That is so ridiculous, that can't be true.' Valentina's body curls over herself and she rocks backwards and forwards while Rosalind strokes her back.

I spin around and face the television to speak to the Judge. 'Based on the limited evidence I have been able to gather in one hour and the fact that Sophia has gone missing, the best assumption I can make is that she is responsible for the death of Jack, either by killing him herself or by inciting someone else to do it.'

Even as I'm speaking I know that I've got it completely wrong; it's a guess made on incomplete evidence.

'So, Kim,' says the Judge. 'Your judgement is that Sophia Dance is behind this. Final answer?'

The honest answer is I don't know but there are two minutes left on the clock.

'Final answer,' I say. The Judge raises the gavel in his right hand and brings it down. There's silence for a moment and we stare, as a collective, at the screen. When nothing happens, I turn to look at the Islanders.

What is going on?

One minute left on the clock.

I sink to my knees, breathing heavily. Relief washes over me; this isn't real, this is not real. It is a challenge. I was being tested for good television. I can't believe how stupid I've been. Jack Peaks isn't dead, I was wrong.

Beeeeeeeeeeeeeeeeeeeeeeeeep.

'You said Sophia killed Jack. That is the wrong answer and now time is up. Another one of your number is dead,' says the Judge. I look from Daniel, to Rosalind, to Mo, to Carly, to Valentina and then back at the Judge. 'You didn't do that good of a job looking for poor Sophia, now, did you? Did you even *bother* to look near the pool?'

Oh my God, oh my God, oh my God. I nearly fall over myself as I run towards the spot where she would have stood had she been the one handing the poisoned shot to Jack. The point is at the back side of the villa, facing away from the main areas we would congregate.

'No,' I cry, falling to my knees beside the lump of blue plastic that would normally cover the pool. Of course I hadn't thought to look here before; I thought we were looking for a person, not a body. I rip the plastic back.

Limbs are sprawled at unnatural angles. Sticky, dark blood has dried in a halo around Sophia's head. I brush away the red curls that cover her face. Her expression is frozen in horror. Sophia Dance lies broken on the earth like a china doll.

Daniel, Carly, Rosalind, Mo and Valentina gather behind me. If they're reacting to Sophia Dance's dead body, I can't hear them. My ears are ringing. My hands shake as I press them against her cold cheeks.

'Sophia,' I call out to her, 'Sophia, it's Kim. Can you hear me?' I grab Sophia's shoulders. Digging my fingers into her flesh, I rattle her shoulders.

'Is she alive?' asks Valentina, coming around to the other side of Sophia's body. Valentina's cheeks are devoid of colour and she presses her hand against her mouth in a way that suggests she's stopping herself from throwing up.

Shaking my head is the only reply I can make.

'What happened to her?' asks Mo.

'It looks like she fell,' says Carly, pointing up to the second floor of the villa; all of us follow the direction of Carly's finger. A perimeter of balcony runs around the second floor of the villa; the panes of glass dividing the balcony from the air aren't high. It would be easy enough to push someone off, especially someone as petite as Sophia Dance.

'Oh my God, Sophia,' says Rosalind, her voice catching.

My mind is spinning with questions. My trembling legs carry me away from her body. I can't look at her, I can't be here. It feels like it's my fault she is dead. I have her blood on my hands, literally. The blood from Sophia's body has sunk into the creases in my palms. I dash to the pool and plunge my hands in, scrubbing them against one another. The blood stains the water crimson, pooling in circles around my hands. I wipe my hands on my trousers; my palms are clean but still tinged with the red.

'You tricked me,' I say, storming towards the outdoor television. 'You said the next murder would occur in one hour, but Sophia was already dead, so you lied.'

'Not really,' says the Judge, his image still on screen. 'If you'd listened carefully, you'd have noticed that I said, "you have one hour to find out who killed Jack Peaks, or you'll find another of your number dead", but I take on board your feedback and I will be clearer for the next time. Sophia Dance is the second victim of the villa. Kimberley, you have one hour until the next death. Better start taking this more seriously.'

Pop.

Chapter Twenty-Five

Sunday 27th July, 13:00

1 Hour And 0 Minutes Until The Next Murder

The screen goes blank and I react in the only way I know how. I run away, dashing towards the perimeter wall of the villa.

'Let me out,' I scream at the top of my lungs. 'Free us.'

'Kim,' calls Daniel. I glance over my shoulder to see him running up behind me. 'Kim, wait.'

'Leave me alone. Please, I can't. I can't do this,' I shout, waving a hand to him. My chest is so tight, I can't catch my breath. I reach the perimeter wall of the villa, push my way through the hedge, and slam my body against the smooth concrete. 'Let me out,' I cry, beating my fists into the hard exterior.

'Kim, calm down, let's talk about this.' He grabs hold of my hand and pulls me to a stop. I don't turn to face him but lean my body away, pressing my forehead against the wall.

'Stop it,' I say, wiping tears from my face with my free hand. 'I don't want your stupid camera in my face.'

'I've turned it off. Come on, talk to me. We need to talk about this.' I twist to look at him. He unclips the camera from its bracket and places it gently on the floor. 'Come here,' he says, opening his arms out wide.

And in contrast to every modicum of police professionalism I once had, I fold myself into him. His muscular arms wrap around me and squeeze me tight against his chest. His beating heart drums against my ear. His warmth envelops me, comforting me. The tears flow freely now, dampening his shirt, but he doesn't say anything, just pulls me in tighter to himself.

'She's dead. Sophia is dead. He murdered her. I should have—'

'This isn't your fault, Kim,' he murmurs, rubbing my back with his hand.

'You're wrong. Everything about this is my fault.' Without warning, a face flashes into my mind; she's linked to this somehow, she's the reason I'm here. After all these years, I'm still not free from it. His fingers grip my arms and he pulls me away from him, so our faces are close to one another's. My eyes scan his face. On anyone else the thickset eyebrows and broad jaw might make them look imposing but Daniel's face is soft and kind. His dark eyes stare into mine.

'This isn't your fault. And you *can* do this.' His fingers squeeze into my arms more tightly. 'I don't want to die here, Kim. I need you to save me. I have faith in you.'

My eyes fill again with tears. How can he have faith in me? I've done nothing to warrant that.

'How can you say that? You don't even know me. You have no idea what I'm capable of,' I say. He pulls me in closer.

'I trust you. You're smart, caring… beautiful,' he whispers. The adrenaline coursing through my body seems to surge, propelling me forward. And without warning, without logic, I press my lips against his and kiss him. A deep, long kiss.

Then, as if electrocuted, I jerk backwards. What the fuck am I doing?

'I'm sorry. I shouldn't have done—'

'Don't,' says Daniel, holding up a hand. 'Don't apologise. I wanted to kiss you since the moment you entered the kitchen last night. And, though I know you're only kissing me because you're frantic and pumped with adrenaline, let me at least pretend it's because you fancy me too.'

I gurgle a laugh and he wipes away my tears with his fingers. I might have only kissed him because I'm frantic, but that doesn't mean I haven't also wanted to do it since yesterday. 'Do you really think this is solvable?' I ask.

He shrugs and pulls me back into a hug. 'OK, if I'm honest, probably not. But you can give it a damn good try.' I sniff and nod my head. I can't give up now. There are people here who need my help.

'Get your camera,' I say. 'And follow me.'

Daniel walks behind me as I head back to where the others are still hovering over Sophia's body.

'Mo, please could you carry Sophia's body to the freezer? Place her next to Jack.'

He nods and slides his hands underneath her tiny, broken body.

'Valentina,' I say. The DJ twists to look at me. 'Please can I talk to you next?' To say she doesn't look happy about it would be an understatement.

'What? Why do you want to talk to me next? I don't have anything to do with this?' She is staring at me incredulously. 'Sophia was about my size, there is no way I have the strength to push her over the balcony.'

'Come with me please,' I say. 'And stop complaining, I'll be speaking to everyone, so I might as well talk to you now.'

154

Valentina opens her mouth to say something but shuts it again. If she was going to argue more she clearly decides it isn't worth doing in front of the others. She huffs loudly and charges into the house ahead of me. Valentina is a lot more petulant than her shy persona sometimes portrays.

'Come on,' I say to Daniel and together we head into the house.

Valentina must have seen the wall of suspects with her own face staring out at her as she entered the living room, but she is pointedly refusing to look at the wall and has instead taken a position on the couch that looks into the room, away from the photographs, the glass wall, and the garden. I sit opposite her and for a moment neither of us speak; the silence between us is broken only by the hum of the air conditioner. Every now and then she glances to Daniel, who lurks in the corner, the red light on his camera now flickering.

Her eyes are puffy, still smeared in make-up. Her lips are downturned like they've been dragged downwards by her feelings.

'Last night, you told me how much you hate this show and how you don't think you're a good fit for it,' I say, cutting right to the chase. There's no time for pleasantries now that the Judge has made it clear how serious he is. 'So, tell me, why do you think you were chosen?' Valentina's face falls at my question.

'Why I was chosen?' she asks as if only now realising this for the first time. 'But I thought it was…'

'Random?' I say, finishing her sentence. 'No, I don't think anything about this is random.'

Her shoulders sag and under her breath she whispers something in Russian.

'What?' I press. 'What is it? Why do you think you were chosen?'

'I...' She shakes her head as if shaking away the thought that rises in her. 'I... I don't know,' she says, lamely.

'So, you hate the show and you don't know why you were chosen. But if your selection came as a surprise and you hate it as much as you say, why on earth did you agree to it? We weren't forced to be here; we were given a choice.'

'Why did I say yes to come?' She gives a bark of laughter and shakes her head at me. 'This is a question I've asked myself from the moment I say yes. My friends, they are cool people, they don't understand why I said yes. They kept using the word "sell-out". The logical part of me doesn't know why I accepted either. I remember I was making myself a cup of coffee early on a Monday morning. Well, early for me; it was probably about lunchtime. Then the doorbell rang, it was the scout Sam Day, that's what he was called. When he told me I had been chosen, I didn't feel anything. I had seen the news that the show was returning, and people would be chosen at random but the thought that I would be chosen never even crossed my mind. *LoveWrecked* is so... not me.' She pauses. 'No, I tell a lie. When I listen to Sam, I did feel something. I feel my heart, how you say in English, sinking.'

'Your heart sank? Why?'

'Because as soon as he told me I had been chosen I wanted to slam the door and never think about it again. But I knew there was no way I could turn down such an opportunity. Not if I am serious about being a DJ. *Love-Wrecked* has millions of viewers. So yes, I have a choice but not really. It was important for my career. Good exposure.'

No choice but to accept, I write on my paper. Valentina felt as if she had no choice. The words ring true for me. I too could have rejected the offer, but the lure of the prize money was strong for me.

'When we were in the kitchen, Jack came over to us and he wasn't exactly friendly. I remember you storming off. But I heard also that you and Jack argued again. What were you arguing about?'

'How do you—'

'Valentina, it doesn't matter how I know. We don't have time for this. What were you arguing about?'

Valentina looks me up and down as if weighing up how trustworthy I am. 'He asked me for drugs.'

'So what? He asked you for drugs when I was standing there too.'

'So, I don't do that any more,' she snaps. 'And because I'm DJ, he made the shitty assumption that I do. That I'd have drugs with me, but I don't. The only drugs I have with me are the ones I take daily for medical reasons.'

'That made you so angry you slapped him? From what I've seen of your personality so far that seems a little out of character,' I prompt.

'I am shy, yes, but I am also tough. Working in a nightclub isn't always easy; I've learned how to defend myself. Last night, Jack was drunk. And pushy. And he, he...' She looks at her hands clasped tightly in her lap. 'He talked like he knew stuff. Stuff about me. And before you ask, stuff not relevant to this place.' Her Russian accent, usually light and almost unnoticeable, gets stronger as she becomes noticeably more upset.

'He talked like he knew something about you? What could he know about you? What have you done?'

Valentina's eyes widen. I can practically see the cogs whirring in her brain as she decides how best to play this.

'I have done nothing. Nothing wrong. Not exactly. But we all have a past, don't we?'

'So, I take that to mean you have a past you'd rather we not know about?'

'You can take it however you want to.' The DJ purses her lips and juts her chin upwards. She is closing ranks; the questioning has taken a route she didn't expect.

I pick up my pen and made a note: *purposefully evasive when asked about her past*. Valentina isn't fooling anyone and certainly not me.

'It would be really helpful if you told me a bit more about it.'

'Why? It doesn't have anything to do with the death of that man. It is my business. I have a past, you have a past, but it doesn't make me a murderer. I didn't kill him.' I raise my eyebrow; Valentina's tone is vicious like a lioness protecting her cubs. 'I'm sorry,' she says, more softly now. 'I don't mean to snap at you, this is all very stressful.'

I laugh hollowly. You're telling me?

'I think,' she says, 'I think you should speak to Carly. Her and Jack have a – how do you say it – exchange last night.'

'Exchange?'

'Yes. I noticed. Jack said something to her. That it had been a long time since he last saw her, and she looked different now. Carly's face went all pale and she told him to shut up.'

My body flutters; I remember this too. Goodness, Jack Peaks was a busy bee last night, upsetting people left, right and centre.

'Can I go now?' asks Valentina.

'Huh?' I say, lost in thought. Valentina tuts and gets up. 'No, wait,' I say, remembering something. 'Just one more question.'

Valentina sighs and flops back down onto the seat. The cushion beneath her lets out a deep exhale as the air is pushed from it, mimicking Valentina's own exhale.

'Did you know Jack or Sophia before you entered the villa?'

'No,' says Valentina sharply.

'Did you know Mo?'

'No.'

'But you and he seem very close. For people who have just met.'

Valentina eyes me suspiciously. 'He and I have much in common. He understands me. Can I go now?'

I make a note. 'For now. Please send Carly in to me.'

Valentina jumps to her feet and saunters off. Well, this at least confirms the theory that Sophia was spreading secrets. Valentina Novak clearly has a secret. But is it a secret so bad she would kill to protect it?

Chapter Twenty-Six

Carly and I sit opposite each other in the living room. I perch on one end of the couch, Carly on the opposite side to me. Carly crosses her slim legs underneath her and rests her clasped hands in her lap.

Carly sits perfectly straight, her back rigid, her chin pointing towards me. Her slender frame manages to be both powerful and fragile at the same time. She's like an assassin lying in wait for her victim.

'Thank you for agreeing to chat with me,' I say. It's uncharacteristically conciliatory of me but I'm trying not to be unnerved by the poise of my interviewee. Carly's only response is a slow blink.

So, as expected, she's not going to go easy on me.

'Could you please tell me a bit about yourself?'

Carly purses her lips.

'My name is Carly Chu. I'm twenty-eight years old. I was born in Kent and I now live in London. I'm an actress.' Her voice is a monotone as she recites her list. 'But,' she adds, nodding her head towards the suspect wall. 'You already know all of this. If you want to know something else, you'll have to be more specific.'

When I was a police officer, the lack of cooperability of interviewees, particularly when it was in their own interest to assist an investigation, never ceased to amaze me. Why did people insist on making themselves look guilty?

It seems that no matter the situation, people will always behave like people, like human beings. Emotional and unpredictable. What can I ask her that will get the conversation flowing? I need to get Carly talking before I zoom in on specifics.

'Why did you apply for *LoveWrecked*?' Shit. As soon as the question leaves my lips I realise it was a stupid one. Carly wrinkles her nose and gives me a smirk.

'I didn't apply,' she says sarcastically. 'None of us did.' Carly folds her arms across her chest and raises an eyebrow. 'No wonder you're no longer a police officer. You don't seem to be very good at your job, do you?'

I force my face to remain impassive, but I can't help feeling off-kilter. I'm really out of practice. I've shown my interviewee a weakness and I've been tripped up on it. I take a deep breath.

'Have you ever applied for *LoveWrecked* in the past?'

Carly narrows her eyes. 'Does it matter?' she asks.

I shrug. 'Have you?'

'Yes,' replies Carly.

Again, I keep the emotion from my face. No commiseration, no celebration. 'So, let me ask you again. Why did you apply for *LoveWrecked*?'

It's Carly's turn to feel the affront and I'm pleased to see the actress, ironically, is worse at hiding it than me. Carly gives me a smile that doesn't reach her eyes.

'Exposure,' says Carly. 'I'm an actress. But not a particularly well known one. Being on a show like this is good for my career. *Should* have been good for my career.' She corrects herself.

'And so, when you were chosen for this year's season, you didn't hesitate to accept?'

'Why would I?' she says. I think back to what Valentina said, about Jack talking like he knew things about her and about the argument she said she witnessed between Jack and Carly.

'There was nothing that you were worried about coming out during your time here? Things you wouldn't want the others to know.'

'Ha, no,' says Carly with a bark of laughter. 'No deep, dark secrets from me, I'm afraid.'

'And did you know any of the other Islanders before entering the villa?'

'No,' she replies.

'You didn't know Jack before?'

'I just told you, I didn't know any of the other Islanders before I got here. We were all chosen at random, remember.' Carly is starting to sound exasperated.

'And what did you think of Jack?' I ask, immediately changing tact.

Carly shrugs. 'Typical man. But he was pretty full-on with me last night.'

'What do you mean?'

'Intense. He kept following me around. Whispering in my ear that we should be a couple.' I notice that Carly gives a little shiver at this, like she can't quite hide her disgust when remembering Jack's behaviour.

'And how did that make you feel?' I ask, leaning into her.

'If you're asking me if I killed him because he came on too strong then you're barking up the wrong tree. Jack's behaviour was nothing I've not seen before.' Carly laughs. 'Seriously, Kim, if I killed every man who had come on too strong, there'd be dead men all over London.'

I raise my eyebrow and ask, 'Are there dead men all over London?'

Carly's mouth falls open into a small O. She looks incredulous at the question, but I won't apologise for it. Joke or not, I wouldn't be doing my job if I didn't at least ask.

'Of course there aren't. If I was some sort of black widow, I'd one, not come on a reality television show. And two, I'd hope to be a hell of a lot richer from all the men I'd married and murdered.' She folds her arms across her chest. 'But as you can see, I'm here and I'm not *that* rich.'

I nod and make a note on my pad about Jack's behaviour. I don't really need to write it down; Jack's brashness and the fact that he seemed to have pissed everyone off is the recurring theme. But the act of writing something down gives me a moment to think about my next question. It has the added bonus of giving Carly a moment to stew over the fact that if she is guilty, I'm somewhat suspicious of her. Even if I don't actually think she is a serial killer.

In interviewing, I've always found that the things that aren't said can be just as valuable and powerful as the things that are. But silence isn't comfortable and it took a lot of practice to fight my natural instinct to fill it. Yet it was a valuable lesson to learn because if the investigating officer isn't filling the silence, often the interviewee does.

I look up from my notepad and am disappointed to find that the trick isn't working here. Carly doesn't say anything, she doesn't fill the silence; she waits dutifully and cleverly to be asked a question.

This isn't going well so far. I've only managed to catch Carly off her guard once and it was with a question that I already knew the answer to. At least, I would have been floored if Carly had admitted to murdering multiple men on national television. I need to dig deeper.

'Last night, witnesses have told me that they saw you and Jack having an argument. Is that true?'

'Witnesses?' she replies with a smirk. 'By witnesses you mean Valentina.'

'Is it true?'

Carly sighs and, sounding bored, says, 'I wouldn't call it an argument. But he... pissed me off.'

'How so?' Carly looks down at her lap and picks at her nail varnish; flecks of black polish fall onto her bare thighs and she brushes them off and onto the linen couch. 'Carly?' I press.

'He...' Her lips twitch and her face softens in a way I've not seen before. It's as if she's letting her guard down. 'I don't really know how to explain it. He talked... talked like he...'

'Talked like he knew stuff?' I question, regurgitating the words Valentina spoke. Carly stares at me, the soft expression gone in an instant.

'Yes, if you want to know. He talked to me like he knew things about me. But before you jump to conclusions, I didn't kill him. I'm not even sure if he did know anything. I can be paranoid sometimes.'

'Paranoid? What's happened to make you paranoid?'

'Nothing that's relevant here,' she snaps. I eye her up. I'm onto something but I'm not sure what. It's an unusual word to use. And from what I've seen, Carly is an unusual person. Her reaction to Jack's death and seeing Jack's body was different from the others too. Like she'd seen it before, like death was nothing new to her, just a normal part of life. Maybe she worked somewhere before where this was a thing.

'How long have you been an actress for?' I ask. Carly considers the question for a moment before replying.

'It's something I've always wanted to do. But I've been paid to be an actress for the last couple of years.'

'And before becoming an actress what did you do?'

'I think people are born to act.'

I grit my teeth. 'OK, before you pursued being an actress professionally, what did you do?'

'Bits and bobs,' she says, pulling a face.

'Such as?' I push.

She flicks bits of her discarded nail varnish from the couch and onto the floor, the black dots looking like ants scuttling across the marble. 'You know, the typical stuff a wannabe actress would do. Bar work, waitressing.'

I nod and note this down. 'Why are you so uncomfortable with me asking about your work? What are you not telling me?'

'There's lots I'm not telling you because none of it is relevant here.'

'Don't you find it weird that you're so uncomfortable now discussing your past and yet seeing a dead body doesn't seem to faze you at all?' I ask.

'No,' says Carly, a little too forcibly. I grip my pen and make a note. 'What are you writing?' she asks, leaning forward. I put the paper down, clasp my hands together under my chin and lean forward. 'Why does not being affected by the sight of a dead body matter here?'

'Because your reaction to seeing Jack's body was that of someone who's seen dead bodies before. It was the reaction of someone for whom death is a simple part of life. I didn't expect to see Jack's body this morning, but my reaction was more surprise than horror and shock. I used to be a police officer; I've seen lots of dead bodies. His body didn't scare me. And it didn't scare you and that makes me think you killed him.' Carly bites her lip and I suspect she's trying to decide how much she should reveal.

'So, because I didn't react like the others, you assume that I killed him?' Carly laughs forcefully. 'That's the most ridiculous thing I've ever heard. But to put your mind at rest, I didn't react like the others because my life hasn't always been so easy. I've been in some dangerous situations before and I learned to control my emotions, especially outwardly.'

I think back to last night, when Jack said something to her and she went completely white. 'So, what about when Jack said he'd missed you when you were gone?'

'What about it?'

'You didn't hide your outward emotions that well then; his words practically drained the colour from you. What was it about what he said that freaked you out?' At my question, Carly turns her face away from me and closes her eyes. She gives her head a little shake.

'I don't know what you're talking about.'

'For God's sake,' I shout, making her jump. 'Why are your purposefully impeding this investigation? Whatever Jack said to you or made you feel could be important. Just tell me.'

Carly grits her teeth and I can tell she doesn't like the audible accusation that she is hindering my investigation.

I get the impression that Carly's reputation is almost as important to her as her life.

'Fine,' she says, eventually, 'but just to show that I'm not impeding this investigation.' Carly leans in closer to me and cups her hands around her mouth, seemingly to avoid her words being caught on camera. 'I used to earn money in a way I'm not proud of,' she whispers, 'but about two years ago I had earned enough to leave it behind me. I changed my appearance, slightly, not dramatically, but I changed my hair, my clothes, took out the coloured contacts I had been wearing. And I moved to a different place. There was something about the way Jack said he'd missed me, as though he knew, and it freaked me. But I was a bit tipsy and therefore more sensitive. If I was really worried about exposure I wouldn't have come on the show.'

Carly pulls away from me and narrows her eyes, as if ready to pounce on any comment or judgement I might make. I don't say anything because I'm thinking about what she has just told me and what it might mean. There is something about the word 'exposure' that gives me room for pause. Both Carly and I have different lives, past lives that we are no longer living. Maybe even past lives that we are running away from. Valentina talked about her past too. Is this an important clue to uncovering who the Judge is and who killed Sophia and Jack?

Beep. Beep. Beep.

Carly and I jump in unison as an alarm blares into the living room. It's a sound I've come to recognise. And whatever it is, it isn't good.

'What the hell is it now?' I say, aloud. Time can't be already up, can it?

Beep. Beep. Beep.

The alarm continues. I press my hands against my ears; it's incessant. It seems to permeate my body and vibrate my bones.

'Islanders, report to the Fire Pit,' shouts a voice like an airport tannoy. I tilt my chin towards the sky; the voice seems to come from above as if from heaven. This is no God, though. This voice is the Devil.

Chapter Twenty-Seven

LoveWrecked @LoveWrecked
1.53m followers

Share your thoughts on this year's season of
LoveWrecked.

@LoveWrecked: Due to events inside the
villa, all UK channels have removed the
show from air. We are cooperating fully
with the British and Greek authorities to get
the Islanders home. Our top priority is the
safety and wellbeing of our Islanders. #Love-
Wrecked #freetheislanders

@madmaddy2002: Channel Z was the last
channel still showing LoveWrecked but
now EVEN THEY have taken it down!
Whyyyyyyyyy? #LoveWrecked

@Skyzthelimit: @madmaddy2002 Because
it's sick what's happening in there. Why do
you want to watch it? #freetheislanders

@JustDeserts: Want to watch Love-
Wrecked? It's streaming live on
www.justdeserts.co.uk/LoveWrecked

@madmaddy2002: Thanks @JustDeserts. Do you know you've spelt desserts wrong? LOL

@JustDeserts: @madmaddy2002, check my blog out and you'll see I didn't get anything wrong ;)

Chapter Twenty-Eight

'Islanders, report to the Fire Pit. Immediately,' the voice repeats.

Nausea squeezes my stomach. Has someone else died? Carly and I lock eyes. I jump from the couch; papers fly everywhere. I race to the door, stopping for a second to hold onto the doorframe. My head swims; I'm dizzy and light-headed.

Beep. Beep. Beep. The alarm continues to blare.

'Islanders, report to the Fire Pit.'

Carly pushes past me, and I follow after her, ignoring her look of scorn at my weakness. I don't need her judgement. Not now, not ever.

The neon countdown timer tells me there are twenty-three minutes to go before the next killing. The countdown timer is a stark reminder of what's at stake. The fearful faces of the other Islanders study me as I walk towards them as if I understand the reason for the alarm.

'Sit down, Kimberley,' says the Judge, screened once again on the outdoor television, his mighty throne. He still wears his costume and his face is still in darkness. Not in the mood to argue any more, I oblige and plonk myself down on the tiered wooden seating area facing the outdoor television.

'Good,' says the Judge. 'You're all here. For now.' His voice mimics that of *LoveWrecked*'s presenter. It's upbeat and chirpy as if everything were absolutely normal and he was speaking to us on a normal day in the villa. 'Stop the clock.' The neon countdown stops. The coloured lights show that there are now twenty-two minutes two seconds left. My heart begins to race; what has he got planned? 'I thought we'd play a little game – wouldn't that be fun?'

The reaction to the Judge's words is immediate. The Islanders and I are now so entwined together by circumstance that we have a single emotional response to the Judge.

The swear word that shoots from my mouth comes out almost in unison with Mo's. My shoulders tense just as Valentina's do. The Judge has made us a unit, united in anger and fear.

Rosalind darts out a hand to grab my arm and, though her squeezes on my flesh are uncomfortable, I don't budge. I want to offer my support in whatever small way I can.

Play a little game? That was what he said. What the fuck does he think we're doing right now? My heart is in my mouth. I shouldn't antagonise him, but I do anyway.

'No, I don't think playing a little game with you sounds fun at all,' I reply with as much sarcasm as I can muster. 'I think that sounds sick; aren't you toying with us enough as it is?'

But the Judge continues as though I haven't spoken, not that I expected him to. 'As you all know, *LoveWrecked* challenges are famous. The British public absolutely love them. So I thought, *Why should this series be any different?*'

My stomach tightens and sweat prickles in my armpits at the thought of another challenge. I have my hands quite full with the first one.

'What if we don't want to participate in your little challenge?' shouts Valentina, speaking aloud the question that formed in my mind. The Judge turns his shadowed face towards Valentina.

'Oh, you will want to participate, because I'm going to make it worth your while.'

'How?' shouts Mo. 'How can you possibly make it worth our while?'

'I'm going to ask Kimberley here a question, a question with three correct answers. For each correct answer Kimberley is able to give to my question, I will add an extra fifteen minutes onto the countdown timer. Surely the chance to live that little bit longer is a good enough incentive?'

There is a flutter of excitement. It doesn't take much for my fellow Islanders to take the Judge's bait. They look to one another with whispers of positivity. Stockholm syndrome has really set in, it seems.

I don't flutter or get excited by his words. My jaw tenses. The Judge is playing with us; he's like a cat holding the tail of a mouse between his claws. He has released us momentarily, allowing us to scramble away from him, but he intends to get us in the end. I'm sure of that.

'And what if we get the answer wrong?' I ask, jutting my chin into the air. I want to know all the facts before I make a deal with this devil. The others sigh collectively, realising later than me that what the Judge says might just be too good to be true.

'You're so suspicious, Kimberley King,' he says in his cool, calculated voice. I narrow my eyes at the screen; I hate that he keeps calling me Kimberley. Nobody calls me Kimberley, not any more. The Judge whistles through his teeth. 'I am feeling generous today. For every wrong answer, I will only drop your time by fifteen minutes,' said the Judge.

'Well, that's no good, we've only got twenty-two minutes left,' says Rosalind. 'What if we get all the answers wrong?'

'Better hope you don't,' replies the Judge matter-of-factly.

'And what if we don't answer at all?' I ask, my fists clenched. The Judge tilts his wigged head towards me.

'I don't understand the question,' says the Judge, feigning intrigue.

'What if we refuse to answer. There's already a gun placed against our heads; what else will compel us to do this?'

'Shut up, Kim, he's offering us extra time,' hisses Valentina.

'So what? An extra fifteen minutes before he kills one of us. That isn't enough incentive for me.' I fold my arms across my body. I'm done being pushed around by an invisible enemy.

'I'm sensing a bit of tension here. Let me put that to rights.' At his words, the Judge's image again diminishes to a small box in the bottom left-hand corner of the screen. The image that replaces him makes my mouth fall open in despair.

It's a photograph of a woman. It's taken from far away; the image is grainy and slightly out of focus.

'Who is that?' ask Mo.

My mouth is dry, and I rise ever so slightly from my seat. I know this woman. I know her dark almond eyes; I know her long, braided hair; I know her warm, friendly smile. The woman in the photograph is laughing at something, completely unaware she is being photographed.

'Zoe,' I whisper.

'That's the problem with people nowadays, they put everything online. And even those who aren't prolific social media users such as yourself, Kimberley, there's still enough there to do stuff with. To find people. To learn about them.'

'Who is that?' asks Rosalind, looking from me to the screen. I can't answer her. I feel as if my anger has snatched my voice away from me. The Judge is displaying an image of my friend.

'If you hurt her—' I start to shout but the Judge interrupts me.

'Who? Zoe Pearce? I wouldn't dream of hurting her. Well, unless you refuse to play with me.'

My nostrils flare. Part of me wishes he'd just kill me, save me this torture. But Zoe's smiling face and her complete lack of knowledge that this photograph is being taken makes her seem so innocent in comparison to this monster. Nothing about this situation is fair, but the Judge wants to play this out and right now, I'm not in a position to stop him.

The Judge claps his hands together; he has me in a bind and he knows it. 'So, I bet you're all dying to know what the question is. Oops,' he says, lifting a hand to cover the place where his mouth would be. He's feigning embarrassment. 'No pun intended.'

His words make me feel as though I'm back on the boat, being thrown around on the open sea. I desperately want the motion to stop.

The more the Judge speaks, the more destructive he sounds. He must be completely unhinged. Is this all nothing more than a madman's vendetta?

Nobody responds to the Judge's remark. How are we meant to respond to words like that? We all sit on the wooden seating around the fire while the afternoon sun beats down on us. Like zombies, we stare, silent and expectant, at the big screen.

I assume that my fellows are saturated, that the shock has consumed them and they're now incapable of reacting. I don't blame them. The Judge beats his hands on his lap, the drumroll sound echoes around the garden, the beat works its way up to a crescendo.

'Kimberley King, you have ten minutes to figure it out. For every right answer, you will gain fifteen minutes. For every wrong answer, you will lose fifteen minutes. Three of your number have killed before – can you tell me who? Ready, steady, go!'

Chapter Twenty-Nine

My jaw slackens at the Judge's words. I don't know what question I was expecting but it certainly wasn't that. It's as if someone has punched me in the stomach. I almost double over from the force of it. Any defiance I felt against the Judge seconds earlier has gone. I'm moment-arily unable to speak.

'Three of you have killed before?' roars Mo, springing to his feet and creating distance between himself and the others. 'Three? No, no it can't be.' His head swings from face to face; his eyes are manic. 'Shit. SHIT. More deaths, more murders.'

I eye him suspiciously. Mo is a man on the edge; the question has touched a nerve. Is he over-egging his anger to compensate for something? Plus, he specifically said 'three of you', not 'three of us'. But Mo, like the Judge, is met with silence by the group.

Nine minutes are left on the clock. The time is slipping through my fingers quicker than I thought possible.

I close my eyes and retreat inside my mind. I should be firing questions at the others; it's in all of our best interests that I do, but I'm paralysed.

If the Judge is right and three of them have killed before then the Judge knows more about us than I could ever have imagined. He knows intimate details about our lives, the most secret details. My stomach clenches. Oh my God, what does he know about me?

Eight minutes on the clock.

Anger, red and hot, surges through my body. I stand and grab Mo by the arm. I point him towards the seating area.

'Mo, sit your arse down,' I instruct in as brisk a tone as possible.

My gaze travels from face to face, locking eyes with each in turn. I look at every single one of them, trying to divine which of them is guilty and staying silent.

Who is stopping us receiving an extra fifteen minutes of reprieve?

'I asked you all for honesty,' I say, placing my hands on my hips. 'Now *really* isn't the time to keep things quiet. The Judge isn't messing around. Clearly he knows things.' The Islanders stare back at me and I feel my cheeks grow warm. Their reluctance confuses me. 'We need more time. Why are you denying us more time?'

I don't even know who to direct my *you* to, so I do my best to scatter my looks across them all.

All sit motionless, waiting for me to question them. Well, all of them except Mo. Mo is blinking a little more than is natural and his knuckles are white from the effort of keeping his shaking legs still. Mo displays all the signs of hiding something.

'Mo,' I say. But before I can continue, my words are cut off. Mo emits a whimper like a dying dog and he digs his fingers so hard into his legs he's in danger of drawing blood.

I've been trained to notice even the smallest indicators of body language, but Mo might as well have a megaphone and be shouting 'I'm hiding something.' I bite my lip; despite myself I feel sorry for him. I have him cornered.

'Mo,' I repeat, more gently this time. 'Did Jack Peaks recognise you?' Remembering Carly's words from earlier.

'He said he did,' replies Mo, still not looking at me. 'But I'm not in his mind, so I don't know if he really did or didn't.' He licks dry lips and shifts uncomfortably in his seat.

'Did you know one another?'

'No,' blurts Mo. 'Before yesterday, I'd never seen him before in my life. Honestly. I hadn't. I don't know the guy.'

'Four minutes on the clock,' says the Judge. I glance up at the screen and narrow my eyes at him. What I wouldn't give to punch the Judge in his hidden face so that his wig falls off. I turn back to Mo. I need to crack this, get at least one name right. We don't have the time on the clock to get more than one wrong.

'Jack knew you, though. He was sure of it. So, if I were to believe you when you say you've never met him before in your life, tell me then how he might have known you or recognised you.'

Mo's eyes dart from me to the floor, from the floor to me. I give him a moment to gather himself and, to stop myself from screaming at him, work through the possible answers in my head.

How might a person be recognisable? Mo is a chef and restaurant owner; maybe he appeared in a marketing campaign. I don't wait for him to answer my previous question – there isn't time. I press on with my newly discovered line of enquiry.

'Have you ever appeared in the papers or online? Maybe advertising your restaurant?' At this he flushes red.

The media. Being in the media is a sensitive topic for him.

For a second time, I press on without waiting for him to answer. My fingers tingle. I'm closing in on the truth, I can feel it. 'Why does the thought of being in the paper make you nervous, Mo?'

Mo sighs and again flops his head into his hands. He murmurs. But he's so quiet I don't catch it.

'Could you repeat that? I didn't hear what you said,' I say.

'It was an accident,' says Mo, louder this time but still directed at his feet. Rosalind inhales sharply and Valentina turns to look at him, her eyes wide.

Oh my God, he's killed someone. He's actually killed someone and he's about to admit it live on television.

I squat down so that my face is level with Mo's.

'What was an accident?' I whisper; I'm so close to the truth that I don't want to scare him.

'Her,' he gulps, his words catching in his throat. The others are silent. The only sound is the click, click, click as the seconds tick away on the countdown clock. Mo clears his throat and speaks again.

'Her death. But I didn't kill her,' he stammers. 'It wasn't my fault, it was an accident.' Mo sniffs and wipes the back of his hand across his nose. I shiver; deeply buried secrets are rising to the surface, whether we want them to or not. I feel another wave of anger against the Judge and his vendetta. 'That will be how Jack knew me. There was an inquiry, after she died. I was acquitted, though, no wrongdoing. But I was on the news and it was online too. Jack must have seen me there but I didn't kill him, not to hide this.'

I nod. I believe him. 'Thank you for being so brave. It can't have been easy to admit that.'

One down, two to go.

There are two and a half minutes on the clock. That leaves Carly, Valentina, Rosalind and Daniel.

'There are four of you here. I need two of you to be as brave as Mo has been.'

'There are five of us,' snaps Carly, her face like thunder. 'Five of us remain.' My brow furrows.

'Five?' I ask, looking around the garden.

'Yes. Five. Why is no one asking if you've killed anyone? You used to be a police officer. Surely you'd have access to weapons. It's on the news every day, police officers killing criminals and innocent people alike. Have you stopped to consider yourself?'

Carly might as well have slapped me. I hadn't thought of myself but now that I do I realise that I'm as good a candidate as the rest of them.

The image of a body flashes, unwelcome, in my mind's eye.

I know what I did. I've killed before. I killed her.

'Kim. Kim!' shouts Rosalind. 'We don't have time, you might as well guess.'

'We can't guess. We'll lose time if we get it wrong,' says Valentina.

'But there is also the right guess to cancel it out,' says Rosalind.

Two minutes to go.

'Do any of you four have anything to add?'

'I haven't killed anyone,' says Valentina defiantly.

'Me neither,' says Carly, folding her arms across her chest.

'Nor have I,' says Rosalind, looking at her hands.

At least one of them is lying but I don't have the heart, energy or the time to press them.

'Mo Khan has *accidentally* killed someone before.'

'Any other names to give me?' says the Judge.

I look from Valentina to Rosalind. From Carly to Daniel.

'Just guess!' Rosalind implores. My mind whirrs with what I've seen and heard. What my instinct tells me about these people. I bite my lip so hard I'm in danger of splitting it.

One minute to go.

'Guess, Kim. Just guess.'

'Mo Khan, Carly Chu, and me, Kimberley King, have all killed before,' I say. Carly gives a loud huff.

Three. Two. One. *Beep, beep, beep.*

'Thank you, Kimberley. Let's see how many right answers you got.' The Judge sounds like a tacky game show host now. 'Mo Khan,' says the Judge and Mo looks up at the screen, his eyes rimmed with red.

Ding. My shoulders drop as the sound associated with correct answers sounds in the garden.

'Correct. Mo Khan has killed someone. Fifteen minutes added to the clock. Next, you said Carly Chu...'

Nuh-uh. The two-beat sound that follows tells me I'm wrong. 'Sadly not. Carly was not the answer I was looking for. Carly has been a naughty girl but not *that* naughty.'

I glance over at Carly. A smile, tight and thin, crosses her lips.

One right. One wrong. Final answer was myself. Something tells me I'm right. The Judge knows about all of us and if he knows things about me he knows what I did.

'And finally, you said yourself, Kimberley King. Very interesting for you to say that, considering you're here investigating what other people may or may not have done.' The correct-answer *ding* sounds again. I let out a sigh and press my hands to my face; so it's true, I'm here because of Emily. 'Two right answers adds half an hour, one wrong deducts fifteen minutes. So you're fifteen minutes up over all. But before I let you go and get back to the fun, shall I give you the right answers?'

'No,' shouts Rosalind. 'Stop it. Stop this.' Her face is pale, but her cheeks are flushed as she shouts at the screen. Does she think he is going to say her name?

'One more of you has killed before. Haven't you, Valentina?'

The silence which surrounds us presses in on me as the Judge's words hang in the air.

'Great,' he continues, breaking the silence. 'Glad that's sorted. You have thirty-seven minutes remaining on the clock before another one of you dies. It is now exactly 2PM, restart the clock.'

The Judge switches himself off from the television screen and the ten-minute challenge timer leaves the screen to be replaced by the red lines of the killing clock. Silence hangs in the garden. Carly, Daniel and Rosalind edge to one side away from us, from Mo, Valentina and me – the murderers. I stand still, my chest rising and falling; my mind is a mess of thoughts. Before the challenge I thought that maybe our captivity was the sick action of a psychopath but now I realise I was wrong: the Judge knows our secrets; he knows about the death I caused.

I flop down on the bench, too shellshocked to speak to the others. The Judge isn't working alone. How could he be? There is no way he could have so much information at his disposal, not without help.

What does the Judge want? To expose us? Humiliate us in front of the world? But why?

What about Jack? Someone was planted here to kill him but what had Jack done that meant he deserved to die?

Oh my God.

'What?' says Daniel, sliding towards me as if noticing the change in my body language. 'What is it, Kim?' He takes my hand and squeezes it.

'I've been so stupid. How could I have missed this? I was wrong, I've been looking in the wrong place, asking the wrong questions. Wrong. Wrong. Wrong,' I say, my lip quivering.

'No,' he says, giving me a tight smile. 'You haven't done anything wrong. He is the one in the wrong.' Daniel jabs his finger towards the television screen, the home of the Judge. 'Did you hear that? You're the one in the wrong.'

'I knew this wasn't random from the beginning, but I didn't know what connected us. I made the wrong assumption.'

'What do you mean?' asks Carly, interested now.

'I kept thinking the Judge wanted to expose us. Expose our secrets, our pasts, to the people watching this show. But I didn't really understand why. I thought maybe for fun or to humiliate us, but it wasn't that.'

'So, what connects us then?' snaps Carly. 'Just tell us.' Her voice rises.

'We're all connected because... no, we're all here because someone wants to punish us.'

Chapter Thirty

Contact Me form

Type your message in the box below. I read every piece of correspondence that comes to me and I will aim to get back to you as soon as I can.

Your Name: Sammy Knight
Your Email Address: sammyknight@blue-skyblue.com

Your Message:
Hi, whoever you are.

I don't know how else to start this, so I'll launch straight in.

I was attacked several years ago by a man, a very drunk man. It was days before Christmas and I was out with my colleagues from the accountancy firm that I worked at, at the time. We'd decided we were going to have a big night, you know: dress up, go to a club, partying until dawn kind of thing. Most of us were all trainee accountants and we'd complained all year about how everyone thinks accountants are boring. Well, we were determined we'd have our Christmas night out to prove we weren't boring. So, we'd all agreed on dressing as slutty Santas, we'd gone to an Italian restaurant for dinner where we'd drunk copious amount of wine, and then we danced for hours and sang Mariah Carey's 'All I Want for Christmas' at the top of our lungs. Multiple times I thought I should probably go home but I remember every time the thought entered my head the song would change, and it would drag me back to the dance floor.

I don't know when he and I started chatting. The man who attacked me, I mean. But I remember that he was on a night out with his football club, they had a shit name, the Essex Eagles they were called. I mean who calls their football team the Essex Eagles, pisses me off even thinking about it now.

Anyway, he was far too sleazy for me to be interested so I gave him the slip and headed outside for a cigarette. I remember slipping out the door underneath the emergency exit sign. It wasn't the official smoking area, but the club had opened those doors in an attempt to cut through the sweaty fog that hung in the air because of the hundreds of sweaty bodies packed in. I remember how cold it was outside, how it hit me like a ton of bricks and set my teeth chattering. I remember how my ears rang at their freedom from the noise inside.

My hands were shaking as I lifted the lighter to the end of the cigarette and I was so busy concentrating on lighting it that I nearly dropped it when he spoke to me.

'Lucky cigarette.' That was what he said to me, his smile was crooked, and his eyes glazed over. They said I was too drunk to possibly be able remember the details as well as I do but I will never forget his glassy eyes.

'Want one?' I asked. Now, that was another thing I got in trouble for, offering the cigarette. But I wasn't really, I was just a bit confused, I thought he was saying Lucky Strike, the brand, and this was his way of asking for one.

'No, lucky cigarette,' he repeated. 'Your cigarette, it's lucky, because it gets to rest between your lips.' I crossed my arms across my chest at that point. I didn't like that he'd said that. I stubbed my cigarette out and turned to head back inside. He grabbed my wrist and kissed me forcibly. His hands went where they had no permission to be. I was frozen to the spot and terrified. It could have been minutes later, it couldn't have been hours but one of the bouncers came around the corner for his own cigarette and he stepped away from me. I went to the police and to give them their due they did take me seriously, treated me respectfully. I pressed charges, but it was quite apparent that I didn't have a cat in hell's chance of it going anywhere. I was drunk that night too and I was wearing a fancy-dress outfit, a provocative fancy dress. Drunk and provocative, that was who they painted me out to be. But that wasn't a true reflection of me, and even if it was it shouldn't matter, being drunk and provocative isn't a crime. Assault is and he broke the law.

That was about three years ago and since then my life has fallen apart. My boyfriend was supportive at first, but it was hard on him too. Eventually, he broke up with me because I couldn't stand him touching me. I've had multiple jobs in the last two years, I can't seem to keep them, nobody wants to employ someone who regularly and randomly breaks down in tears.

I feel like the only thing I can control in my life is my weight which I do by starving myself. The people who knew me before are quite horrified by what I've become and they've all fallen away, they don't understand that I can't just get over it.

I hate myself and my body no longer feels like my own. I'm a shell of the woman I once was, and it is all his fault.

I wanted to let you know how much you've helped me. You helped me see that what I need is for him to know exactly what he has done to me and for him to feel the pain I have. I think I will only get peace once he knows that. From one victim to another, please help me...

Chapter Thirty-One

When I realise that we were all chosen for *LoveWrecked* because we have something for which we needed to be punished, I feel a moment of acceptance. I should be punished; I want to be punished. I've been punishing myself for long enough. A calm settles over me. I won't fight it any more; I won't run away from it; I will do what is asked of me because that is my punishment.

I get to my feet and stand on the wooden seating. 'Everyone, we may have been granted some extra time but there are still only thirty-seven minutes left before the next killing and I'm no closer to finding out what happened to Jack. Mo, we haven't spoken yet; will you come and have a chat with me? In private.'

Mo gives a hollow bark of disbelief. 'Private?' he says, folding his arms across his chest. 'There is nothing private here. There's no effing way I'm talking to you. You've seen what they've done to me. Look at what they're saying about me, about Valentina, about you. You've killed someone, so why should I talk to you.' Mo points his arm towards the outdoor television screen.

I scrunch my eyes to read some of the messages and my muscles tense at the inhumanity of it. The words that can come from people shielded by the protection of their computers. People are telling Mo, Valentina and me that we deserve to die like the people we've killed. That they hope one of us is the next victim.

Someone even go so far as to ask if they can vote for who they want to die, because if they could vote, we'd be the first to go.

I shudder; I hope the Judge doesn't get any ideas from this. This sounds exactly like the type of thing he'd love to introduce.

How the hell am I going to convince any of them to talk to me now?

'Mo, please,' I say.

In the real world, I've encountered people who don't want to speak with me but back then I had the authority of being a police officer. Life inside this villa is a law unto itself.

'No, I don't really feel like speaking with you,' he replies, the distaste as evident in his voice as it is in his face.

'I understand that this is difficult and uncomfortable but—'

'You understand?' he spits out. 'Have you not just seen what happened to me when I mentioned one thing to you? There's no way I'm putting myself at risk like that. I have a reputation to think about.'

Carly scoffs loudly at this and I can't help but empathise with her; his selfishness is astounding.

'We're all at risk,' I reply as calmly as I can because under the surface I'm seething. 'Listen to me, please. If

you all refuse, then I can't push forward with this investigation and the deaths will continue.'

'Do you know what?' says Mo, getting to his feet. 'I'm
not convinced any more that this is a real threat. Maybe
Jack isn't really dead. And this, all of this...' – he spreads
his arms out wide and gestures to the surrounding villa
garden – '...is just a ploy to get us to admit something,
creating drama to get the producers great ratings. Maybe
LoveWrecked is taking advantage of us to make good television. I refuse to give in to that. I *refuse* to be made to
look like a fool and allow them to line their pockets at my
expense.'

'This isn't a ploy,' says Rosalind, her voice heavy and
her body shaking. 'Don't you think that if this was real,
I, the producer, would know about it? I didn't know
anything about it. And I'm absolutely fucking terrified.'

'She's right, Mo,' I say. 'You need to believe me when
I say this is real.'

Mo laughs at this. 'Do you think I'd believe you? You're
a murderer. Who did you kill, hey? And what's to say
you've not killed again? Or that she has?' He jabs his finger
towards Valentina.

Valentina's lip trembles and a fat tear slides down her
cheek.

'Cool it, Mo,' says Rosalind, putting her arm around
Valentina. 'There is no need to use that tone.'

'No need to use that tone – are you all crazy? There
are people here who've just been exposed as murderers.
I'm not a murderer. I wasn't even convicted.' He turns to
me. 'Why don't you interview Valentina or yourself?'

Valentina stands up. 'Talk to me again. Please, I need
to explain what happened, what really happened; it isn't
like the Judge is making it sound. I didn't kill anyone.'

'No, I want to speak to Mo next.' I'm determined about this; I haven't chatted to Mo yet and his mood has been up and down like a yo-yo since we discovered Jack's body.

'Mo doesn't want to speak to you. I do. The Judge has explained things wrong. I'm not a murderer but I did hurt someone, and I will tell you about it all.'

'Sit down, Valentina. Mo, I want to speak to you next.'

'And I don't want to speak to you,' roars Mo. 'You have no authority over me.'

'Why are you stopping this investigation?'

There's a spark in Mo's eyes.

'You call this, this, an investigation? If I were in charge I'd be looking at the murderer first.' He jabs his finger towards Valentina. 'She's even bloody admitting it.'

Valentina's fists clench and she launches herself at Mo. 'I never said I was a murderer. I'm not a murderer.' She beats her tiny hands against his chest. He pushes her off him like a lion swatting away a bird.

'Don't push her around like that,' shouts Rosalind, taking a step closer to Mo.

Valentina is undeterred by Mo's force and takes a step towards me instead. 'Kim, I need to tell you something. I can explain everything. I should have told you before. But I didn't and I'm sorry. Jack knew too.'

I swivel to face her. 'What?'

'Jack, he came up to me last night. After he asked me for drugs and he said he only asked me for drugs because he knew what I did. And he wouldn't let it go when I didn't want to talk about it. I don't know how he knew. It must be in my file. Maybe Sophia knew.'

'So you killed him and Sophia to shut them up?' interjects Mo.

'No,' shouts Valentina. 'I didn't kill Jack and I didn't kill Sophia.' Valentina's eyes are wild now and her jaw is clenched so tight she's in danger of breaking her teeth.

'So Jack knew your secret. Maybe he knew mine, Kimberley's and Rosalind's. And yours, Mo. Any of us could have done it to shut him up,' says Carly, clearly deciding it is time for her to enter the argument.

'Everyone,' I say, my hands raised in what I hope is a calming gesture. 'Please, calm down.'

'But what I want to know is how come the Judge knows so much about us?' asks Carly. She turns around and takes a large step towards Rosalind. 'I didn't trust you much before, Rosalind, and I definitely don't trust you now.' Carly's finger is pointed in Rosalind's direction and Rosalind takes a step back, looking as if she's been slapped.

'Do you think I wanted this to happen? If I don't die here, what kind of life is left for me?' asks Rosalind, her eyes red.

Valentina grabs the hand that Carly is pointing at Rosalind. 'What does the Judge know about you, Carly Chu? What are you hiding?'

Carly yanks her hand free. 'Fuck off.'

'Don't tell me to fuck off. Nobody thinks you're innocent. You're just as guilty as the rest of us,' shouts Valentina, her face contorted with anger.

'I'll tell you to fuck off if I want to,' replies Carly, giving Valentina a hard shove.

'Hey!' I shout. 'Both of you, all of you. Stop it.' But I'm ignored; Valentina pushes Carly back. Carly stumbles, tripping over her feet, and tumbles to the ground.

This does it. The tension that has been building in the villa since the morning erupts. A fight breaks out. Valentina has Carly by the hair. Rosalind tries to pull them apart but gets slapped across the cheek by Carly's windmilling arms. She yelps in pain. Daniel steps forward and grabs Valentina around the middle in the way he did earlier this morning and pulls her away from Carly.

'Ouch,' she cries. 'Get off me, Daniel, you're hurting me.'

'And you,' says Mo, pointing at Daniel. 'Why is no one questioning you more? Doesn't anyone else think it is weird that this guy is filming all of this and is clearly involved?'

'I didn't kill anyone, unlike you!'

'It was an accident,' shouts Mo, charging towards Daniel, like a bull to a red rag. It's like a twig has finally snapped in Mo and he is on the rampage. I'm terrified someone is going to get hurt.

Everything is chaos.

'Stop,' I scream. 'Stop it, all of you.' There are only twenty-five minutes on the clock. They're wasting valuable time with their petty squabbles.

'Mo,' I call over the noise. Mo doesn't look away from his altercation with Daniel but continues to wag his finger in Daniel's face. 'Mo,' I say, more forcefully this time. Again, I'm ignored. 'Mo, you say you're not a murderer. This is your chance to explain it to me and to the world.' Mo stops and takes a step back from Daniel. Daniel storms away from him, shaking his head angrily. The restaurant owner turns towards me. His shoulders curl around, closing in his chest. Mo Khan looks exhausted and defeated. 'Please, Mo, let's have a conversation and talk about this?'

Mo's fight is gone now, and he shrugs as if to say, *What is the worst that can happen?* Now that the accusation that he has killed before has been announced to whatever people are still watching *LoveWrecked*, he seems to have decided things can't really get worse.

I want to go easy on him, he's suffered quite enough in this villa but I'm not afraid to push harder if need be. I can't forget that our lives are at stake.

'Let's chat over here' I say, gesturing for Mo to follow me. I don't want to discuss this inside; I prefer to stay close to the others.

On the far side of the garden there is an area made up of several sun loungers. It is removed from the others and relatively secluded but still enables me to keep an eye on Rosalind, Valentina, Carly and Daniel.

From here, I can see that the three women continue their squabble but not with the same vehemence as before. Valentina sits slumped back on the wooden seating, watching as Carly and Rosalind bicker. They're arguing with words now, not violence, which I'm grateful for.

I sit down on one of the loungers and watch as Mo trudges towards me. I try not to take too much delight in how Mo's state of mind right now makes him the perfect interviewee. He's tired and emotional. People often say more than they mean to when they're in this state. That's assuming he really feels as awful as he looks.

Someone is lying to me. And despite the death and the horror, I can't let my own emotions get in the way of my investigation.

'I've never applied for the show before, no. I've barely even watched it before,' says Mo, answering the same question that I posed to Carly an hour ago.

'So, what did you think when you were approached?'

'My first thought was that there was no way I was going on the show.'

'Why did you think that?' I can predict the answer. Someone who's killed someone, accidentally or not, probably doesn't want to put themselves in the spotlight if they don't have to.

'Because of my past. Which, for the record,' Mo tilts his head upwards, searching for the camera, 'I was acquitted of all wrongdoing.'

'And yet you're here; why is that?'

'I was reluctant; I didn't want to expose myself, I didn't want more people to know what I'd...' Mo hung his head. '...what I'd done. But my business partner thought it would be good publicity. Me being on television, people would hear about our restaurant, and we'd get more customers.' After a pause Mo added, 'The restaurant isn't in any trouble or anything; we've got lots of loyal customers but as they usually say, no publicity is bad publicity.' Mo scoffs at this. 'I think everything happening here in the villa is the exception to the rule. I mean, not that publicity matters if you're dead.'

'Last night,' I say, remembering the exchange I intervened in. 'Jack Peaks said he recognised you. You protested, quite forcefully. What was that about?'

'Your theory being Sophia told Jack about me and the person I killed. Jack made a huge show about recognising me to put me on edge, and eventually, I killed him to shut him up?' He laughs humourlessly.

'Did you kill him to shut him up?' I ask.

'No,' explodes Mo and I almost lean back at the force of his words. 'When Jack said he recognised me, it sent me into a panic, I didn't want to be remembered on the show for – for that. I was acquitted but there was publicity and many people thought I shouldn't have been acquitted. I came on this show to move on from my past and generate good publicity for my new restaurant.'

'And so how did you feel when Jack Peaks posed a potential threat to this good publicity?'

'I was worried, but—'

'And did you find out that Sophia was the one who told him? I've heard she was good at digging up information about people's pasts.'

'No, I didn't know Sophia knew anything.'

'What would you be willing to do to keep your past hidden?'

'A lot. But I wouldn't kill someone.'

'That's interesting, because if the Judge's game has taught me anything, it is that you did kill someone.'

'No, not like that. This was different. That was an accident.' Mo twists his hands, intertwining them nervously.

'Do you have categories of killing someone?'

'No, I mean, yes. This is different. I didn't kill Jack Peaks. I was frightened he recognised me and would tell everyone about what I'd done but I didn't kill him. It is nobody else's business, but I wouldn't kill to keep it a secret.' Mo slams his hands on the sun lounger in frustration. His hands bounce off the plump cushion back into the air; the effect is almost comical.

'Tell me about the person you did kill.'

Mo's eyes widen. 'It was five years ago. In my restaurant. It was a busy night. There was a huge table of men out on their annual boys' night. There was another table, a family dinner.' He rubs his forehead. 'The family was four. Mum, Dad, son and daughter. The daughter had an allergy, a peanut allergy. And they told me about it. They did. But I was so distracted with the large table that I... I didn't write it down. The daughter had an EpiPen with her but the amount that was in the food was too much. She died.' Mo drops his head between his hands and he sobs, almost uncontrollably. 'And it's ridiculous because I have allergies too. I'm severely allergic to shell-fish. So it's something I take seriously, but that night I lost it.'

I reach out and squeeze his shoulder, all the while thinking that if this is true, then Mo too is definitely here to be punished and it is, therefore, unlikely that he's guilty. 'Tell me about last night. What were your movements?'

'Dinner, dancing, bed. You were with me for most of it.'

'What time did you go to bed?'

'I don't know, I'd had too much to drink. Do you remember what time you went to bed?' I smooth down my hair in an attempt to deflect the question; I don't remember what time I went to bed.

'Well, then,' says Mo, taking my lack of response to mean that things are as hazy for me as they are for him.

'You came on this show to move on from your past?'

'Yes.'

I know I can't trust anyone. I know that everything Mo is telling me might be a lie. But my instinct tells me his story rings true. His frustration and panic that I might think he committed this crime feels real to me.

I open my mouth to ask another question, but my words are drowned out by another sound. My question is stopped by a scream. I jump up from the sun lounger to look over at the others. Rosalind is screaming. Valentina has wrapped her arms around herself. Carly is staring wide-eyed. Daniel pushes away his camera and takes a step towards the women.

I dash towards them. What is happening? Who is hurt?

My question is answered almost immediately. Valentina's knees buckle and, with a hard thud, she hits the floor. Her eyes are wide and for a second, we stare at one another. Then she flops backwards, collapsing in a heap.

Chapter Thirty-Two

To: sammyknight@blueskyblue.com
From: contactme@jd.co.uk
Subject: Reply to Contact Me form

Message:

Hi Sammy,

Thank you for getting in touch and for sharing your story. I want you to know I think you're really brave to reach out to me. It's an absolutely horrible thing to have your life taken away by someone else but I want you to know that you're not alone. I'm working on a plan to help others like you and I'd be delighted for you to be involved. But before that I think it might be better to meet in person – let me know if you're interested.

Best wishes,
JD

Chapter Thirty-Three

I sprint towards Valentina, who lies on the paving, frighteningly still. Her legs are sprawled, and her arms jut out beside her. When I reach her, I crash to my knees.

'Valentina!' I call, wrapping my hands around her arms, and shake her. Under my grip, her head rolls to one side and hangs there at an odd uncomfortable angle. Her mouth falls open slackly. But it is the colour of her skin that sends electricity coursing through my body.

'Please,' I beg, hovering my ear above Valentina's mouth. It's impossible for me to tell if Valentina is breathing. The sounds of the garden and my own ragged breathing overpower any sound coming from her. The others clamour around us.

'Get away. She needs space.' I flap my arms to get them to step away. I turn back to Valentina. 'Please be alive. Please.'

I stretch two fingers to Valentina's neck. My stomach tightens as I hope against hope that Valentina is still alive. My fingers are like a hot poker as I press them against Valentina's neck. Her skin is like ice and I pull my hand away.

'No, no, no, please no.' The cold of Valentina's body sends a shiver through me.

Tentatively, I press my fingers against Valentina's neck once more and feel for a pulse. I close my eyes, hoping against hope.

Oh my God.

I pull my fingers back in alarm. All the signs point otherwise but Valentina isn't dead; there is a pulse. A slow, erratic pulse but it is there, signalling that we haven't lost her yet.

'She's alive,' I shout to more than just the other Islanders, to an audience unseen. 'Valentina. Can you hear me, Valentina?' Valentina gives no response, not even so much as a gurgle. I bite my lip; she's on the cusp. We are so close to losing her. But not if I can help it.

'Valentina, it's Kimberley. I'm going to help you, OK?'

Valentina's cold skin, erratic heartbeat, limp body are all the signals of someone who's taken an overdose, so she may have been poisoned. I don't know how or with what, or how long she has got before it kills her. But I know what I need to do.

I lean over Valentina. Her body looks as small and fragile as it is possible for her to look; she's like a baby bird that's fallen from its nest. I grit my teeth. I have to save her. Balling my fist, I press it against Valentina's chest. Using my knuckles, I rub hard over Valentina's sternum. My hope is that the pain will stimulate Valentina to consciousness.

My knuckles grow warm from the friction of skin on skin. I clench my teeth, biting back the searing pain in my hand. The movement is beginning to burn.

'Valentina. Valentina!' I shout, my voice getting louder the longer Valentina remains unresponsive.

'What's happened to her?' says a voice from behind me but I ignore it. I need to focus on Valentina, on saving Valentina.

'What can I do? Tell me what I need to do,' says Rosalind; her voice flutters as she speaks. I ignore her – I know she's trying to help but all I see is Valentina. My knuckles sear as I continue to rub them over her bony chest. But I don't stop, I can't stop. My chest tightens with a sadness that threatens to consume me. It's too late. I can't save her. Valentina is dead.

I glance at the countdown timer; there are still eight minutes left on the clock but Valentina is dead. The clock flashes and the time changes.

Three.

Two.

One.

Beeeeeeeeeeeeeeeeeep. The countdown timer ends.

'No!' I whisper, placing my forehead onto Valentina's still chest. Her chest is red and hot from the force of my rubbing. My body is heavy, weighed down my failure. My tears fall and splash against Valentina's skin. A scream builds in my throat and I clamp my mouth shut as hard as I can to stop it from erupting.

I've had over an hour to solve this thing with only five suspects. What haven't I figured it out? Thoughts I've had many, many times before surge through my body. I've failed. I am a failure and I have cost an innocent woman her life. My breathing increases; I feel my chest rise and fall jaggedly as I struggle to catch my breath. I've never had a panic attack before, but I feel as if I'm on the precipice of one right now.

The others gather behind me. I know they're there. I hear their yelps of horror and tears of shock, but I don't acknowledge them. It's as if I'm separated from the others by a sheet of glass. I'm completely alone in my grief.

It is no one else's fault but mine. Valentina is dead. Dead! And now I will have to add her name to the baggage I lug around with me every single day. My eyes blur with tears and I slump onto my bum, pressing my face into my hands.

'What… should… we… do?' someone asks, each word interspersed with a sob. The question is directed at me, but my ears feel as if they've been stuffed with cotton wool.

Why are they asking me? What do I know? I know nothing, nothing except this fresh pain that stabs in my heart like a knife.

'Come on, darling,' says a gentle voice close to me. I feel a warm, soft hand clasp my own. 'Let's go and sit down.'

My eyes find Daniel, who is crouched beside me. The camera operator's face, too, is wet with tears. He looks as shellshocked as I feel. I blink at him, barely able to register his words. My arm tugs as Daniel tries to coax me into a standing position. But I make no effort to move myself. I don't want to move. I want to stay here guarding over Valentina's body until I shrivel away from lack of sleep and lack of food.

Without warning, a sound so violent rips through the haze that has settled upon me. I open my eyes to see a violent shake take over Daniel's body. Bile rises in my throat. So powerful and evil is that sound to me now. It's the alarm that signals the return of the Judge and whatever hateful message he has to deliver.

Beep. Beep. Beep. 'All remaining Islanders, please report to the Fire Pit.'

Daniel tugs at my arm again and this time I allow myself to be dragged. The others sit like zombies around the Fire Pit, their faces pointed towards the screen.

As we've obeyed the Judge's request without complaint, the alarm stops, and the garden is completely silent. The aftermath of Valentina's death is different to that of Jack's. Gone are the shouts of disbelief.

'How can this be happening?' whispers Rosalind, more to herself than anyone else.

'Hello, everyone,' says the Judge. His image looms over us like an evil god. 'How are we all?' The Judge's question rings out, but no one answers. My head has been commandeered by a tension headache so intense I can barely think, let alone speak. 'Silly question, I guess.'

The Judge shifts his focus, so his pixelated eyes are directed more towards me. It's an effort to lift my head to look at him; my head is heavy and my temples throb. My eyes linger over his face and I realise that the anger that has consumed me for the last few hours has passed.

No, not passed, numbed. Apart from my headache I feel nothing.

'Kimberley,' says the Judge with a sigh. 'Here we are. Another hour later and because you didn't solve it, Valentina Novak is dead.'

'She died before the timer ended. You said we had extra time; yet again, you lied to us.'

'It isn't easy to time these things, Kimberley. Valentina regularly takes medication for her anxiety and, given the stress of this situation, my little helper recommended she take one of her pills about an hour ago to help her keep calm and focused. We'd tampered with her medication. Based on the dose and her size, an hour seemed about right but poison really isn't a great choice for murder

– very unpredictable. I'm sure the audience will forgive me eight minutes; you've got to admit, it was close.'

'And what would you have done if I'd solved it? If I'd figured out who killed Jack,' I ask.

'Then Valentina would have been an unfortunate victim of my lack of faith in you. It's not nice when people don't believe in you, is it, Kimberley?'

I know what he's getting at and it's impossible for me to muster any reaction apart from a curt nod. This is my fault, but I know that already. There's no way the Judge can make me feel worse about it. The heaviness in my body threatens to crush me. I place my hands on the seat and lock my elbows, using my straight arms to keep me upright. I want to crumble, to fall to pieces, but I refuse to give the Judge the satisfaction.

'I can see how upset you all are by Valentina's death, but I really don't want you feeling too bad about it. Between you and me, she wasn't that nice of a person anyway.' The Judge pauses. 'It is two thirty-five in the afternoon. There will be one hour to the next death. Start the clock.'

Pop. The Judge vanishes from the screen.

Chapter Thirty-Four

Contact Me form

Type your message in the box below. I read every piece of correspondence that comes to me and I will aim to get back to you as soon as I can.

Your Name: Tristram Campbell
Your Email Address: tristram@thecampbellfamily.com

Your Message:

By all accounts, I'd say I'm a pragmatic man, someone who believes in the law and the verdicts that it gives us but here, the law has failed me and my family and allowed the manipulation of a young woman to win the day. Let me start by saying, I loved my father and despite my anger at what has happened I don't blame him at all. He was a vulnerable old man who could not resist her charms and she took advantage of him in the worst way.

My father, Philip Campbell, was a well-respected and, at his retirement, a high-ranking public servant. Upon his retirement he was looking forward to spending the wealth he accumulated over years of hard work and intended to travel, eat at all the best restaurants and just generally live his life to the fullest. Unfortunately, and it breaks my heart to write it, he fell ill quite soon afterwards and became housebound. My wife and I arranged for a carer for him, someone who would come in the morning and help him around the house but would also be there in case he hurt himself. As time went on we noticed a change in my father; he looked at us differently and was more distant than usual. When I confronted him about it, he said he knew about the affairs and that he was disappointed. I was shocked at this; I'd never had any affairs in my life.

As it transpires, the carer was also a budding social media celebrity or whatever the appropriate terminology is here. She liked to dig for gossip and, unfortunately for my family, there were secrets to be found. Nobody is perfect, you have to understand that, but I could never have imagined that my private life would have become fodder for a young woman's pursuit of fame. She discovered that early on in our marriage my wife had strayed and that my eldest son was in fact not my son and as such, my father was of the opinion, my son should be cut from the will. I should stress that although my father was unwell he had a strong moral compass and infidelity, especially on the woman's side, was a treasonable offence. So, my son was cut off and the funds that should have gone to him were redirected to this truth-teller. This girl used the indiscretions of my family as a subject for her YouTube channel and as a means to turn my father against us. Naturally, when I discovered this I fired her, but it was too late, my father had made up his mind and no matter how much I reasoned with the lawyer that he was not of sound mind it did nothing to change it. My father was determined to give her something to 'pursue her passion', if exposing other people's secrets for money can healthily be called a passion but there we are.

My father died over a year ago now, but I have recently discovered this girl's Internet success has only gone from strength to strength. I find it astonishing that she has made her money exposing other people's secrets for entertainment when she exploited a man at the most vulnerable stage in his life. I am of the opinion that someone needs to expose her for what she truly is, and I think you could be the person to help me. I did inherit something from my father, even if it wasn't money, and that is the propensity to be a workaholic. This means that even without the money I am an extremely wealthy man and I'd certainly be willing to pay you for your troubles.

Chapter Thirty-Five

Kimberley
Sunday 27th July, 14:35
60 Minutes Until Next Murder

Valentina is dead, murdered right in front of me, and I could do absolutely nothing to stop it. A feeling of shame creeps over me. I turn my back to my fellow Islanders and walk away from them. My legs carry me to the dining table and I sit down, my chin resting in my hands. Rosalind and Mo join me, mirroring my position. Without warning, my stomach growls and I place a hand to it. 'Sorry,' I say to them, 'my stomach seems to have forgotten that I have a murder to investigate.' Rosalind gives me a pained smile; she clearly doesn't understand how I can be hungry at a time like this. We sit for a couple of minutes in silence and I will my stomach to stay quiet too.

'Well, that settles it,' says Mo, pushing his chair back and standing up. 'I have decided to cook us all a late lunch.' His voice is stronger than it has been in hours. He has devised a plan, he has something to focus on, and that clearly gives him comfort.

'No wonder you're hungry, Kim,' he continues. 'None of us have eaten all day, and I need to do something to keep myself occupied. As a chef and restaurant owner, I'd never forgive myself if we all died of hunger.' He laughs. It's a forced, awkward laugh. The gallows humour doesn't sit well with him. He's probably not seen as much as I have. He's never needed it before. None of the others around the table join in with Mo's joke, if it could really be called that.

'I'll help, it would be good to have something to do,' says Carly, heading towards us from the garden, her voice uncharacteristically gentle.

'Me too,' says Rosalind, twisting her neck to look up at Mo.

The three of them retreat to the kitchen. Daniel, who has relieved himself of his camera, also heads to the kitchen, but it isn't to help the others. Instead, he heads straight for the fridge. His fingers curl around its smooth round handle; he jerks it open and darts his hand inside, grabbing a bottle of wine. He then plonks the bottle down – the glass clinks loudly as it collides with the table – and slides an empty glass in my direction. Unscrewing the top, he pours a measure in my glass and a measure in his own.

'To Jack,' he says before downing the entirety of the glass in one gulp. I hesitate for a moment; alcohol doesn't seem like a good idea right now. Mo, Rosalind and Carly turn to watch Daniel's first toast but all three of them refuse to participate. They're too worried and I understand that. I look down at the wine-filled glass and pause. If I'm meant to die next, I'm meant to die next. Wordlessly, I mirror him. Daniel lifts the bottle again and pours another toast. 'To Sophia.' Again, we both down our drinks. 'To Valentina.' Another toast. 'And finally,' he says, placing a hand on my arm, 'to us.' We clink our glasses against one another's and then drink.

The four small wine toasts go some way to loosen the tension I've carried for the last five hours. The truth of it is that I'm lost. I don't have any idea what I should do next; I thought that by obeying the Judge's demands I might be able to save them but the attempt I made was a complete and utter disaster. I'm no closer to figuring out who killed Jack than I was when I first discovered the body. And now the path is littered with the deaths of Sophia and Valentina and there will be more.

Forty-one minutes remain on the clock. Maybe toasting my failure is the only way to go. I reach out to grab the bottle and pour myself another glass.

'No more,' says Daniel. 'We need you to be sober.' I can't help but scoff at this. What is he talking about?

'Daniel, none of you need me. The only thing you need me for is if you all want to die more quickly than you biologically should.'

I shrug Daniel's hand off my arm. I wish he'd stop trying to help me; doesn't he know I'm not safe to be around? I reach again for the bottle but Daniel removes it from the table and stands up.

'Oh go away then, Daniel,' I snap. 'Go to the kitchen. Help the others. I want to be alone.'

'Fine but I'm taking the bottle with me.' He trudges away from me, his back turned.

'Fine—' My lame remark is interrupted by a shriek from the kitchen. I'm on my feet in a flash, stepping alongside Daniel, who has stopped in his tracks.

'What is it, Carly?' asks Rosalind, looking at her but not moving any closer to her. Mo, who is standing next to the fridge, reaches out a hand to grab the handle and support himself; he looks like he might faint.

'Is someone hurt?' calls Daniel, his arm out in front stopping me from moving any closer in case there is danger. I loop under it and approach the scene. Carly looks at us and swallows.

'There were three this morning and now there are only two.'

'Only two what?' asks Daniel.

'Knives,' says Carly. 'One of the incredibly sharp Japanese knives is missing.'

'It is what it is,' says Mo, opening the fridge and retrieving a handful of blood-red tomatoes from it.

'It is what it is?' replies Carly, staring at him incredulously. 'That's alright for you to say, you're a man. If someone comes at you with a knife you can at least defend yourself but look at the size of me!'

'How do we know you didn't take it?' asks Mo, looking at Carly. 'And have announced it to cover your tracks.'

'You're unbelievable,' she shouts back. But Mo is unaffected by her shouts. Instead, he stalks past her, pulls one of the remaining knives from its holder and starts chopping the tomatoes.

'I have decided to cook, so that is what I'm going to do and if someone wants to stab me in the back while I'm doing it, they can for all I care right now. You can either help me or you can go somewhere else.'

Carly's jaw tightens, and she crosses her slender arms across her chest. 'I'll stay here, thank you. Now, give me something to do.'

Mo gives her and Rosalind instructions to gather all the necessary ingredients and lay them next to the pot; he also asks Daniel to make a salad, which he does without argument. I perch on one of the bar stools and am treated to another small glass of wine by Daniel. For 'good behaviour', he says.

A further twenty minutes pass as Mo, Carly, Rosalind and Daniel move around the kitchen chopping, stirring, seasoning or cleaning until the smell of meatballs in a rich tomato sauce tickles my nostrils. My stomach rumbles again and as a group we head to the table, each carrying a steaming plate of warm food.

With the toasting and cooking, there are now only twenty-one minutes until the next murder. I wonder how the Judge feels about my lack of engagement. Is he annoyed that I'm not trying to figure it out? Or maybe he's happy that I've so obviously failed?

Fear and nausea had staved away the feeling of hunger but now, relaxed by alcohol and the smell of the dish, my stomach makes it clear just how much it demands payment.

Not stopping to think about my actions, I grab my fork and plunge it into one of the meatballs and, picking it up, I shove it, whole, into my mouth. The heat of it sears my tongue but I don't care. I barely chew it before swallowing. At the same time, I reach for a hunk of bread to mop up some of the sauce. There's a small part of my brain that reminds me that people are watching. But I ignore the fact that I probably look like a caveman, devouring the food without airs and graces and as if I haven't eaten in weeks. People can think what they like; our audience has probably already made their opinion of me.

It's obvious that the food that's been prepared is excellent but for my hungry body it's sustenance and little more.

Using another piece of bread, I scrape all the remaining sauce from my plate and put it into my mouth. Once I'm finished, I look up. I furrow my eyebrows; none of the other Islanders have made much of a dent in their own meals. The Islanders are all looking at me: Mo's eyes are wide; Carly's arms are crossed; Rosalind's mouth hangs open; and even Daniel looks a little shocked as he raises his eyebrow at me. There's an awkwardness around the table. My undeterred appetite came as a shock to them; even hunger won't allow them to forget the horrors of the day.

Rosalind leans forward and rests her chin atop her intertwined fingers. 'There's only twenty minutes left on the clock. Maybe now would be a good time for us to try to, to…' Rosalind stumbles over her words. 'To reset. To plan what we should do next and how to…' She pauses.

'How to stay alive, you mean?' says Mo, finishing her sentence. Everyone avoids looking at me. It is clear how uncomfortable the others feel around me. It's understand-able – any interaction with me could mean an expedited death sentence. Annoyance pricks at me; is it really my fault we're all at risk of being murdered? Nobody's inno-cent here.

'Eat,' I say, unsure what else to offer them. 'It isn't easy to think on an empty stomach.' The Islanders give me weak smiles and begin to take meaningful bites this time. It's as if all they needed was permission to proceed, to be told it is OK to be fearful and to grieve and for your body to still want to go about its normal functions. The small glasses of wine gave me permission and I'm only too glad to pass that on to the others.

'Thank you, Mo,' says Rosalind. 'This is really deli-cious.'

'You're welcome,' he says and raises his glass.

'To our last supper,' I say. I'm the only one who raises my glass to clink with Mo. As our glasses connect, there's a sound, much louder than is warranted by glass on glass.

What was that?

I narrow my eyes; Mo's mouth falls open in a silent scream, gawping at something behind me. Carly mirrors Mo. Rosalind spins around in her seat, following their gaze.

What is it this time?

The question lacks the same intense concern as it would have earlier. I slam my glass onto the table, let out an exaggerated sigh and turn around, ready to once again attend an audience with the judge. I'm wrong to treat this so lightly.

The image that awaits me sends a shiver down my spine. The Judge sits there, still wearing his black gown and his white wig. His face is still pixelated but he's holding something in his left hand. It's an hourglass. Golden sand slips from the top half into the bottom half; there's barely any sand left. Another reminder that time's almost up.

'Kimberley, I'm disappointed in you. The viewers are disappointed in you. Drinking wine during an investigation? If that's what they taught you in the police force, then it's no wonder our justice system is on its knees.'

The sound of silverware rings out. My blood runs cold and I whirl around. My eyes scan the others: Rosalind, Carly, Mo and Daniel. It's Mo. Everyone's eyes are on Mo, like he's an unexploded bomb. There's something very wrong in his expression.

Mo sinks lower in his chair; his knees graze the ground. Two hands clasped around his throat. His mouth flaps, making him look like a fish that's been dragged out of the water and left to suffocate on dry land. His breathing is ragged as he gasps for air.

My chair is flung behind me as I leap upwards and run to him, pushing him onto his back. It looks like he's having an allergic reaction; he's going into anaphylactic shock.

My heart is beating wildly and the meal churns in my belly, but the adrenaline focuses me, cutting through the effects of the food and wine.

'Adrenaline,' I shout.

'What? What should we do?'

'Rosalind, where's the first aid kit? He's having an allergic reaction. We need an EpiPen.' Rosalind's on her feet. She says something to me, but I can't hear her. All I hear is the sound of my own heartbeat. 'Rosalind, get the first aid kit. Now. Carly, go and check Mo's bag, he's sure to have brought his own with him. Mo, can you hear me? It's Kim.'

But Mo doesn't respond. He's lost consciousness. I place the heel of my hand on Mo's chest. Then positioning myself so I'm hovering over him, I press down hard and fast.

My breathing gets heavy from the effort of pumping. Where the hell are the others? As if on cue, Rosalind comes running toward me. Her cheeks are flushed and her hair flies wildly about her as she sprints towards me. But it's her hands I notice. Her hands are empty save for a small packet.

'The pens are gone. But there were antihistamines.'

'Antihistamines? Have you seen him?' I snap at her.

'I thought…' Rosalind stops short and lets her hands drop to her sides.

'Go and find Carly, she might have them.' She nods and scurries away. I was too sharp with her; she was only trying to help. The muscles in my arms are burning. I don't know how much longer I can continue this.

'Here,' says Daniel. 'Let me.' Daniel kneels beside me and slips his hands in underneath mine. I pull away but stay close, to guide Daniel through this. But he doesn't need my guidance. His hands pump downwards, short and sharp.

'Come on, Mo. Don't give up.' Daniel is panting now as he continues to pump up and down, up and down. I switch with him. 'Come on, buddy.' Tears pool in my eyes, splashing further down my face with each movement. The flush that appeared in Mo's cheeks in the first stages of his anaphylaxis have gone, the colour dying with him.

I can't help myself, but I glance up at the countdown clock. There is less than one minute remaining but it doesn't matter. One minute won't save Mo; neither will another hour. Without proper medical help, Mo is never going to survive.

I slump forward and rest my head on Mo's broad chest. His chest is warm, from the shock and our aggressive attempts at resuscitation. The warmth will soon leave it, never to return. Mo is dead and there are now only four of us.

Chapter Thirty-Six

To: tristram@thecampbellfamily.com
From: contactme@jd.co.uk
Subject: Reply to Contact Me form

Message:

Hi Tristram,

Thank you for getting in touch. I'm very sorry to hear what happened to you and your family, what a horrible thing for a person to do, especially one whom you let into your home. I'm currently working on something that I think you might be interested in, do let me know if you still want to get your own back.

Best,
JD

Chapter Thirty-Seven

The alarm sounds, signalling that our hour is over. Pushing myself to my feet, I don't look at the others but storm to the kitchen.

The cauldron-sized pot Mo used to prepare the meatballs sits on the steel hob. Around its rim the remaining bits of the tomato sauce cling, dried and crusty. But, aside from this one dish, the marble work surface around the hob is spotless. It would almost be impossible to know that someone has cooked.

'Why is everything so clean? Where are the empty packages or the chopping boards?'

Daniel's forehead crumples in confusion as if he thinks I've completely lost my mind.

'Why are you asking this?'

'Because I want to know what the hell in a meal prepared by Mo killed him. It was meatballs, for God's sake – Mo was allergic to shellfish.'

'Mo asked us to tidy up as he cooked,' says Rosalind, taking a step backwards so half her body is covered by Daniel's. 'I did the washing up and Carly was clearing everything up.'

'Where's the bin?' I snap and Carly points towards a spot at the end of the kitchen. I storm towards it, rip off its lid, and peer inside. There are empty tins of chopped tomatoes, garlic peel, bottle top after bottle top. Deeper into the bin I go, throwing the bulkier items over my shoulder to get them out of my way. Then I find what I'm looking for: a miniature glass bottle, empty of its contents. I pull it out and thrust it towards the others. 'This is what killed him. My God, this one was so simple. Slip in oyster sauce to the meal and boom, goodbye Mo.'

The others stand motionless. The survivors – Daniel Oni, Carly Chu and Rosalind Jenkins – stare at me. Daniel's forehead is cut with deep frown lines as he narrows his eyes at me; Carly's lips are drawn so thin they've almost disappeared; and Rosalind's face is as white as a sheet and she edges ever closer to Daniel.

'What?' I ask. 'What is it?' My hair stands on end. The horror of the other three isn't directed at Mo's lifeless body or the bottle I'm holding in my hand. I can feel that their horror is directed at me. The three of them look at one another as if of one mind.

'What's happening?' I ask again, my voice fluttering.

Why are they looking at me like this? I scan my eyes down over my own body. Am I dying too? Is that what they're looking at? But there are no wounds; physically, I feel unchanged.

'You,' whimpers Rosalind, lifting a trembling finger to point at my chest. 'You told him. Us.' If Rosalind expects me to understand what she means by this, I don't. Carly's mouth pulls even tighter and she reaches out a hand to grab Rosalind's wrist.

'What are you talking about?' I stare at the three of them, trying to decipher the meaning behind their horrified expressions.

'You,' bellows Rosalind. 'You said you were hungry, you practically instructed Mo to cook. And then when he did you told us to eat. You said it would be easier to think once we'd eaten.'

'Oh my God,' I whisper, my shoulders tensing at the accusation. 'I didn't... I wasn't even cooking. How can you think this is me?'

'It's been you,' says Daniel, his face slack. 'It's been you all along.'

My skin grows hot as if it can feel Daniel's disappointment. Daniel was my ally, the only person who truly tried to help me and now even he's betrayed me.

'You knew Mo was having an allergic reaction and you sent them to get EpiPens that you knew weren't there. Did you enjoy watching us panic?'

'All this time, I thought you were trying to help us,' says Carly.

'No—' I try to stop them, but I'm interrupted.

'Save it,' says Rosalind, her nostrils flaring. 'I trusted you. We all trusted you.'

'What the hell are you talking about? And Carly, less than an hour ago you didn't want anything to do with Mo. Suddenly you're mourning his death?'

'The Judge has shown me that the truth can change depending on the angle,' snarls Carly. 'But from every angle, you look guilty. The Judge even said it. You're a murderer.'

My throat is dry, and I wring my hands together in a move that probably makes me look guilty. How can they think this of me? It's so wrong.

Carly, Rosalind and Daniel crowd together and I'm forced to watch as they whisper among themselves. They're deciding my fate and there's nothing I can do to stop them. We're one step away from descending into *Lord of the Flies* and the death of poor Piggy.

I almost wince at the irony that the victim in that crime had the same name as the worst nickname given to my people, police officers. To them, I too am nothing more than a pig.

The group breaks apart and Daniel marches towards me. He wraps his fingers around my arm and I inhale sharply as his nails dig into me.

'Ow, what are you doing? Let go of me!'

Daniel looks down at me; his eyes are wild like a horse startled by a bird flying up out of long grass. And, like a horse, his fear makes him dangerous. I soften my tone; I need to be gentle with him before he completely loses control. 'Daniel,' I say softly, 'please, you know I wouldn't do this. Please let go of me, you're hurting me.'

'What shall we do with her?' he shouts over my head to the others, ignoring my plea. His hand is warm against my skin and he holds on so tightly that my arm begins to throb. The connection we built in this hellhole has gone, snuffed out like a short-lived candle.

'What?' I twist to look up at him, thrown off-kilter by his words. And for a split second of blind panic I think they want to harm me. Get rid of me to save themselves. Rosalind and Carly exchange glances, as clueless as Daniel.

'We can lock her in the bedroom. The private one,' says Rosalind, forcefully looking at Daniel and not at me. 'That one's got a real lock, not an electrical one.'

'No.' I'm shouting now. They can't lock me away; I need to find a way to defend myself. They need me, I see that now. Granted, I haven't done a great job at protecting them up until now, but my gut tells me that without me, things will be worse. I twist my arm, trying to wrench it free from Daniel's grip. My skin burns as it stretches under his fingers. But the pain's overwhelmed by a fear of what might happen without me. They need me. They need me to save them.

'No,' I shout again, my voice stronger with each shout. I have more conviction. 'You can't lock me up. You've got this wrong. You need me, you know you do.'

'It's you, you're doing this,' shouts Rosalind, her hands on her head, her fingers knotting into her hair. She's in danger of ripping it out; she looks so frantic.

'You can't possibly think I'm responsible for this,' I say to them. But Carly and Rosalind turn away as Daniel drags me from the pool area. 'This is ridiculous. You need me.'

I stick my feet into the grass, making it as difficult as possible for Daniel to pull me; I won't comply with him. I need them to understand. I'm not responsible for this and I won't abandon them without a fight.

It becomes increasingly apparent that I will need to fight. I let my legs go slack, using the weight of them to drag myself towards the ground, making it more difficult for Daniel to hold me up by the arm.

'Listen, this is not me. This is bigger than me, bigger than any of us. We need to stick together. To work through this together.'

'I don't want you anywhere near me,' yells Carly. Rosalind places a hand on Carly's arm as if to keep Carly at a safe distance, as if I'm an uncaged animal that could fly at them at any moment.

'I am not a murderer. I am a police officer.'

'A police officer who left the force under a cloud,' spits Rosalind. 'Why aren't you being honest with us, Kim? We've all been honest with you.'

'You're a liar and you're dangerous,' shouts Daniel breathlessly. He's tiring against my struggle. He loosens his grip on my arm for a split second and I take advantage of it. I scramble to my feet, launching myself away from him and head towards the pool. They need to understand.

'Ow!' I cry as something strikes my ankle and I trip. A sharp pain shoots through my knees as they collide forcefully with the floor. Daniel had swung his leg out to trip me over and he succeeded. I crumple on the floor, pulling my knees into my chest. I'm winded from the shock as much as the pain. I lie on the grass, breathing heavily, unable to right myself, letting the grass prick my cheeks uncomfortably.

Daniel's hands hook my armpits roughly and he pulls me away like a limp ragdoll. He drags me away from Carly and Rosalind, across the grass, across the flagstones, past the kitchen and into the villa.

'Ros, where am I taking her?' asks Daniel.

'I'll show you.' Rosalind hurries behind us. I stare at her, trying to get her attention, trying to get her to understand.

'Daniel, Rosalind, please,' I cry. 'Look at me. I wouldn't do this. You know I wouldn't do this.' Rosalind keeps her chin held high, purposefully avoiding my gaze, directing Daniel through the villa to the site of the private bedroom. 'Daniel,' I say again. If anyone is going to listen to me, the man I shared a kiss with is my best bet.

'I don't know you wouldn't do this,' whispers Daniel in an angry breath. 'I don't know you at all.' I crane my neck up at him. His fingers dig deeper into my flesh. His lip quivers almost imperceptibly and his eyes shine, glazed by tears. My stomach clenches; I've seen that look before.

I've failed him, betrayed him. And the worst part is, maybe he's right. I might not have killed Jack, Valentina, Sophia or Mo but I sure as hell did a shitty job at protecting them.

I can't let it end like this. Like a lightning bolt to the brain, I know with absolute certainty that if they lock me in the bedroom, I will never see them alive again and there's no room in my conscience for any more deaths.

So I've got two choices: give up or fight. And this time, I decide to fight. I will find out who is doing this, and I will save the others. I screw my face up and clench my stomach and with all the power I can muster I kick, launching my legs up into the air. Daniel huffs from the effort of restraining me and I kick again.

'Listen to me,' I cry out. 'This is madness. I didn't do this. Ow!' Daniel digs his fingernails hard into my skin. 'Daniel, stop it.'

'Shut up,' growls Rosalind, her eyes blazing with renewed anger.

'This is a huge risk. You... need... me. We're guilty. We're all guilty of something. That's what the Judge wants me to find out.' The effort of shouting and kicking makes me pant but I don't relent. I won't relent, not until they listen to me.

We're inside the villa now. The smooth marble floor made it impossible for me to find anything to slow our progress. I kick my legs outwards, trying to use them to wedge my body in between the walls but it has zero effect. Instead the skin on my feet tears as they scrape along the wall. Daniel stops, and Rosalind tries to slip past me to open the bedroom door. I kick out my leg at her. It collides with Rosalind's soft stomach. Rosalind doubles over and groans, her hand clutching her middle.

'You bitch,' spits Rosalind.

'Sorry, that was an accident,' I splutter. I wasn't trying to hurt her, but it doesn't look good. Striking Rosalind in the stomach doesn't exactly help my cause. 'I wanted to stop her; you can't lock me up. It's a mistake. It's a huge mistake.' In my desperation to get them to listen to me, I'm only making matters worse.

Daniel pulls me further, past the door, so that Rosalind can slip the key into the lock.

The door creaks open. I cry out as pain rips through my shoulders.

'Not that it matters at all. But I really did like you,' says Daniel. And with that, he hoists me into the air and throws me onto the bed.

Thwack.

White-hot pain sears through my brain as the back of my head strikes against something solid. Through the haze of my disorientation, a fuzzy body grabs the handle of the door. It swings shut. My body sways and, like curtains closing, everything goes dark.

Chapter Thirty-Eight

Contact Me form

Type your message in the box below. I read every piece of correspondence that comes to me and I will aim to get back to you as soon as I can.

Your Name: Dr Joanna Upton
Your Email Address: drjupton@thesurgery-.com

Your Message:

Hi JD (I don't know what else to call you, so we'll go with this)

Honestly, I can't really believe I'm getting in touch with you, I'm not very good at social media but something in me is compelled to contact you.

I do want to start by saying thank you. Your words have been a comfort, more than a comfort, a lifeline, these past couple of months. You see, I've been struggling to cope with the anger I feel after the death of my son. Nobody else seems to understand my anger. I think it's because they think it was his own fault that he is dead. That he killed himself because of a reckless choice. But he didn't. She killed him. Without her, he would very likely still be alive.

My son Eddy was the perfect son. As a child and teenager, he was quiet, respectful and completely dedicated to his studies. He had his sights set on studying economics and had his eye on the top universities in the country. Well, you wouldn't believe how thrilled I was to find out he had been offered a place at none other than the London School of Economics – I was very much the proud mother hen. His first year passed without incident. Eddy was still the young man I had raised; he did well in his first-year exams. Not exceedingly well, mind you, but that is always expected when one takes the step up from school to university. His second year was the same, but I did start to notice something in him. The desire to get out and see the world. This didn't worry me, in fact the opposite: I was quite excited to see him venturing away from the library and exploring the big world. At the end of his second year, he got a job working in a bar in Menorca, not necessarily the summer job I would have chosen for him, but I decided it wasn't my place to get involved. It was during his time in Spain that he met her. To say he was besotted would be an understatement. I remember the emails he used to send me. He wrote that she was like no one he had ever met before, that she was cool and sexy, that she liked to party but loved reading books about philosophy. I could go on, but I won't.

Anyway, the summer was over and Eddy was devasted to have to leave Spain and her but I was of the opinion that it was a summer romance (I say romance; Eddy never indicated that she reciprocated his affection) and what might or might not have happened between them had come to an end. If only things had ended there.

I heard nothing of her from Eddy for a while. He'd returned to university for his third and final year and, by all accounts, was doing well. He messaged me from time to time but with nothing of note on the girl front. That was, until November.

Eddy messaged me full of excitement that she was moving to London and had invited him to her housewarming party. Saturday night, I'd given him a call to wish him luck and he'd thanked me and said he would call me the next day.

Eddy never made that call. Instead I received a very different message at 2 the following morning. My beautiful boy was dead. Drugs. I couldn't believe it – Eddy had never done drugs in his life and I'm not just saying that as his mother. His friends said the same and even she attested to that, when she was questioned. Eddy had arrived at the party, far earlier than everyone else. Eddy wasn't a party person, hence his ignorance of the 'don't arrive early' rule. She was getting ready still and decided to pop a pill to get her in the mood. Ecstasy, apparently, but from what the coroner said the drugs weren't exactly premium. She was a part-time waitress while trying to pursue her dream of being famous, so she couldn't afford anything of quality. She said she took one of the pills and that Eddy had asked for one too. She claims she tried to discourage him but that he took it out of the bag and swallowed it. She then left to go and get set up for the party. She said she was 'giving him some space to let the drug kick in'. He died at some point between then and three hours later when she finally realised he hadn't come to the living room. She found him slumped on her dirty, threadbare carpet.

My lovely, kind, gentle Eddy died in a bedroom of a disgusting London houseshare after taking a pill that a good-for-nothing bitch gave to him and not a day goes by when I don't think about what I want to do to her.

To look at me, you wouldn't think I am the type of person to get angry. If you saw me, what you'd see is a sixty-year-old woman in smart trousers and an expensive set of pearls hanging over a buttoned-up cardigan. 'She looks well-to-do' is what you'd probably think. Not that that isn't true but underneath it all, beneath the cashmere, is a soul consumed.

I cannot tell you how life-changing it is to know that you exist and feel the same as I do. A kindred spirit if you will.

Reading your work has made me think. I'm starting to see what I need to do to fix things, but I can't do it alone. I need your help.

Looking forward to hearing from you.

Kind regards,
Dr Joanna Upton

Chapter Thirty-Nine

Kimberley
Sunday 27th July, Time Unknown

The pain is what eventually wakes me. I have no idea how long I was gone for but my respite from the horror of this place is violated by the pain. It roars in my head, shooting behind my eyes and making my eyelids flutter. It pulsates rhythmically. Like a baton on a drum, the pain strikes the back of my head, its waves reverberating around my skull. In the darkness, I reach a hand to my head and locate the source. The lump is coming along nicely. A gently rolling hilltop that served to knock me out quite successfully.

The bed is soft beneath me and slowly I shift myself upright. I sit in darkness as the memory of everything comes crashing down on me once again.

The villa. The Judge. The deaths of Jack, Sophia, Valentina and Mo. And they think I'm behind everything. They trusted me, and I've failed them.

How long have I been out for? Long enough for the Judge to have finished what he started?

'Fuck,' I shout into the darkness. The shout only serves to set my headache off further.

An ache creeps through my body. My arms throb from Daniel's grip. Being in this villa, trying to satisfy the Judge's sick agenda has left me exhausted. I sit up further and press my back against the headboard, leaning my weary body against it. I relish the darkness and quiet of the bedroom, letting my breathing and heart rate slow.

I give myself permission to wallow in my failure. It seems to gather in the pit of my stomach, making me feel sick. But maybe this is what the Judge wanted all along. The Judge wanted me to fail on national television, so he could prove what he said from the start: police officers are incompetent.

Well, the Judge picked the perfect person because I've already established how incompetent I am as a police officer and a person.

I reach my hand out to my left and walk my fingers along the side table. They brush the smooth base of what I hope is a lamp. Finding the cord, I guide my fingers down it and switch it on. The light sears my eyes for a moment and I'm reminded of the morning when I stepped outside, hungover and feeling sorry for myself. The memory of me this morning is as foreign and removed for me as thinking about a character in a film.

That Kim was an idiot, thinking the only problem she had was getting over a hangover. The Kim of the last five years has been stupid.

As my eyes adjust, I survey my prison.

Had this been any other moment, my jaw might have dropped. Had the circumstances been different, I might have squealed and broken into a smile. Had I been awarded a night in this room to get to know one of her fellow Islanders better, I might have been excited, there might have been butterflies in my stomach wondering what the night might hold. Had I not touched the skin of four dead people, I would have been impressed by this private room, or the boudoir as a sign above the door names it.

But instead, it all makes me queasy.

The walls and ceiling are painted a midnight blue. On the ceiling, golden stars that have been stencilled in a cluster above the bed are waiting to twinkle down at the bed's occupiers.

The lighting in the room consists of a golden tube that runs across the middle of the wall and culminates in a giant golden heart above the headboard of the bed.

The bed itself is huge and circular; plastic rose petals are scattered across it. They stick to the bare skin on my arm.

Subtle.

My stomach churns. The heart only serves as a reminder of the four that stopped beating in the villa and the rose petals are the colour of spilled blood. The perfect presentation of it all jars with the events I've seen.

I can't look at this. I lurch forward and grab fistfuls of petals in my hands, throwing them indiscriminately on the floor.

The violence of my movement makes my head sway. I don't want to be in this room, full of petals and neon light. There's a door on the opposite side of the room. Hopefully the bathroom will offer some relief from this horror. I wrench the door open and wrap my fingers around the cool rim of the sink, taking deep, steadying breaths.

When I've composed myself, I run the tap; cupping my hands under the water, I splash it on my face. The icy temperature of it makes me gasp but serves its purpose. The tears that have collected in my eyes are washed away along with the fire of my panic.

I pause before drying my face and, with my hands planted on the surface either side of the sink, I stare at my own reflection. Water clings to my cheeks and my dark eyebrows but the droplets don't hide the truth of what I've become. The skin underneath my eyes has darkened and my eyes themselves are sunken. Their usual brightness is dulled as if covered over by a yellow film, streaks of red cut across them. My lips are cracked, desperate for moisture and care. My usual full cheeks have hollowed; I'm gaunt and drawn. It really is amazing the toll one day of stress can do to a person.

But then again, at least I'm alive. I am alive. I grip the sink harder and make a resolution. While I'm alive and breathing I will give everything I can to save the others, whether they want my help or not.

I roughly dry my face and, turning my back on my reflection, leave the bathroom. I stride to the door. I ball my hands into fists and bang them against the door, but the door barely shakes beneath my battering.

'Rosalind, Daniel, Carly. Let me out. Please, don't do this to me.' I only realise I'm crying when I feel a warm tear roll down my cheek. It collects at the edge of my mouth and I lick my lips, tasting its saltiness. It doesn't matter how much I strike the door or how much I protest. It does me no good. They've locked me in. Like it or not, I'm stuck here. The three survivors don't want me anywhere near them.

But they're not all survivors. One of them is a murderer.

I let my hands slide down the door and rest my forehead on it, taking some time to catch my breath.

If I want to help them, I need to break out of this room. I won't be much help to anyone sitting on a bedroom floor. The door is locked, so the solution is simple, in theory: break out.

I stride across the room and flop down by the door, my eye line hovering next to the handle.

From inspection, it looks like a standard mechanism lock. If it were anything modern needing an electronic key card or anything older and lacking the mechanism, I'd be screwed. But there is a glimmer of hope; seems I'm not all out of luck yet.

A buffed brass rectangle houses a handle in the shape of a small fist and beneath it is a circular disc, within which there is a slim slit, the gateway to a lock that could be picked. If only I knew how.

Think, Kimberley, what would I need to pick a lock?

I scan the room; it isn't exactly a treasure trove of items that would help me escape. The bed is covered in throws and cushions scrawled across with letters spelling the word 'love'.

The room has a table in the far corner, champagne flutes, wine glasses and tall tumblers standing to attention, waiting to be the vessel for the lucky couple to drink from. Beneath is a small fridge. I head towards it. Sparkling water, still water, and bottles of white wine, red wine and Prosecco lie, their tops facing towards the glass fridge door.

Well, if I fail miserably, there's enough alcohol here to sufficiently drink my sorrows away.

Ha! If there are bottles, there must be a bottle opener. It might be the perfect item to help me escape. Not that at this point I'm exactly sure how I'd use it.

A cursory glance, however, tells me that there is no bottle opener. Crouching down, I inspect the contents of the fridge more closely.

Damn. I smack my hand against the fridge door.

They're all screw tops. No corks, no corkscrew.

I can't stop myself wondering if this is a health and safety thing, which nearly makes me bellow at the irony of it. Neither health nor safety have been a concern in this house after the Judge took control. Quite the opposite.

I stop myself from being disappointed by the lack of bottle opener. It probably wouldn't have worked anyway; the corkscrew would have been too large to even fit into the lock's slit. I'm a fool for even thinking it was possible.

What am I going to do? I need to get out of this room.

As a police officer, I never needed to pick a lock. If I was ever presented with a locked door I'd simply order for it to be rammed down. But, unsurprisingly, I don't have a battering ram or a team to drive it at my disposal. I exhale; I don't have anything.

'Stop it,' I say aloud. I won't allow myself to give up this early. If my hours are numbered, I refuse to go down without a fight.

But the only frame of reference I have for lock picking is on television or in the movies. What do they do then?

My eyes shoot open. It is so obvious, and simple, and stupid. A hair grip. I'm forced to remember this item particularly because it often so annoys me how the only value women bring to heist films, aside from their bodies, are their hair accessories.

I pat my hands along my head, feeling for the bumpy metal surface of the grip. I ease it out and smile. This innocuous, brown hair accessory that regularly clogs my vacuum cleaner is transformed into the key of my escape.

'No. Get your hands off me.'

A scream blasts into the room, coming through the speakers embedded in the wall. I jerk up, more alert than ever before. 'Get off me. Please, please don't hurt me.'

The voice belongs to Rosalind. The desire to escape intensifies within me. Rosalind is in danger. Serious danger.

I slot my nail into the gap between the grip's teeth and wrench it open to create a U shape. I use my teeth to peel off the rubber coating at the end of each part of the grip. While the coating helped the grip slide into my hair, something tells me it will inhibit my ability to do this properly. If the lock mechanism is metal, I don't want it sliding off the rubber.

Armed with my makeshift key, I proceed to the lock. I know that locks are multi-layer mechanisms, so the most important thing will be the positioning of my hair grip. I need to weave it through; I can't just stab it in. In the movies, they usually jiggle it about.

'Help me, please, someone, help me,' screams Rosalind from within the villa. Her voice sounds closer now. My heart thuds and sweat prickles in my armpits. I'm running out of time to save her. And what about the others?

My fingers tremble. I feel them swelling from the increased blood flow surging through my body. Their dexterity is being dampened just as I need them more than ever. I hold the hair grip in my left and dominant hand. I lift it above the lock, pointing it downwards. With my right hand, I guide the hair grip into the lock. Once inside, I lower my hands, attempting to lever the mechanism. Millimetre by millimetre, I edge the hair grip further into the bowels of the keyhole, manoeuvring up and down. I'm unable to tell if it's making any difference. I'm completely blind to the effects of my work. Dampness collects on my forehead, but I don't dare spare a hand to wipe the sweat away.

'Come on,' I growl. There's been no scream from Rosalind for several minutes and the rising nausea in my stomach makes it hard to concentrate on anything else. Does her silence mean she's dead? I lean in closer to the hair grip and keyhole. It is working its way slowly further inside but is it even doing any good?

Then, suddenly, with a sound like a tongue smacking against teeth, the lock clicks.

'Oh my God,' I gasp under my breath. I can't believe I did it. That it worked. Scrambling to my feet, I grasp the ludicrous fist-shaped handle in my own fist and twist. The newly unlocked door swings open without issue. Ha! I give a small, involuntary bark of laughter. I'm free.

The corridor looms to my left beyond the threshold of this room. And suddenly, I'm hesitant. It's like when someone has been working their whole life to achieve a goal and then when they finally succeed and get what they want they're suddenly not sure if they want it after all. Winning my fight against the lock became my focus and what would happen when the door actually opened melted away.

I stand for a moment, hovering at the threshold, the dividing line between a place of safety and security and a place of danger and fear. I can't help but wonder: *What awaits me outside of this room?*

Chapter Forty

To: drjupton@thesurgery.com
From: contactme@jd.co.uk
Subject: Reply to Contact Me form

Message:

Hi Joanna,

Thank you for getting in touch with me. It took great courage for you to reach out. I know my blog is a bit of an acquired taste but it's an honour to hear how much my words have helped you. I'm so very sorry to hear about the death of your son and I completely understand the anger you are feeling. Losing a loved one is hard at the best of times, but it is almost unbearable if someone else is to blame for their death, if someone else took them away from you.

I have an idea of what I need to do to feel better and it could help you too, if you want to be involved?

Speak soon and stay strong,
JD

Chapter Forty-One

Kimberley
Sunday 27th July, Time Unknown

The door is cool when I wrap my fingers around it and lean outwards. My ears strain for whatever sound they might pick up but there's nothing. The villa is completely silent. There are no more screams or shouts of pain. The quiet hangs in the air. The silence feels dangerous.

Gingerly, I place a foot into the corridor. The marble stones are cold against the bare sole of my foot. Swiftly, I follow it with my other foot. I exhale, relieved. I'm not sure what I was expecting, as if exiting would blow me up or something.

I shake myself. Now isn't the time to hesitate. Now is the time for action. Find them. Save them. *Find them, save them* is the mantra that propels me forward. My feet slap against the marble floor as I march down the corridor.

My first task is to find them. Find the Islanders. I pass the communal bedroom and pop my head in. The beds are unmade, the block colour pillows strewn on the floor as they were in the morning. My neon green bikini is curled on the floor where I chucked it before I got into bed. There are no people here, though. Next I move to the living room, where all the remnants of my makeshift operations room remain. Some of the photographs have escaped their binds and have fallen to the floor. Jack's face looks at me from the wall. His wide smile no longer feels cheery but sinister.

But aside from the still, photographed faces, the living room is empty.

I exit and proceed towards the double glass doors leading to the garden. The villa is quiet, eerily quiet. Reaching the end of the corridor, I pull the door open and step out into the garden.

The sun has set and night, with its darkness, has taken hold. I have no idea how late it is; it could even be the middle of the night. The remaining Islanders must be outside. Perhaps too fearful to sleep. Perhaps they thought it better to crowd around the outdoor Fire Pit, keeping warm and staying together. But that doesn't make sense. I heard Rosalind screaming, which means the killer is either Daniel or Carly. One of them is innocent and one of them is guilty.

My arms wrap around my chest; the tank top I chose to wear this morning is no longer suitable for the coolness that has deposited itself over the garden. It isn't cold, but the absence of the blazing heat of the sun is noticeable. My skin pricks with goose bumps.

The garden is dark, lit only by the spotlights shining in the depths of the pool. The Fire Pit isn't in use.

Are they out here?

I open my mouth to call out for them, but something holds me back. My shout would shatter the silence of the evening. If, for some reason, they are asleep, I don't want to wake them. I edge closer to the Fire Pit and the pool, to the tiered seating where the Judge announced his horrors. If they were going to sleep anywhere outside, it would be here.

But they're not here. I spin around the empty garden, my heartbeat picking up with every turn. Panic rises in my throat, overriding my worry of disturbing them. Of course they're not asleep; why would they be asleep? I need to find them.

'Rosalind?' I call. 'Daniel? Carly? Where are you?'

I scan around me, hoping one of them will pop up. When that doesn't happen, I tear around the garden, passing the flagstone cracked by Sophia's falling body. Her body is gone, and, for an insane moment, I doubt the fact that she is dead. But then I remember we moved her to the freezer. Sophia, Jack and Valentina were all moved. I can only assume the others moved Mo because his body is no longer where it lay after dinner. I loop around into the kitchen area.

'Ouch,' I cry out as something sharp spikes against my foot. I bend down to see what it is. A piece of the coffee mug I shattered this morning sticks out the bottom of my foot. Bright red blood forms a thick bubble before rolling down my sole. Kicking the piece away, I place my foot delicately back on the floor. I don't have time to fix the wound or be distracted by the needling sting.

But as I'm leaving, something catches my eye. Where there were three, there is now one. Another knife is missing.

I need to find the others. The longer it takes to find them, the more I dread what I will find when I do. But they might still be alive. There might be time to save them.

'Daniel? Carly?' I shout. 'Rosalind? Where are you?' I speed from the kitchen back into the villa. Tearing around it like a woman possessed, I continue to shout. But there's no answer. No matter where I look, I can't find them. They're nowhere to be found.

My ears ring at the silence that hangs over the villa. In the absence of my shouts, there's nothing. No sign of life.

I leave the villa once more and slump down on the wooden seating around the Fire Pit in the garden, my chest heaving up and down.

Where are they? I've looked everywhere.

'Argh,' I scream and slam my hand against the wood. The frustration at my own inadequacies gnaws at me. But above everything else, I'm really, really worried.

Jack Peaks dead. Sophia Dance dead. Valentina Novak dead. Mo Khan dead. Is it only a matter of time before I find the others dead too?

'Where the hell are you?' I shout. The bush nearby me shakes and I jump to my feet. 'Who is it? Who's there?' There's no answer. 'Show yourself,' I shout, and the bush shakes again. This time the culprit shows himself as he flies off up into the air. I exhale loudly. A bird, just a bird.

My palms are slick with sweat and I wipe them against my thighs. I need to work methodically. Running about like a headless chicken is helping no one, especially not the others.

Where haven't I looked yet? What have I missed? They're not in the garden, the bedroom, the kitchen, the bathroom, or the living room. Where could they be?

'Of course.' I slap my hand against my forehead. There is one place I haven't looked yet. It isn't exactly part of the villa, but it has borne witness to a major turning point in our story.

The place where we realised we were trapped and Mo vented his fury as he slammed a chair again and again against the immovable door.

The entrance gates.

I sprint from the garden, wishing with every fibre of my being that Carly, Daniel and Rosalind have escaped. I hope that I'll arrive at the entrance gate and security hut to find the doors wide open, signalling the freedom that they've found. In my mind's eye, I can almost see them dragging their exhausted bodies through the dense Greek forest in search of safety.

I retrace my footsteps, back into the house and towards the spare bedroom that was my prison. I glance inside just in case they slipped inside after I left. It's unlikely but nothing is as it seems in the *LoveWrecked* villa. It is, as I suspected, empty.

I pick up my pace. They have to be there. They have to be at the entrance gate. It is the only place in this godforsaken villa that I haven't looked.

The sliding door at the end of the corridor is shut and I press my wet palm against it and drag the door open. I step out into the dark of the night, hoping against hope that everything will be alright.

The entrance area of the villa is dimly lit. It's as silent as the rest of the house. As if even the crickets don't chirp so as to pay their respects to the dead.

Or maybe they've been driven away by the horror?

Despite the warmth of the evening, a cold chill runs through me. My shiver is a reaction to the sight that greets me.

The strong, steel entrance gate remains firmly closed but the door to the security hut is ever so slightly ajar. My breath catches in my throat. The silence seems to consume me. There's something about the silence that tells me everything is wrong. This isn't the escape route I hoped to find.

My feet crunch along the gravel as I step towards the security hut. My reflection looms larger in the glass door as I approach. The effect is eerie, like a ghost emerging from the darkness.

My heart pounds against my chest. My fingers tremble as I lift my hand towards the door handle. The feeling of trepidation crashes over me like an angry ocean wave.

I pause, my hand resting on the handle. The inside of the hut is in darkness, my view obscured by my own reflection. I take a deep breath, steadying myself for what I might find. I grit my teeth, and in one swift movement, wrench the door open.

The smell inside makes me gag. It hits my nostrils and seems to travel down to my mouth, so within seconds I can practically taste the blood.

As my eyes adjust to the darkness inside the hut, the mass that lies slumped over the table comes into view.

The skin on her neck is bunched as her head twists uncomfortably away from me. One hand is pressed against the wall in front of me and the other dangles, limp, over the edge of the table.

The blood, almost unnoticeable against her dark clothes, has streamed from a source on her back, staining the light oak table that supports her.

There's so much blood; how many times must she have been stabbed to be covered like this? Nobody could survive losing that much blood. A small whimper leaves my lips. Rosalind Jenkins is dead.

Chapter Forty-Two

Contact Me form

Type your message in the box below. I read every piece of correspondence that comes to me and I will aim to get back to you as soon as I can.

Your Name: Matteo De Luca
Your Email Address: matt@deluca.com

Your Message:

Hi,

I wanted to get in touch because I want to say you're not alone. I, too, feel like you feel. I know how lucky I am to be writing this and to be able to say that I haven't lost someone, but someone close to me has had their life significantly changed by the recklessness of another.

Six months ago, my wife and I were driving home after a lovely evening at one of our favourite restaurants when our car was hit by another. I swerved to avoid the collision, but the other car struck the passenger side, resulting in my wife receiving life-altering injuries. For my part in this, I will never forgive myself. But what is even harder to forgive is that the driver was acquitted because apparently the investigators couldn't say for sure how fast she was driving before the crash. The investigators also found no evidence of braking or skidding so the judge felt that the testimony was all too imprecise and that it was no one's fault. This is despite the fact the driver was over the legal alcohol limit. The driver was fined and had their licence suspended but that was it. I can barely type this I am so angry. We're appealing, of course, but my rage has taken a hold of me; it has wrapped its way around my heart and I know I won't feel happiness again until I have my hands wrapped around the driver's neck and I can squeeze the life out of her in exchange for the life she took from us.

Chapter Forty-Three

I dash away from Rosalind's lifeless body and towards the Fire Pit, not stopping to think where I am going. I need to find Carly and Daniel and get us all off this island.

My head spins; where can I look? I've already scoured the villa. I've already gone over every inch of it.

I force myself to take a deep inhale and a slow exhale. I close my eyes and try to shut everything out. It takes all my strength to push aside the images of the dead Islanders that appear in my mind once my eyes are closed. Bile rises in my throat as the grisly sight of Rosalind's wounded corpse resurfaces. I shake my head, telling my brain I'll have plenty of time to dwell on the deaths later. Right now – right now I need to focus.

What did Rosalind say when we first arrived? The villa was designed for the show. There are corridors, secret corridors for the camera crew to traverse. How could I have forgotten this?

And if there are secret corridors there must be secret rooms. Rooms that allow the crew to live and work out of sight of the day-to-day life in the villa.

My eyes snap open. This is where Carly and Daniel will be. It's the only option.

I tear through the garden and enter the villa. I walk along the corridors and spread my arms out wide, running my fingers along the walls. If there are more hidden doors, there will be grooves in the wall that indicate it.

As my fingers scrape across the smooth wall, I smear flecks of Rosalind's blood along it. I wrinkle my nose at the sight of it. Now more than ever the villa looks like something out of a horror film.

The hallway gives me nothing apart from the entrance to the producer's corridor where Rosalind's production room is. But perhaps there's more here than meets the eye.

I peer into the corridor. The way is dark. My fingers feel for a light switch, but I fail to find one. But there's no time to worry about this now so I step forward into the abyss.

'Carly,' I call out, my voice shaking. 'Daniel.' It's not like me to be afraid of the dark but somehow, it's as if the last twenty-four hours have been leading me to this moment.

Step by step, I edge along the corridor. My heartbeat and footsteps are the only sounds keeping me company.

Ahead, there's a strip of light. It looms in the distance, growing brighter with each step I take. Or are my eyes deceiving me? There's no light; my eyes are simply adjusting to the darkness. No, it's definitely a strip of light which means that somewhere ahead there's a door. I slow my footsteps, my heart in my mouth. The light is less than a metre away now, shining through the gap left from a slightly open door. My heart thumps so hard against my chest it seems to reverberate around my body.

This is it. The final two are here.

'Please let them be alive, please let them be alive,' I pray, bringing the palms of my hands together.

I reach out and curl my fingers around the door; it's the type that slides along tracks in the floor. Steeling myself against what I might find, I slide the door aside and step into the room.

'What the hell are you saying?' The voice of Carly cuts through the silence, making me jolt. I twirl on my heels, taking in the full aspect of the room, but there's no one in here and neither is the light I saw. Instead the room is lit from the far side, where at the corner is a door with a window, through which the jungle is visible. Carly's voice is coming from over here as well. I'm about to charge towards the door and announce myself but the response that comes makes me stop.

'I'm saying I know who you are, and I know what you've done.' Daniel's reply, though muffled by the door, is loud and angry enough for me to hear. My footsteps are silent against the floor as I edge closer.

'And what have I done?' replies Carly. Though I can't see her expression or body language, her tone is enough to expose her defensiveness.

'You killed him, and I won't let you get away with it.' I can't believe what I'm hearing. I'm near the door now and edge myself as close to it as possible so I can peer around it without letting them see me. Carly's back is pressed up against the wall of the villa to my left and Daniel stands less than a metre away from her, his hands balled into fists, facing her.

'Daniel, you've got this completely wrong.' Daniel laughs at this. 'I—' Carly's word is cut off as Daniel steps towards her, his broad hands wrapping around her throat. Carly's mouth falls open as Daniel squeezes.

'No,' I shout, grabbing hold of the handle and pulling it but the door won't budge. Red light flickers to the left, telling me it's locked. At my shout, Daniel turns his head to face me and bares his teeth, the anger in him palpable even through a pane of glass. The expression on his face changes in a flash; his mouth falls open as he shouts and steps back from Carly, who is holding a kitchen knife in her hand. Carly had the knife all along; so, she killed Rosalind. Daniel turns away from me and back to Carly, ripping the knife from her and throwing it to the ground. For the second time he wraps his fingers around her throat as he shouts, 'This is for all of your victims.'

Carly's eyes are wide with fear and her gaze darts from Daniel to the floor where he has thrown the knife; her tongue protrudes from her open mouth and her cheeks flush red. She reaches her delicate hands and claws at Daniel's, trying in vain to pull him off her.

My fists bang against the glass of the door and my voice screeches as I scream for Daniel to stop, but he doesn't, and what seems like only seconds later he releases Carly and she slides down the wall into a heap on the floor.

The light above the door turns green, signalling to me that it's been opened. My sweaty palms wrap around the handle and I yank it open.

'Daniel,' I shout as I move towards him. His eyes are wild. He stoops to pick up the knife from the floor and brandishes it at me, forcing me to stop.

'Get away from me, Kim.' He takes several steps away from me, the knife still held aloft.

'Carly has paid the price for what she did, and I need to get away from this island.' At that he turns and runs towards the thicket of jungle and steps onto a narrow path that cuts a small gap in the leaves. Not pausing to think about what I'm doing, I follow him, calling for him to stop. The darkness in the forest is impenetrable and branches scratch at my arms as I run. Daniel thrashes ahead of me, using the knife to cut at anything that gets in his way.

Then the thrashing stops and the jungle ends abruptly. Moonlight bounces off the dark water and the waves lap gently against the sand. To my right, Daniel bounds along the beach, holding the knife tightly in his hand as he runs. I follow him.

'Daniel. Stop.' At my words, Daniel suddenly halts as if I've cast a spell over him. But I quickly realise that he hasn't stopped because of me; he crouches down and unties a knotted rope that is keeping a tiny fishing boat from floating away. Water splashes into the air as he pushes the boat out into the sea, pulling at the string of a motor as he goes. The engine purrs and Daniel launches himself into the boat. Daniel's words come back to me. *Carly has paid the price for what she did*; so it was her all along? No, it can't have been her. If it was, why is Daniel escaping?

'Daniel, it's over.' I don't know whether I'm telling him the ordeal is over or that it's game over for him. I still can't point the finger of blame. 'Daniel,' I call again but the smell of petrol catches in my throat, making me cough.

'Goodbye, Kim,' he says, and with that his hand grips the handle of the engine and he sails off into the night and away from the island of horror.

Chapter Forty-Four

To: matt@deluca.com
From: contactme@jd.co.uk
Subject: Reply to Contact Me form

Message:

Hello Matteo,

What an awful story but sadly not one I haven't heard before. I'm working on a plan that may help you satisfy your rage. I'll be in touch soon!

Best,
JD

Chapter Forty-Five

Spyland.co.uk – News, Scandals and all the latest Gossip from your favourite celebrities

BREAKING NEWS: Location of the real LoveWrecked villa sent to police from unknown email account

Posted on Sunday 27th July, 10:01 p.m.

In the last twelve hours, the British and Greek governments have been on a frantic, race-against-time search for the island which has played host to this year's season of *Love-Wrecked*. They've been looking in vain, until now.

Less than thirty minutes ago, *SpyLand* received information that the location was sent to a British police officer in an email.

Around ten minutes ago, the *LoveWrecked* villa screened its final image. That of former police officer Kimberley King, the only known survivor of the tragedy, sitting in front of the outdoor television screen and the Judge as he, in his words, 'delivered his final verdict'. He chastised Kim for failing to catch the perpetrator of these crimes and said it was a stinging indictment on the whole of the British police force. He also said that the challenge was now over and that he had sent the island's location to the police. In one of the most harrowing turns yet, he instructed Kim to one of the rooms where there were two things. The first was a book, none other than Agatha Christie's *And Then There Were None*, a story about massacre and vengeance. And the second is almost too horrible to report, but *SpyLand* is committed to bringing our readers the truth. Above the book was a noose. The ending prepared for Kim is reminiscent of the last one standing in Christie's book. Her name was Vera Claythorne and she let an innocent child die on her watch.

The final image we have from the villa is from the CCTV cameras. Though the image is grainy, it is unmistakably Kimberley King walking towards the noose. It is at this point that the filming was cut.

The whereabouts of Rosalind, Carly and Daniel are also currently unknown.

Little is known about whether the island has yet been found but for those of us who've been watching the drama unfold, we only hope that the police get there before it's too late for Kimberley. Fans across the world have reacted in terror and sadness to this horror movie come true and our thoughts go out to those who've lost their lives.

As always, *SpyLand* promises to keep you updated with the latest as and when we have it.

Comments section

@trashqueen2000: Oh good God, it's a mass murder-suicide

@gormlessguy: if anyone ever needed a reason to get rid of their tv. This is it! Death to modern media.

@curlywurlyhurly: OMG what happened to Rosalind, Daniel and Carly? Why aren't they showing what happened to them. I hope they're all OK

@trashqueen2000: Errrr… have you been watching any of this? It is highly likely they are NOT OK.

@queenjulia: So, do we know who did it?

@Scandalina: I'd put money on it being Kimberley all along

@queenjulia: that'd be a twist eh?

Chapter Forty-Six

The smooth white frame of my front doors stands resolute in front of me. I press my hand against it, trying to steady myself. I hold my key outstretched like a dagger but, no matter how much I try, it seems to be repelled by the lock like a magnet facing a magnet. Every time the tip of the key nears the lock, my hand trembles so violently that it slips sideways. There's nothing wrong with the key, nor the lock, just me and my trembling hands.

It's only been a week since I last walked through this door. One short week since I left England for Greece. One week since the deaths of my fellow Islanders. And it was for just under a week that I was held in a Greek prison while my fate was decided. Then one day, a police officer came to my cell and told me a flight had been booked and I was to head home, that the UK government had made it clear they wanted to deal with me themselves, whatever the heck that means. I've turned over and over in my mind the events that took place and am certain now that Daniel's survival and subsequent escape is the signal of his guilt. In that final moment, I had thought he had discovered Carly was behind it but time away from the panic has cleared my mind; Carly was there to be punished and Daniel was the hand that delivered it.

Less than three hours ago I landed in Liverpool John Lennon airport and was greeted by a torrent of reporters and photographers practically climbing the barriers at arrivals, all clamouring to get their shouts above their neighbours'. Some shouted an offer of cash, others offered me the opportunity to tell my side of the story. I didn't like the latter, as though there is more to tell than what the world has witnessed. I hopped around all of them and managed to squeeze myself into a taxi. I knew I don't really have the cash to spare for such a journey but the attention I received made it clear I couldn't exactly jump on the bus. Plus, it's not like there's anyone I could have called. And even if there was someone, my phone was smashed and left in the villa, so I couldn't call anyone even if I wanted to.

Finally, the key slips into the lock and with a click the door to my apartment unlocks.

After a week of complete hell, I finally cross the threshold of my home. The place I dreamed about every single night in prison. My own bed called to me like a siren on the rocks.

But it's as if even my homecoming has been soured. As I enter, my nose wrinkles; one week is a long time to not have a window open in this heatwave. The air is thick and sweat creeps down my back.

I march along the cream-coloured carpet of the hallway, straight into the living room, and crack open the window. Thankfully, the evening is cool and has brought with it a light breeze which cuts through the stagnant air. That done, I walk zombie-like to my bedroom.

I stand for a moment, staring at my room. The room is as tidy as I left it, my modern floral bedspread slightly wrinkled because I never bother to iron the sheets, matching pillows piled high against the studded headboard. My dressing table is practically bare, housing only the perfume I chose to leave behind because I deemed it too wintery a scent for the summer. The magazine I'd been reading the night before I left for Greece lies at a jaunty angle on my bedside table. The main topic was, unsurprisingly, the upcoming series of *LoveWrecked*. When the magazine went to print it was part of the wave of excitement for the new series that had swept the country; nobody knew that that wave was about to turn into a tsunami of terror. The sight of it turns my stomach and I flip it over to hide the cover.

Everything in my bedroom is the same as it was when I left. Only once before have I experienced the feeling I have right now, but I'd forgotten the power of it. Nothing prepares you for the feeling of disbelief that comes when the entirety of your world has changed. When something so monumental has happened, you know in that instant that you're a different person than you were before. And yet, bizarrely, unbelievably, the world around you remains exactly the same.

It's as if my bedroom is chiding me for leaving. It's mocking me; it's as if my bedroom refuses to change despite what's happened. My safe haven has turned on me.

My body shakes, expelling the huge tears that have been welling inside me for the days that have felt more like decades. I'm completely exhausted and my body aches from head to toe.

Pulling my T-shirt over my head, I let it drop onto the floor and rummage around my drawers for some pyjamas.

My bed calls to me and I collapse onto it, pressing my head against the pillow and squeezing my eyes shut. Yet despite all the sleep my body is screaming for, my mind won't let go. It hasn't been able to let go for a single second since Jack's body was found floating in the pool.

Suddenly, my bedroom door slams shut, forcing my eyes to ping open.

'Who's there?' I call but my question is met with silence. Then I remember the window. The door slammed because the window is open; it happens all the time. I sigh in relief and, pushing my feet into my slippers, I shuffle to the living room. My bare skin tightens as the cool air makes its way into my home. I wrap my fingers around the handle of the window and am ready to pull it shut when something stops me. In the dark street below me, I see something that makes my heart feel like a hand has closed around it. Standing on the opposite pavement is a person, their body pointed directly towards my window, towards me. Someone is watching me.

The unknown figure is encased in a huge, black Puffa jacket with a baseball cap pulled low over their head. The evening is definitely not cold enough for such a large jacket but if their goal is disguising themselves it does the trick. Under the darkness of their baseball cap, it's impossible for me to make out their face and from this distance I can't even tell their height, their gender or the tone of their skin. My feet remain rooted to the spot with my hand still curled around the handle of the window. I have no idea who this person is but I'm certain that this person is watching me; why else would they be standing there at this time of the night staring at my window?

Thunk. I slam the window shut, cutting off the sound of the wind passing through the trees, and dash to my bedroom. I rummage through the bottom drawer of my bedside table, grab my old and slightly battered digital camera from it, and run back to the window, readying the camera to get a photo of my stalker. But as I lift the camera to the window, I see that the camera's screen can only capture a dark and deserted street. There's no figure standing there, not any more. The stark white eyes sparkling in the black night have gone.

Sweat gathers in my armpits and despite my skimpy attire, my pyjamas suddenly feel too warm and too tight like they're suffocating me. My hands fall to my sides and my camera slips to the floor, thudding gently on the carpet. Not being able to see this person is more alarming to me than seeing them.

It's probably a photographer, I say to myself, forcing myself to be calm. Photographers and reporters have followed me everywhere since I was rescued from the villa: they were there as I entered the prison and were there as I left, and the memory of them clamouring around me at the airport is still fresh in my mind. So far, I'm the biggest story of the year and they're buzzing around me like wasps at a picnic.

I pull down the blinds to make sure no unwanted snaps of me in my pyjamas end up on the Internet overnight. Up until now, I've not seen the news or checked social media; something tells me the content about me won't be kind.

Turning away from the window, I'm determined to put the photographer out of my mind. I head to the kitchen to make myself a hot drink, opting for a chamomile tea. Considering I can't sleep, coffee would be a terrible idea.

As the kettle boils I try not to dwell on how weird it feels to be doing something so normal as making myself a tea in my own kitchen, like discovering that there is a world outside of the villa or prison. I turn on the radio, hoping for some music to soothe me and make me feel more normal. The song that blasts into my kitchen is a high-octane pop song whose lyrics are focused on summer sun and romance. The juxtaposition of its tone with my mood is almost too ironic to bear.

'If you weren't dancing before,' says the radio host, his voice almost as energetic as the song, 'I hope you're up on the tables now. That is without a doubt the hottest tune of the summer and wherever you are listening to us tonight I hope it's helping you kick yourself into weekend mode.'

The kettle clicks and steams billows from the spout and the radio host's voice is replaced by the beeps indicating that it's 10 o'clock.

'Now, for a quick lowdown of the latest news.'

I grab a tea bag and, dropping it in a mug, lift the kettle and pour the boiling water over it.

'The search for Daniel Oni is over.' My body convulses in shock at the sound of Daniel's name and my hand jerks away from the mug, splattering boiling hot water all over the counter. I leap backwards to avoid the drips spilling over my exposed legs. Before *LoveWrecked*, I was able to control my fear, able to push it aside so I could focus on the job in hand. But my time imprisoned in the villa seems to have changed everything and, for a moment, I'm paralysed, rooted to the spot and quivering, like a child after a nightmare. I lean around the puddle of water and jab the button to increase the radio's volume; Daniel Oni is on the news.

'Police have confirmed that Daniel Oni, one of the men trapped inside the *LoveWrecked* villa has been found. Greek fishermen happened upon what they thought to be an abandoned motorboat and found Daniel's body slumped in the bottom, dead.'

Chapter Forty-Seven

Contact Me form

Type your message in the box below. I read every piece of correspondence that comes to me and I will aim to get back to you as soon as I can.

Your Name: Daniel Oni
Your Email Address: cameramandan@hotmail.co.uk

Your Message:

I will never forget the two times I set eyes on the woman who ruined my life and the lives of my family. I was twenty-one years old and had just started working as a cameraman on a new reality television show following the life of a former reality television show star (sometimes I try not to think too deeply about how ridiculous all of this is). Anyway, I wasn't earning much, so I was still living at home. I remember that Dad had been acting strangely for weeks. He was coming home earlier than usual; he worked at an investment bank, so early nights weren't normal. And then he was sneaking out late at night. He was jumpy and distracted. My mother tried to pretend nothing was happening – she always was one to put her head in the sand, much preferring to ignore than deal with things. I, however, am not like my mother at all. So, one night, I followed him and discovered he was meeting with a young woman. She was probably in her early twenties, about the same age as me. My father handed her an envelope which she accepted with a smile. I assumed the envelope contained money but at the time I didn't know what for. A month later, I found out when pictures of my father, laid out on a bed surrounded by cash and an array of illegal substances, were posted through the front door. It turns out they were posted to his work too. He lost his job and his reputation and eventually fled the country to return to his hometown in Nigeria. I never saw him again.

But I did see her. Years later, still a camera operator, but financially in a much worse position, I was filming audition tapes for a new series of a soap opera. She walked in, sat down, and smiled at me from behind the camera. I couldn't believe it. But even more unbelievable, I couldn't believe the anger that rose inside me. From that moment on I was determined that Carly Chu wouldn't get away with what she did.

Chapter Forty-Eight

Kimberley
Sunday 3rd August, 22:15

Daniel Oni is dead. Dead? Everything that I've been turning over and over in my mind for the last week is shattered into a thousand pieces. I totter to the living room and crash down on the couch.

Daniel was found dead, slumped in the bottom of the motorboat I'd seen him escaping in. But how did he die? What killed him? I remember the tussle he and Carly had with the knife; maybe she wounded him more dangerously than it appeared. If he was killed by Carly, did she do it by accident, nothing more than a fatal result of her struggle for survival? Or did Daniel die another way? Maybe Daniel was always meant to die and he, like the rest of us, was there to be punished. But if this is true then that means one of the others is the killer and that person might still be alive.

I jump from the couch and march to the other side of my living room. I tug open the top drawer of one of my cabinets and pull out my laptop and its charger. Plugging the laptop into the wall, I switch it on. It whirs noisily as if resurrected from the dead. The laptop seems to take an age to boot up. I chew my fingernails to stop myself manically tapping the keys. Come on, why is it taking so long?

I want to find out who of the seven in the villa with me is confirmed dead and, if my hunch is correct, who isn't.

After what feels like a lifetime, the laptop screen shines, greeting me with a photograph of me with my two sisters. My heart squeezes at the image.

The photo was taken at my little sister's university graduation. My younger sister stands in the middle, her head thrown back in a laugh. Me and my older sister stand either side, pulling puzzled expressions, like we've missed the joke. I love this photograph, I love my family and I hate how much I've separated myself from them. I promise that once this is all over I'll get back in touch. I know they'll be anxious to hear from me. Guilt pangs in my stomach when I think of the terror my family have probably gone through over all of this.

I'm relieved my grandmother is no longer alive to witness the decline my life has gone through. Disgraced police officer, party-hard waitress, an Islander at the centre of a media frenzy, and now suspected of executing a plan to commit multiple murders.

I brush aside a solitary tear and tap in my log-in details. As soon as I'm in, I drag my cursor to the Internet browser and pull it up.

'Shit,' I say to my computer. It isn't connected. I click the Wi-Fi button and search for my home wi-fi. But it isn't there. I place my laptop down and walk to the router. It looks fine, but I turn it off at the wall and back on again.

It doesn't do the trick. My connection still isn't showing. What is going on? Then I remember, my bill was due the day I left for Greece and I didn't have the money to pay for it so they've probably cut me off. I've got no Wi-Fi and no chance of 4G since I left my smashed phone in the villa. But I need to get onto the Internet, I need to find out what the rest of the world probably already knows. Who did this?

I glance at the clock hanging on my living room wall. It's almost 11 o'clock; most of the cafes will be shut. Where would be open at this time for me to get Wi-Fi? Oh, the irony of needing the Internet to google and find out where would be open at this time and has Internet.

I could go and ask my neighbour. But Mrs Rahman is in her seventies; would she even have Wi-Fi? And it's probably not fair or appropriate to knock on her door at this time. There's also the fact that the entire country potentially thinks I'm a mass murderer. I don't want to scare Mrs Rahman to death by turning up demanding Wi-Fi that I don't even know she has. No, that won't work. I need to go out.

There has to be an Internet cafe or something on the high street.

My body aches from tiredness as I change out of my pyjamas. I pull on a pair of jeans; they hang loose around my hips and I'm forced to keep them up with a belt. Evidently, I've lost quite a bit of weight during my ordeal. I pack my laptop and charger into my backpack and, zipping up my jacket, I head out into the night.

As the door to the street swings open, the evening wind hits my cheeks and I pull my coat a little closer. The heat of the day has completely evaporated now and it's colder than I thought. Why am I doing this? It would be so much nicer to just curl up in bed and wait for the police to solve it.

It was my task to find the killer. I need to know who did this. It isn't just my reputation at stake; if I am the only known survivor, perhaps my innocence is too. The cold and tiredness are nothing in comparison to the indignity I feel at being forced into the centre of all of this. It's a twenty-minute walk to the city centre and every moment that passes makes it more unlikely there'll be somewhere for me to get Wi-Fi.

The streets are dark and deserted, the only light coming from the orange glow of the streetlamps. I glance behind me, half expecting to see the figure beneath my window following me. But it's only my imagination; the street is completely empty.

Turning back around, I keep my eyes trained ahead. I'm close to the high street now. End of this street and it's there on my left. I speed up. I'm nearly there; soon I will know who was lying to me.

When I reach the high street, I'm relieved to see some signs of life. Light glows through glass-fronted restaurants filled with people sharing tables and bottles of wine. I stand for a moment, mesmerised by the normality of it all. Will I ever feel normal again? Normal enough to sit in a restaurant with a bottle of wine without worrying what might happen to me. I continue onwards; right now I don't have time to dwell on what I've lost. I continue down the high street but the only places open are restaurants. Given my current notoriety, I don't feel like I can just waltz in, take a seat and open my laptop. Surely there is an Internet cafe. There has to be. Doesn't every high street have one? Somewhere.

A side street comes up on my left. I peer down it and my heart does a little leap. A sign sticks out from the wall, swinging stiffly in the brisk wind. *TJ's T'Internet Temple*, reads the sign. The ridiculousness of the name doesn't deter me. I step into the side street and march towards the sign.

I push the door open. It doesn't budge. A sticker in the door says *Closed*. Closed. No, no, it can't be closed. But there's a light on inside. I rap impatiently on the door. A man, youthful and chubby, walks to the door.

'We're closed,' he mouths at me through the door. I press my hands together in prayer.

'Please,' I mouth back. 'Please it's really important. Fifteen minutes. I only need fifteen minutes.' I press my face up close to the glass, hoping he will see the desperation in my face and take pity on me.

The man's eyes widen as he registers my face. He unlocks the door and pulls it open a fraction. 'Aren't you that girl? That girl from *LoveWrecked*? Kimberley King?' His breath smells of beer and cigarettes. I can't decide if saying yes will make him more or less likely to accept my request and let me in. But there's something in his hungry expression that makes me think it's the former.

'Yes,' I say. 'I'm Kimberley King. And if you know who I am, you probably know what I'm accused of. But I didn't do it. That's why I'm here. I'm here to find proof.'

The man breaks into a smile and he gives a deep chuckle. 'Well, ain't that exciting. Fine, I'll let you in. On one condition.'

'What?'

'You let me take a Polaroid of you at one of our computers and you sign it. I've always wanted to have one of those walls of celebrities who've visited.'

'Right. Who else do you have?' I don't really know why I ask this; I guess it's because I want to know what company I will be among. Does TJ of TJ's T'Internet Temple have a host of notorious visitors?

'No one. You'd be the first.'

I don't really want to do it, but I've come all this way and I don't want to turn back now.

'Fine,' I say.

'Nice one. Come on in then, let me get you set up.'

TJ pulls open the door to reveal his bulging belly over which a large *Games of Thrones* T-shirt hangs loosely. Computers are lined up in a row on all three sides of the shop. The many screens are dark. My heartbeat quickens as I'm reminded of the *LoveWrecked* producer's room. My legs go wobbly and I reach a hand out to grab the back of one of the computer chairs.

'You're not in the villa. You're OK,' I whisper to myself.

'What?' asks TJ.

'Nothing. I'm fine,' I say but my fluttering voice gives me away. TJ just grunts and gets back to the computer.

'Right, it's ready,' he says, gesturing to the seat. With every step I take closer to the computer, my heart thuds more forcefully against my chest. Who was lying to me?

I roll the chair back and take my seat. The search engine is open and at the ready. The cursor blinks expect-antly. I glance over my shoulder and see that TJ is sitting in front of the counter watching me. He clears his throat.

'Better leave you to it,' he says, turning away.

My fingers hover over the keyboard. What should I search for first? I think about typing in the names of the Islanders, but I don't. My invitation to the island was personal and I realise to uncover the truth I need to look where all of this started. The thought of this trip down memory lane isn't a welcome one but I take a deep breath and type *Emily Cadman* into the search tool.

Chapter Forty-Nine

Spyland.co.uk – News, Scandals and all the latest Gossip from your favourite celebrities

Emily Cadman: the police failings that led to the death of a young woman

Since the murder of Emily Cadman, her friends, family and boyfriend have called for an investigation into the circumstances that led up to her death. They want to understand why the police failed to take her reports of harassment by her former colleague seriously.

Earlier this year, Emily Cadman was stabbed by her former colleague Roger Bartlett, who was later sentenced to life for her murder. Bartlett, with whom Emily had been on two dates, refused to accept her decision not to take their relationship any further and began what became months of harassment.

Emily was murdered just days after she reported him to police for constantly ringing and texting her, as well as bombarding her with gifts. Emily also reported that her car and house keys had gone missing and that she suspected Bartlett had taken them to stop her travelling. She felt that he wanted to stop her from seeing her new boyfriend with whom she had recently started up a serious relationship. Emily only went to the police that one time, as she was murdered by Bartlett in her home soon afterwards.

Following Emily's murder, an investigation was conducted to review the police officer's handling of Emily's complaint and whilst 'no further action will be taken', the investigation did find that although the officer's actions were proportionate, they did not report that Emily's car keys had been stolen but rather the officer believed that Miss Cadman had simply 'misplaced' them. In the inquiry, the officer defended her actions by stating that Miss Cadman 'by her own admission was absent-minded' and 'although she thought Bartlett had stolen her keys she really couldn't be sure'. Emily's family believe that had the officer taken Emily more seriously and believed Bartlett had stolen her keys then the matter might have been investigated more thoroughly and Emily might still be alive.

Jeffrey Goodrum, one of the investigators handling the complaint, said: 'My sympathies remain with Emily's loved ones following her tragic murder. It is clear that the handling of Emily's complaint was inadequate, and the police officer was ill-equipped to properly assess the threat to Emily's life. Our investigation gives recommendations for the force on how to provide a better response to victims in the future.'

Chapter Fifty

Within seconds, the search returns thousands of results. The feeling of nausea that always comes when I think about Emily and the mistakes I made rises in my stomach.

Man, guilty of Emily Cadman's murder, 'acted because of police intervention'.

What should the police learn from the death of Emily Cadman?

There is no need for me to read the articles; I know what they say, and how I'm the police officer they all refer to. Instead, I click on the header that says *Images*, and instantly photograph after photograph of Emily Cadman fills the screen: her face is heart-shaped; her dark brown hair hangs long and straight, draping over the front of her shirt; her skin is pale, and the whiteness of her face is broken up by her thick, dark eyebrows and plump pink lips. The memory of that young woman and the tragedy surrounding her death comes rushing back like a flood.

I feel as if I've been winded and I fight the urge to look away.

I don't need to see photos of Emily. I know what Emily looked like because her face will be forever branded in my mind. But it isn't Emily that I'm looking for; it is the people that surrounded her: her friends, her colleagues, her family. One of them is responsible for this; one of them sought revenge.

My eyes gloss over the images of Emily until I find what I'm looking for. I move the mouse and select the image to enlarge it. The image is of a group of people standing in a huddle behind a man whose bony fingers are wrapped around a piece of paper. The man is grey-haired and grey-skinned, and I remember that at the time he was in his mid-fifties, although in this image he looks like one of the undead. It's a picture of Emily's father as he read his statement following the verdict against her killer. A hand clings to his suit, hanging off his upper arm. A woman, with hollow cheeks and hair scraped back in a low bun, stands just behind him. Her thin, lipsticked mouth is clamped together in a way that makes her look as if she is stoppering a scream. Joan Cadman, Emily's mother, is the exemplification of a picture speaking a thousand words.

There are other people huddled around; will I recognise any of them? I click on the image again; I need to enlarge it further because I can't quite make out the background faces. The page changes and I realise that I've accidentally selected to move to a webpage. It's a newspaper's digital site. The headline of the article reads: *Father speaks out against police failures that killed daughter*, and underneath it is the image. Except, I now see that it isn't an image but rather a still from a video. A large red play button is slashed across the image, partly obscuring

Alan and Joan Cadman from view. My finger trembles as I move the cursor and press the play button.

Alan speaks in a slow, monotonous voice, conveying the extent to which reading from his pre-prepared statement is an effort. The paper shakes as he grips it fiercely.

The waves of sadness I felt when I heard this speech live come over me again and I'm transported back to that moment. I stood shoulder to shoulder with Zoe, watching from the background, just out of shot of the cameras. Every word Alan spoke was like a knife to the heart. My heart broke as Emily's dad thanked the jurors for placing the maximum penalty on the man guilty of murdering his daughter and then my sadness turned to horror and I fought to keep my face neutral as Alan continued on to place the blame of his daughter's death on the police that stood around him and who watched from afar. He chastised our faults and failings and highlighted not only our inability to stop the man, the murderer, from being captured before he could inflict the worst of crimes on his daughter but the fact that we, and he meant me, in the course of our investigation had alerted Bartlett to the fact that Emily had reported him. Alan Cadman concluded that he would never ever forgive us for it and I knew then that I'd never forgive myself either.

My chest tightens, and I feel my breath become ragged as the sadness and horror hit me again almost as powerfully as it did then. I inhale slowly through my nose, trying to master my emotions, but as I breathe out I realise that my emotions are accompanied by another feeling.

Recognition.

I pause the video and lean forward, my nose almost touching the screen. Is this who I think it is? Standing behind Alan Cadman is someone that I've met before.

Someone that looks very different now but there in that face is the glimmer of the person I met in the villa. A person who, I think, must be very much alive. My suspicions are confirmed when I read an article about the Islanders. There, in black and white, is the name I'm looking for.

'So,' I whisper, 'it was you, all along.'

Chapter Fifty-One

The computer screen goes black from my inaction. I move the mouse, bringing the image back. I feel like I should tell someone, but who? It's not as if I can call anyone. No, I need to finish this myself and to finish it, I need to go to the place where it all started. Something tells me that is where my assailant is.

'Time to go, Kim,' says TJ. I give him a curt nod, log off quickly and push myself away from the computer.

'Could you please call a taxi for me?' He gives my request a thumbs up. 'Oh, and there's something else I need.' I can't believe I'm going to go to the house at this time, but this can't wait. Every second that the killer is free is a second too long. TJ nods as I tell him what I need and reaches for one of the shelves to retrieve the package.

'Look, this is none of my business,' he says, shaking his shaggy head of hair as he helps me get set up. 'But are you sure you want to do this?'

'Yes, I'm sure. And if I don't come back, you know what to do?'

'I'm not super happy about this,' he says with a look that seems to say he is actually thrilled to be involved in my scheme. 'But yeah, if I don't hear from you in one week, I know what to do.'

'Thanks, TJ,' I say, reaching out and shaking his hand before exiting the shop. The bell tinkles above me and once the door has closed, I hear TJ bolting it behind me.

The night is colder than before but that could be due to the chills making their way down my spine. It is only a couple of minutes before the taxi pulls up outside the Internet cafe and I bundle myself into the back. The thirty minutes it takes to get to the address seems to drag onwards. It is as if time is purposefully trying to eke out every moment, giving my adrenaline time to course through the entirety of my body.

'Here you are, love,' says the driver. I tap my card against the reader.

I slide out of the car, slamming the door behind me. The taxi speeds off, not waiting for so much as a wave from me.

The road is deadly silent. The street lamps are few and far between and the nearest one flickers jumpily. Every breath brings icy air into my lungs, stabbing at my chest like a knife. Standing here, in front of it, makes my body turn to ice.

21 Beech Drive is a small, unassuming bungalow. It looks exactly like the bungalow on its left and exactly like the bungalow on its right. Pale red bricks; a grey, tiled roof; black-rimmed windows and matching front door.

The bungalow had belonged to Emily's grandmother and she left it to her two granddaughters in her will. This is where Emily's body was found, murdered. This is where it all began and ended for me. This was the crime that made me realise how awful I was as a police officer and what a horrifying result my failings had for that innocent woman.

My mind pulls me back to that time.

The door creaked as I pushed it open. Ominous, like it knew. My chest tightened. The noise of activity buzzed around me, but the sound of my heart drowned it out. Step by step I walked down the corridor. An arm pointed me to the room where it was. Where she was. I nodded at the arm's owner. I knew him; we'd worked together before. Our paths never crossed under pleasant circumstances, but of all of them, this seemed like the worst. I reached the threshold of the room, the safety of the wooden-floored hallway distinctly separate from the horror of the carpeted living room. The tightness in my chest closed in further. My foot raised and stepped forward. My boss was talking to me, his hands gesturing to different points in the room and then down. My eyes followed his fingers and I looked at her. Her pale wrists were bound in fraying rope. Her eyes were wide and vacant as she stared at the ceiling. Blood pounded in my temples so hard I could barely think. But two things were clear. The young woman was dead. And it was entirely my fault.

A strong gust of icy cold wind shunts me back to the present day, back to my current reality.

What am I doing? I shouldn't be here; this is so dangerous. But I've come all this way so maybe I shouldn't run, maybe I should go in. This might be the only chance I have to find out the truth.

Before I have time to contemplate my decision any further, something hard and circular presses against my back.

'I wondered how long it would be until we met again. In you go.'

Chapter Fifty-Two

From: contactme@jd.co.uk
BCC:
Subject: The Islanders

Message:

Dear Joanna, Sammy, Tristram, Matteo, Kevin and Daniel,

Thank you for all of your messages. I am so sorry to hear about the difficulties you have faced and how let down you feel by a system that refused to properly punish those who brought you harm. I have connected with you all on an individual level but now we have all agreed it is time to move forward as a collective. But before we do, I want to say another thank you also for your honesty; it can't have been easy to share your stories with me and I think it is only right that I share my story with you. Well, I'm going to tell you. I hope you're sitting comfortably. This won't make easy reading but, given what you've all been through, I'm sure you will be able to handle it.

It all began in the early nineties. I was two years old and in an instant my life changed.

Though, of course, I didn't know it at the time, and wouldn't really know it for a while. But when I was two years old someone was born who would go on to completely change my life. She changed the course of my life then and eleven months ago she changed the course of my life again. This woman was very, very important to me.

What can I say about her that will properly do her justice? For starters, she was beautiful; just looking at her could make you smile. I acknowledge that it isn't fair to judge someone on their beauty alone, it's conventional and boring of me, but I'm trying to paint a picture. More than that, though, she was kind, likeable, and funny. Everything that I wasn't. She was the day, I was the night but we fitted together. I'd tell her when she was being naive and stupidly optimistic, which she was a lot, and she'd tell me was when I was being an arsehole, which I was a lot. Of course, her being her she'd never have used the word 'arsehole'. Grump, she'd call me a grump. When I would work late, she'd slip into my apartment and leave dinner on my worktop. All I had to do was come home and heat it up. And unlike other people in my life she never moaned when I worked late into the evenings or at weekends. She knew my job was important to me and she not only respected that but actively supported it. She really was one of a kind.

She had always dreamed of being a teacher and she was thrilled when she got a job as a teaching assistant at a school in the city centre. She loved working with children and they loved her. Reading this you might think I'm exaggerating but I'm as cynical as they come and I can guarantee it was like Miss Honey stepped off the pages of *Matilda* and bounced into the classroom.

All of the staff loved her too. After a couple of months working there one of the staff, the sports teacher, approached her and asked if she fancied going for a drink with him. I remember her telling me she was a bit uncomfortable about mixing business with pleasure but she hadn't been out with anyone all year and I wanted her to meet someone nice. Ever since she hit her twenties she was desperate to have a child and she wouldn't make much progress if she refused to go on any dates. After a bit of persuading she agreed. She called me on her way home to tell me that he was nice but, perhaps, a little too keen for her. She said that he had a look about him that said he was the type of man who liked to have an object of adoration. I remember thinking this was typical her; she was humble and as such was often surprised that people loved her. I told her that she deserved be adored and that a second date wouldn't hurt. How stupid I was.

She did go on that second date; it was right before the Christmas holidays and I remember her telling me she thought he seemed a bit miffed that she wouldn't be able to see him again until January. School finished for the holidays and that was when the texting began. Text after text, call after call. She hadn't officially broken it off with him but she thought ignoring him might help him get the message. In January, she decided she didn't want to return to school. Luckily her contract was only temporary and she was able to find another role at another school. She never told the headmistress her reasons for moving.

About a month passed and the messages and calls had stopped and she was relieved and believed that he had probably given up. This coincided with her friend setting her up with one of her colleagues and she instantly knew this had a future. Her friend, pleased about her own success in matchmaking, posted a picture on Facebook, tagging them both in it and that was when Roger saw it. The calls and texts started again, along with gifts. I didn't realise how bad things had become; I was working long, tiresome hours and wasn't regularly checking my phone or when I did I'd see a missed call from her, followed by a text telling me not to worry. She never liked to worry anyone. And then her keys went missing.

She went to the police, where she was met by a police officer who took her statement and a full report of the harassment and made a note about her missing keys. The police officer wasn't convinced they'd been stolen so it was just 'noted'.

The very next evening, Roger Bartlett let himself into her flat and killed her because if he couldn't have her, no one could. I will never, ever forgive myself for not answering the phone all those times she called in the lead-up and I will never, ever forgive the police officer who so obviously failed to protect her.

She was twenty-seven years old and her life was cut short by a man who was screwed in the head and a police officer who didn't do her job properly. He's in prison now where he'll rot unless someone kills him in there first; stalking and murdering a young woman won't exactly make you popular in prison. So, I live in hope on that side of things. But what about the police officer? Three words haunt me: no further action. No further action was taken because the police force believed that the officer's response was proportionate.

Therefore, I will take action and I am hoping that you as a group want to take action too.

Joanna – Valentina Novak should be punished for the drugs she gave to an unsuspecting young man.

Tristram – Sophia Dance should be punished for meddling and for stealing money that was not hers to steal.

Daniel – Carly Chu for entrapping men unfairly and blackmailing them until they bled dry.

Sammy – Jack Peaks for raping an innocent woman and robbing her of a happy future.

Kevin – Mo Khan, whose carelessness killed a beloved daughter.

Matteo – Rosalind Jenkins for the drunk-driving that has forever changed a couple's life.

And for myself, Kimberley King, for failing to protect my sister.

Chapter Fifty-Three

The feel of the gun against my back makes me inhale sharply and I follow its instruction to move forward towards the door. I push against it and it creaks, just like it did the last time I was here. The house is dark and, unlike the last time, completely silent.

'How did you know I was coming here?' I ask the gun's owner as I cross the threshold of the house.

'I've been following you since you arrived back in the UK yesterday. Not that you went many places: home, an Internet cafe, here. But after you left the Internet cafe, I followed in my car and it quickly became apparent where you were going so I sped ahead and waited for you to get out of the taxi. Go to the end of the corridor,' says the voice. It's familiar but different to before. Where previously the accent was neutral, belonging to nowhere in particular, it's morphed into one distinctly more local.

Without argument I walk down the hallway. The sound of the door being closed and locked behind me makes me tense and I hurry to the end of the corridor, and turn to press my back up against the wall. I don't want to be ambushed from behind. I run shaking fingers along the wall, feeling for a light switch. The wallpaper is bumpy to the touch and I'm reminded of the vintage wallpaper that covered the walls all those years before. My fingers brush a plastic square; finding the switch, I flick it. Despite the change, the hallway remains in darkness.

'It won't work,' says the voice. 'Electricity has been switched off for years. Go through the door at the end of the hall.'

I don't want to obey the order but I'm not the one holding a gun. My arms reach out in front of me, feeling for the gap in the wall. When I find it, I step into another room of complete darkness.

'You'll be familiar with this room, I believe.' The voice is closer now and I gulp. 'This is where she was found. Emily, I mean. Murdered by Roger Bartlett. But she shouldn't have been. Should she? He should have been arrested and charged but he wasn't because of shitty police work.'

Light flares in front of me as a match is struck and, in spite of my fear, I can't help but admire this ability to create an atmosphere. The match connects with a candle, then another, then another. Light glows at different spots in the room. Back then the room looked very different to the hall, as Emily, I learned, had been decorating one room at a time. The living room was her first achievement: the carpet was new, and it wasn't long since the walls had been given a fresh coat of paint. Now, the carpet has clumps of dust on it and the smell of fresh paint is replaced by the smell of damp mingled with the smell of struck matches. The candles illuminate more than just the signs of decay; out of the darkness looms the face of Rosalind Jenkins.

'I come here sometimes to think about her, hence the candles,' says Rosalind, answering a question I didn't ask. The light is strong enough now for me to see her properly.

She wears lace-up military-style boots, dark skinny jeans and roll-neck top, and a black denim jacket. Under a dark baseball cap, long auburn hair flows in front of her shoulders. It's a colour that looks much more natural and striking on her than the mousy colour she opted for in the villa. Even though it's only been about a week since we last saw one another she too has lost weight; the loss makes her cheeks appear sharper and her jawline more angular.

The disguise of Rosalind Jenkins has melted away and now she looks like she did back then. Up close, the realisation makes my stomach drop. I see her more clearly than I ever saw her in Greece and I can't believe she was staring me in the face this whole time. Her real appearance, I'm now aware, makes her look very like her sister. She isn't really Rosalind Jenkins and she never was: she is Beth Cadman.

'What should I call you?' I snarl.

A smile crosses her lips; it twists her thin face. 'So, you do remember me,' she says, keeping the gun pointed directly at my chest. 'It took you a while to figure it out. I'd prefer Beth, if you don't mind.' Beth takes a step closer to me. 'I did think you'd go for it,' says Beth, taking a step closer to me. 'The noose, I mean.'

I stare at her.

Of all the places she could have started our conversation, this is what she chooses and she does it with such nonchalance that I'm stunned into silence. I don't need to reply; Beth continues regardless of my silence.

'Your life took a path that suggested you blamed yourself for Emily's death. Quitting the police, abandoning your friends and family, drinking yourself silly. I thought that once I'd shown you that you caused destruction wherever you went it would be enough to push you to do it.' Beth tilts her head to one side like a curious Jack Russell terrier. 'And yet you didn't. Why?'

'Sorry, you're asking me why I didn't kill myself?' I ask with all the scorn I can muster. Beth's cold, unemotional exterior makes me want to slap her; she must be a psychopath. That's the only way to explain how she can talk about death in such a cruel and forthright way.

'Yes. That's exactly what I'm asking. Why didn't you kill yourself? You know you deserve to die for what you did, and I gave you the means. So why didn't you do it?'

Beth's voice is monotone, unfeeling. Involuntarily, I give a bark of laughter. It's such a harrowing yet simple question it's almost ridiculous.

I feel offended to even have been asked this question let alone to have to answer it. But as much as I hate the woman standing in front of me for everything that she's done, I can't deny the guilt that I've carried with me about what happened to Emily. Guilt that forced me to consider myself unworthy of joy, of love and sometimes of life. And, in my darkest moments, when the guilt threatened to consume me, I did think about ending my life.

Yet when it was presented to me by Beth in the form of a noose, I realised I couldn't do it. No, it was more than that: I didn't want to do it. I realised in that moment that I had life in me and I was determined to live it and stop feeling sorry for myself. I lick my lips, dry and cracked.

'I will answer your question once you've answered mine,' I say, wanting to get her talking, otherwise my purchase from TJ will be a complete waste of time. 'You want to kill me, I know that. You could have done it already but you brought me inside because I think you want to tell me how you did everything, I think you want to show me how much cleverer you are than me, a lowly police officer.'

The light flickers under Beth's chin as she gives me a narrow smile. 'I know,' she says. 'I have an idea — why don't you interview me? Like one of your suspects; that would be fun.'

Before I can reply Beth strides towards one of the couches and flops down on it. Clouds of dust billow into the air and she waves them away. I'm willing to play along if it will get me what I need.

The room is still very dark, but I can just make out a dining table surrounded by wooden chairs. I grab one of them and drag it towards the couch. I position it so it faces opposite to where Beth is sitting. The need to get proper answers from Beth is accompanied now by a need to prove myself to her, a chance for me to display the investigative skills that Beth so clearly thinks I'm lacking, and I'm determined to do it properly. I clear my throat.

'Jack Peaks, Sophia Dance, Mo Khan, Valentina Novak, Carly Chu and Daniel Oni were all invited to a villa in Greece where they were murdered; did you kill them?'

'I didn't murder Daniel,' says Beth, narrowing her eyes at me. 'He was never meant to die. The papers reported that he was stabbed, so if it wasn't you then it must have been Carly. And I didn't murder Carly either, that was Daniel.'

'OK, you didn't kill Daniel or Carly but there's still Jack, Sophia, Mo and Valentina. Are you responsible for their deaths?'

Beth's brow furrows as if she needs to contemplate her answer. 'Yes... and no.'

I keep my face passive as I would for anyone I was interviewing. 'Could you elaborate on what you mean, Beth? How are you both responsible but also not for their deaths?'

She chuckles. 'It's a simple one really. I killed them. For example, I encouraged Sophia to give Jack the shot and then come and meet me upstairs afterwards. When I pointed out what was happening to Jack she was so distracted by what she had done she didn't notice me sneak up behind her and give her a big old shove. I put the oyster sauce in the meal. Carly, unknowingly but helpfully, drew attention away from me when she was screaming about the missing knife and I tampered with Valentina's medication. But anyway, as I say, yes I murdered them but they were responsible for their own demise, really. I saw they were punished for their crimes, but they committed crimes in the first place, so they need to take responsibility for their own deaths, you understand?'

I lean away from her at these words and say, 'I understand we were there to be punished but I don't understand why that means you're not responsible.'

'Well then, that's where we're different,' she says with a shrug.

'I don't remember this from when Emily was murdered because your job wasn't really relevant but are you even a producer?'

'Yes, actually I am a producer. In fact, *LoveWrecked* is my show. It was my idea over ten years ago.'

'What? You created *LoveWrecked*?'

'Yes, I'm surprised you didn't know that, but then you're not a great police officer. I created *LoveWrecked* and let me tell you, it made me a lot of money.'

'If it was making you loads of money, why stop? Why did the show take a hiatus?'

Beth rolls her eyes at this. 'Come on, Kimberley. It's staring you in the face.'

I nearly slap myself in the forehead. She's right, it's obvious. The show stopped five years ago. 'Emily. You stopped the show because of Emily?'

'My sister was murdered; I didn't have the bandwidth to think about it, and I didn't want anyone else producing it. So, I stopped it.'

I rub my eyes. Hundreds of questions crowd my brain and I can't stop them from coming out.

'So you're telling me you restarted the show for the sole purpose of revenge against me? Why would the production company agree to it and not want Beth Cadman involved? Why would they hire Rosalind Jenkins out of nowhere? And wouldn't they recognise you on the show?'

Beth smiles again, her head nodding with every question I ask. 'All good questions. Yes, for five years I stewed, letting my anger build inside me, until the desire for revenge became too strong. I was reading a lot about revenge at the time and I realised, like Agatha Christie's book, I too had the capability to lure people to an island to kill them. It all spiralled from there really. I made a telephone call, as Beth Cadman, to the management of the channel that usually shows *LoveWrecked* and told them I'd been approached by a production company who wanted to restart the show. I told them that I was ready for the show to be restarted and liked the vision this company had. I said I wouldn't be involved but that I had every faith in the production company as I'd talked with them in depth about their plans. The channel was so desperate to get *LoveWrecked* back that they didn't ask any more questions. That's what happens when you have talent; something you wouldn't understand.' I ignore the dig. 'Also, the channel was only streaming the show; with my assurances they were quite happy to let this production company be in charge of everything else. And so the production started. And when it all went wrong the management team at the channel weren't close enough to the show to interfere.'

I stare at her in disbelief, everything she has said is ludicrous and yet, she did it. She stands before me having pulled it all off.

'And it went is exactly as you intended?' I ask, strangely desperate to see some weakness in her plan. She clicks her tongue at my question.

'Close to it but not exactly,' she replies, crossing one leg over the other. 'I hadn't intended to appear on the show. Rosalind Jenkins was meant to be an Islander, she even worked in production. But the real Rosalind Jenkins died in a car accident before I could invite her to work on the show; she always was a reckless driver. There was nothing else to be done, the show must go on, so I took her name and pretended to be her. We weren't hugely dissimilar looking, she had a background in production and, luckily, I had only spoken with the television channel on the telephone. I've changed a lot in the last five years, aged in advance of my years from the grief and the stress. I doubt they recognised me on screen. Then, I picked Daniel Oni as my camera operator and off I went. If I'm honest with myself, I don't think it will be too long before the police piece it all together, if they haven't already. Rosalind Jenkins, the producer, on *LoveWrecked* might ring alarm bells for her family, and add to that the fact that fake-Rosalind's body has gone walkabout. I'm also sure the police are looking for Beth Cadman to speak to about this mysterious new production company. But what can I say? It was fun while it lasted. And,' she says, nodding her head towards me. 'I should say aside from not doing what I wanted of you at the end, overall, I thought you did a pretty good job in there.'

'By good job, you mean I didn't solve it and everyone was killed?' I spit out.

'Yes, you were as useless as I had expected you to be.'

The game was rigged. I want to shout it from the rooftops, but I bite back my retort. This is meant to be an interview, not a discussion. I clear my throat; there's one question that's still bugging me.

'You chose me because of Emily. What about the other Islanders, how did you find them?'

At this Beth gives me her most sinister smile yet. 'Interestingly enough, they found me. Or more accurately, their victims did.'

Chapter Fifty-Four

JustDeserts.co.uk – the blog that keeps me sane

Revenge isn't a dish to be served. Unless that dish in question is hard enough to crack open a skull...

ARCHIVED POST, originally posted five years ago

I am a person who refuses to 'let it go' or 'move on' or 'heal'. A person who will not forget the wrongs I've been done and will spend every waking moment of my life dreaming of the opportunity to get my own back.

They say don't get mad, get even. But I am mad, and I don't want to get even. 'Even' is too kind; I won't rest until they're in the negative, until their loss is my gain.

This is the reason for my blog... revenge on all the bullshit forced on me by this world... revenge for all my people that have endured the failures of our society.

Revenge is for when the punishment doesn't meet the crime.

Did you know that in this country only the worst of crimes are actually punished? Our prison system is on its knees and so if the crime isn't 'too bad', criminals are released with nothing more than a slap on the wrist.

THIS IS WRONG. But what's the solution?

The dictionary meaning of 'revenge' is 'to inflict hurt or harm on someone for an injury or wrong done to oneself or others'. It is such a dirty word, but the great philosopher Francis Bacon actually called revenge 'wild justice' that 'put the law out of office'. I think he's right and wrong. I think revenge is justice even if it is a bit wild. But I don't think revenge puts the law out of office; I think the law put itself out of office, meaning we need revenge. When our justice system fails us (and boy, it does), isn't it only right that we step in? Isn't it only fair that we do something, even the score? I think we should exact punishment where others have failed.

But I'm interested in what you think. Which side of revenge do you fall on?

Comments

@KatyBakes: This was an appalling thing to read. I came here thinking this would be a nice baking blog and instead I read this. You're sick. You need help. And change the name of your blog, you're misleading readers.

@JustDeserts: @KatyBakes, you should learn how to spell. You are a complete and utter idiot.

@Slasha: Revenge is natural. Humans aren't the only species that do it, you know. I read once that camels, elephants and lions seek revenge too. Although in the animal kingdom, chimpanzees are the most sophisticated at it.

Chapter Fifty-Five

Kimberley
Monday 4th August, 00:53

I stare at Beth. The fear and anger that have risen in me are crowded out by confusion. I acknowledge that it would have been impossible for her to have done this alone but her turn of phrase is a strange one. Like she's a magnet for revenge-ridden souls.

'The Islanders' victims found you,' I repeat. 'How?'

'Through my blog,' she replies. 'Just Deserts.'

'Just Deserts? What are you talking about?'

'When Emily died, I started a blog. I called it Just Deserts, you know like the expression: to get one's just deserts. I know, not particularly imaginative,' she says, voicing something I'm not even thinking about. When I don't say anything, she carries on. 'I had absolutely zero expectations for it and to be honest, I can't even remember the spark that drove me to start it in the first place. All I was was rage and I needed a place, a public place, to vent my fury about how the failings of Police Officer A had killed my sister.' I flinch at the memory of how the papers reported the story. 'But what started as nothing more than a repository for the hate I had for you and for the world soon become the thing that fuelled me. The thing that gave me a purpose when I had thought I would never have purpose again.' Beth is on a roll, telling me everything, and I hold my body still so as not to disturb her. Everything she is telling me will clear my name and I don't want her to stop. 'In only a couple of months and without any prompting or conscious effort on my part, my blog grew and gained a modest selection of followers. You wouldn't believe my surprise when one day I saw that my posts had likes and comments. And, even better, the majority of the comments weren't telling me I was evil or should seek professional help. These comments were in my favour; these people were on my side. After a while, I even started to receive direct messages from people who had suffered the wrongs like I had, who had been let down by a justice system that they were forced to pay for.

'I was tentative to reply at first but it soon became clear to me that I couldn't ignore them; they needed me. Soon, my blog became a community and I connected with these people in a way far better than I connected with anyone in the real world. They became my allies and as my anger showed no sign of burning out and I retreated further from the world outside, these people became my friends. And why not? They understood me more than anyone in the real world.

'By day, I worked hard at a production company in a job that I used to love but which had soured; by night, I typed furiously at my computer, replying to the comments and messages my blog received.

'A better person than me might have replied with messages of peace, love and comfort in order to help these people move past their pain and allow them to get on with their lives. I had always thought of myself as a sensible, reasonable person, but my sister's murder had flipped a switch in my head. So, when a mother contacted me about how a DJ named Valentina Novak had supplied her son with drugs that killed him or how Sophia Dance, the upstart wannabe, had ruined a family with her nosiness, I found that I didn't have it in me to tell them to accept this as part of a bigger plan. No, I couldn't do that to my followers or those who had lost their lives. How could I preach peace when I would never feel peace again? For me there was only anger and discontent. So I acted in the only way I knew how: I used my messages to stoke the fires of revenge in myself and others.'

'So the victims of the other Islanders are involved in this?'

'Urgh, keep up, Kimberley,' scoffs Beth. 'But let me tell you, I had my pick of options. You wouldn't believe how many people in the UK alone want revenge. People in this country are really dedicated to justice.'

The admiration in Beth's voice makes me feel sick.

'If revenge is so popular, how did you pick the *successful* candidates for your scheme, then?'

'First things first, they had to be a viable option for the show. They needed to be young and relatively attractive, otherwise the public wouldn't be as interested to watch. This group were, in my opinion, also more likely to watch the show and, therefore, be tempted to go on it. And secondly, perhaps more importantly, my associates, be they the actual victims or relatives of the victims, needed to be helpful to me in some way.'

'What do you mean, "helpful"?' I ask.

'The parents of Mo Khan's victim, for example, own a villa rental company with houses across Europe. One of the bookings was put on the "books" but wasn't the real location so the channel thought we were in one villa when we were actually in another one, miles away and much more hidden. Another clue for the police, of course, but I knew I'd never be able to pull it off without any traces to me. Anyway, the villa we all went to was regularly used by the mafia for their summer holidays, meaning it had the necessary security features. Then there is the victim of Jack Peaks; she is a very technically savvy woman. She knew how to control the outdoor television and ensure that the Just Deserts channel was able to keep showing the live feed. The victim of Sophia Dance played the part of our Judge and, along with myself, financially contributed to this scheme. And the mother of Valentina Novak's victim is a doctor so she helped me...' Beth pauses and bites her lip. 'How do I put this? Understand the more logistical side of murder as well as having good access to drugs and blood. The doctor actually came to the villa with us; she came here a couple of months ago under the pretence of volunteering at a hospital. This is where she stole the blood needed for my disguise and she helped me make it look believable enough to fool you.'

A knot tightens in my stomach. It's amazing what people can achieve when they have the drive to.

'And Carly's victim was Daniel,' I say. 'Who I assume was helpful because he knew how to work a camera?' Beth nods.

'Precisely, and it was helpful to have someone nearby to help me. Carly, who, by the way, entrapped men by attracting them over for a drink, drugging them and taking compromising photographs of them and then blackmailing them for money, had forced Daniel's father to flee the country and ruined his reputation. It was always our agreement that he could be the one to kill her. Sadly, he didn't factor in that she might be armed.'

I used to earn money in a way I'm not proud of; I remember Carly's words now.

'How did you get off the island?'

'When the police arrived, we fled out the back door where Carly was. I'd arranged for the driver who ferried you across to come back.'

'At what point did it become this, Beth? At what point did you decide that mass murder was the only way you could seek revenge?'

'Oh, Kimberley, I've been thinking about killing you for a very, very long time. The others were just a bit of fun really. I wanted to expose you for what the police in this country really are: third-rate investigators who are more of a danger to the public than a help.'

'How could I have shown anything different when the game was rigged?' My voice breaks its neutrality now and I realise I'm shouting.

'The game is always rigged, Kimberley,' Beth shouts back at me, jabbing the gun as she does so. 'Rigged in favour of the guilty. And I wouldn't go so far as to say it was rigged. I was there, I was present, waiting for you to discover who I really was. I'd have been mightily impressed if you'd done it but you didn't.'

I open my mouth to ask another question, but Beth cuts me off.

'No, my question now; you owe me a real answer.'

'I don't owe you anything,' I say, my jaw tightening. 'You took enough from me in the villa.'

'Oh, but you do, you know you do, because you...' Beth pauses; her face is white with anger, her teeth are bared. I'm about to feel her bite as well as her bark. My muscles tense and I prepare myself for what Beth is about to say. I know with all my being that it will involve Emily.

'You killed my sister,' explodes Beth.

My chest tightens so hard and so sharply that it feels as if I'm having a heart attack; my hands wrap around the seat of the chair and I squeeze, as if trying to control the power of the guilt that washes over me like a tidal wave.

For years, I've told myself over and over again that it was my fault that Emily Cadman died, that I might as well have killed Emily myself. Hearing Beth say it, hearing her confirm it, makes it feel truer than it has ever felt.

'So, tell me, why didn't you kill yourself? You'd been disgraced in front of the world and your failures meant you should have felt you were responsible for the deaths of five people, so why didn't you do it?'

I pause, thinking back to Emily and that horrible time in my life. The errors I made and the guilt I carried. Why didn't I do it? The answer comes to me like an epiphany. And despite the pain and guilt that I carry, I know the answer. It is an answer that Beth won't like.

'I didn't do it, Beth, I didn't kill myself, because I realised that one mistake doesn't define me.'

As the words come out of my mouth, I can see on her face they're not what Beth wants to hear. Something flashes in her eyes. She gets to her feet and walks so she's standing to my right. She leans down and whispers in my ear.

'You're wrong about that. One mistake does define you. Just like your mistake defined me. My life will forever be defined by the fact that my sister was murdered. I am changed. You changed me.'

It's as if she's pouring out her hatred onto me. The grief within her has curdled over the years, morphed into something unpalatable and dangerous.

307

Beth's hand raises the gun and points it at my head. I stiffen. My pulse pounds in my ears, the sound roaring in my head. But I won't grovel. I won't beg for forgiveness. There's life in me yet.

'No,' I whisper. 'I am not responsible for what you've become. And the mistakes you have made will haunt you forever.'

I grip the chair and, in one swift movement, swing it from under me. The gun flies from Beth's hand and she screeches. I go to hit her again but she's too quick; she scrambles after the gun. I dart from the living room and dive towards the bedroom, slamming the door behind me.

Bang.

A gunshot blows the mechanism straight off the door and it swings open. I retreat further into the room, my back to the window. Beth stands in the doorway. Gun held aloft.

Step by step, I edge away from her. I'm backed into a corner; there's no way out. I feel my knees knock together as they tremble.

I take a deep breath and close my eyes. It's over.

There's a scream.

Then a shot.

White-hot pain sears my arm as the bullet brushes it.

The window behind me shatters.

Beth's auburn hair flashes like a firebrand as she falls.

The pain and force of the shot makes me stumble backwards. My foot catches on the leg of Emily's dressing table and I topple over. The edges of my vision blur.

My fingers squeeze the top of my arm, squelching against my moist top. Blood is seeping from my wound. The blurred edges of my vision close in, fuzzing it more and more.

Paramedic and police sirens blare.

There are voices calling to me, calling my name, but they sound increasingly further away.

I don't fight the hands that grab me; I'm about to close my eyes and give in to the pain.

But before I do, the face of my old friend Zoe Pearce swims in front of me.

Chapter Fifty-Six

Spyland.co.uk – News, Scandals and all the latest Gossip from your favourite celebrities

BREAKING NEWS: How did Just Deserts get their Just Deserts?

Posted on Tuesday 5th August

SpyLand have just found out that Beth Cadman was arrested yesterday for the murders of Jack Peaks, Sophia Dance, Valentina Novak and Mo Khan. She is also charged with conspiracy to commit murder for the role she played in the murder of Carly Chu. Carly, whose death was not shown as part of the livestream, is now thought to have been killed by Daniel Oni. Daniel himself, we have heard, died from a stab wound inflicted by Carly Chu in self-defence.

The woman we knew as Rosalind Jenkins was actually Beth Cadman, sister of the murdered Emily Cadman. Beth, this year's producer of reality television show *Love-Wrecked*, was the ringleader of a plot to lure victims to the villa and kill them in a plot centred on revenge and retribution. Her victims were sourced through her co-conspirators who connected with her on the blog, Just Deserts, where she vented her rage over her sister's murder at the hands of her former colleague. We believe the police are still focused on hunting down her co-conspirators, but we don't think it will be long until they too face justice.

This finally answers the question of why *LoveWrecked* took a hiatus! Beth Cadman, creator of the show as well as producer, was too busy plotting this to think about making money.

The *LoveWrecked* management team are likely to be prosecuted for failing to properly protect the contestants on their show and were ordered to give £6 million in compensation to the families of the show's victims.

But despite this, little is still known about what contributed to Beth and the group's arrests and the police are keeping a tight lid on it.

SpyLand don't like being kept in the dark, though, do we? We are appealing for any information about how Beth was caught. Heck, we're even offering a reward of £1,000 for anyone who can share more information. Do you know what led to their arrest? If so, email us at justdeserts@spyland.co.uk and put us ALL out of our misery.

Chapter Fifty-Seven

Kimberley
Wednesday 6th August, 9:33

I wince as I push myself into a sitting position; the wound I sustained during my fight with Beth Cadman three days ago is still tender. The bullet from Beth's gun grazed the side of my arm but I know it could have been much worse had Zoe not shown up and pushed Beth to the ground. Zoe and I haven't spoken properly since I arrived at the hospital so I have no idea how she knew where I was but I know from the note accompanying the large bunch of flowers she sent me that when I'm allowed out, she will come and collect me and explain everything. All being well, that should be today.

Thanks to the quick arrival of the paramedics and the work of the doctors and nurses at Liverpool Hospital who cleaned and stitched me up, the wound should heal without any problems and is unlikely to cause any long-term issues. Having me as a patient hasn't been an easy task for the hospital. The media attention has been so intense these past few days that the hospital was forced to give me a private room. But not only that, they had no choice but to put a security guard outside that door.

I heard from one of the guards that the hospital staff struggled to cope with the journalists and photographers crowding the corridors. It eventually got so bad that the hospital put a ban on them even entering. Not that that stopped them.

I swear I saw one of the presenters of a crappy Sunday morning TV show creep past my window. The woman clearly hadn't done her homework because not only could the corner of a pillow be seen sneaking out of the bottom of her fashioned 'baby bump' but the hospital doesn't even have a maternity ward.

The attention I've garnered after my time in the villa shows no sign of abating and is as clear a signal as any that my life will never be the same again. I know that now and I also know that I have to accept it. Regardless of how hard it is, I have to find a way to accept what I've seen and what I've lost.

This time I won't repress my feelings like I did after the death of Emily Cadman. This time I'll deal with them properly and sensibly. The hospital was even so kind as to send round one of their therapists for a conversation. We talked about how, although I only knew them for one day, my fellow Islanders will always be a part of my life. I'm one of them. The only difference is that I survived. As time goes on, I know we'll work together on dealing with the guilt I feel about surviving and maybe I'll find ways to accept that I couldn't have done any more than I did to save them. There's a knock on the window of my room. Today's guard gives me a wave. I wave back, signalling for him to come in.

He pops his head around the door and gives me a smile.

'Good morning, Kimberley, how are we today?' His gentle Caribbean accent always makes me smile when I hear it.

'Morning, Winston. Getting better every day,' I reply.

313

'Excellent news. Are you ready to get out of this place then?' he asks. I pause to think about it. I've gone from *LoveWrecked* villa, to prison, to hospital; there's not been much interaction with the outside world.

'Yes,' I say, with a nod. 'I think it's time I finally entered the real world, don't you?'

'I hope the real world is ready for you, miss.' He chuckles as he helps me into a wheelchair.

Winston wheels me through the hospital, past ward after ward of patients. The double doors at the front of the hospital whoosh open. I glance around suddenly realising I don't know what car I'm looking for. But I'm spared a panic as a silver Renault chugs its way towards us, stopping a couple of metres away. The driver gets out and waves to me before rushing round to open the passenger door.

'Stay safe now,' says Winston and I blow him a kiss as he retreats to the hospital, pushing the empty wheelchair. I lower myself into the passenger seat slowly, keeping my face straight, trying not to convey the pain that comes with the movement.

'Thank you,' I say, turning to Zoe. 'Thank you for coming to get me. And for saving my life.'

'You're welcome,' she replies, giving my hand a squeeze. 'And I'm sorry. So, so, so sorry.'

'For what?' I ask, looking at her.

'For everything that happened to you, for not being able to stop it sooner, for falling out of touch for all these years.' Her words speed out of her and I can tell she's been wanting to say them for the past few days. She twists in her seat to look at me, her expression pained.

'How on earth did you find me?' I ask, more interested in this than discussing the years past.

'I was worried about you so when I heard that you were back at home I thought I'd come and check on you. I wasn't involved in the *LoveWrecked* investigation so I didn't want to knock in case I got in trouble for interfering but then I saw you leave your house, and I don't know what possessed me but I followed you.'

'You weren't the only one,' I say; I had quite the tail that night. 'Thank you though, it was stupid of me to go there alone.'

'Yeah, it was. When I saw you heading inside Emily's abandoned house with someone I must admit you had me confused, I swayed between wondering if you had been lured there or this was the place you'd plotted the scheme. I just couldn't understand what you were doing there. Regardless, I called for back-up and crept inside the house after you.' Zoe bites her lip. 'I'm sorry, I should never have suspected you for one minute but...' She trails off and shakes her head. 'I've missed you, so, so much. Work hasn't been the same without you.' Zoe turns to face me, her smile and words are genuine, her concern real.

'I've missed you too,' I say, squeezing her hand back. Zoe's eyes glisten and she clears her throat before putting the car into gear; she never was one for emotions.

'The others are asking about you,' she says as we drive towards the exit of the hospital car park. 'Even the Detective Chief Inspector.' I turn my face to look at her, feeling a look of disbelief cross my face.

'Who is the Detective Chief Inspector nowadays?' I ask.

'Sunita Kheri.'

'She is asking about me?.'

Back when I worked with Zoe, I never really got the impression that Sunita Kheri had a high opinion of me and I think, in the end, she was relieved when I handed in my resignation.

'Why is she asking about me?'

'Well,' says Zoe, biting her lip and giving me a sideways glance. 'As much as I'm glad to see you and wanted to collect you, I'd be lying if I didn't say I do also have an ulterior motive. Sunita has a proposition. Which, I should add, I agree with.'

'OK…' I say, slightly worried now.

'I think you should come back to us, to the force.'

My mouth falls open; she's asking me to re-join the police force, after my performance on *LoveWrecked*.

'You can't be serious.'

'Don't answer straight away. Think about it.'

Being a police officer had been such an important part of who I was and stepping away from it was one of the hardest things I've ever done. And I'd be lying to myself if I denied that in the past week, lying in this hospital bed, I didn't think about it. But I dismissed it quite quickly because when I left I hadn't exactly reviewed the policy on returning and I know that it is a bit of a taboo subject. The police force isn't exactly something people swan in and out of; it is typically a for-life sort of arrangement.

'OK,' I say as Zoe stops the car at a red light. 'Since you saved my life, I promise that I will at least think about it.'

Zoe lets out a cheer, which nearly gives an elderly lady toddling past the car window a heart attack. We apologise to her before dissolving into laughter; it's as if the past five years never happened.

As we turn onto the main road that leads back towards the town centre, Zoe says, 'You're a free woman now so where do you want to go first? Home? McDonald's? Your mum's house?'

'All great options but there's something I need to do before I go home or visit Mum.'

'My wish is your command,' says Zoe, though I don't suspect she will be as willing when she knows what I have planned and I'm not about to tell her.

'Head towards the city centre, I'll give you directions from there.'

'OK…' says Zoe, sounding slightly suspicious but she follows my instructions without question.

'There,' I say, ten minutes later, pointing out my stop on the right. Zoe stops the car on the pavement and I get out.

'I'll be five minutes,' I say, slamming the door behind me. Zoe gives me a confused look but says nothing. Pressing my hand against the cold glass door, I push it open. A man, Pringle tube in hand, turns around to look at me. TJ of TJ's T'Internet Temple gives me a wide grin.

'Hi, Kim, I heard about your adventures on the news. Since you're here and alive, I assume Plan A is on.'

'Plan A is on,' I say, with a smile.

His eyes register my sling. 'It's true then, she shot you?'

'She shot me.'

'Nice,' he says and nothing more. TJ stomps over to one of the vacant computers and sits down; the seat groans under his weight. 'Give it here.' The tiny camera that I purchased from him before I went to meet Beth has been hidden in my pocket ever since I woke up in the hospital and found it still attached to my jacket. 'Are you sure you want to do this?' he asks, uncharacteristically inquisitive, but I chose to come back to TJ because I was sure his years of working in an Internet cafe have probably made him less judgemental and more discreet than others. Plus he'd already agreed to hack into Just Deserts for me when I first bought the camera from him. If I didn't survive, I'd asked him to go the police and tell them about the camera and where I'd placed it. If Beth had seen it, it would never have worked but I hadn't had much time to devise Plan A, let alone a particularly comprehensive Plan B.

'I'm sure,' I say to him defiantly. 'It's the right ending. Rosalind wanted me to solve the murder live on television, but she was never going to let me do it; the game was rigged from the start. I know this video isn't me solving it, but it is my video that I made. And it is one of the only portrayals of myself that I am in control of. Plus, Beth started it on camera, so I'm ending it on camera.'

TJ takes a deep breath but says nothing. I know his silence is his way of remaining neutral on the matter, to neither give nor deny permission. In many ways, it is better this way. I don't need anyone telling me what the right or wrong way is to handle this.

'OK,' he says, 'I need a bit of time to access the website, etc., but it should be loaded on there at some point today.'

'Thanks, TJ. And I haven't forgotten about that photo, but maybe it can wait until I've removed my sling?'

He gives me a thumbs up and focuses his attention back on the computer. As I turn my back on TJ and exit the shop, I smile because there is a part of me that thinks Beth Cadman will be pleased. Something tells me that for her, too, this will feel like a fitting ending.

'All done?' asks Zoe as I get into the car.

'All done. Home, please.'

Epilogue

Spyland.co.uk — News, Scandals and all the latest Gossip from your favourite celebrities

BREAKING NEWS: The infamous revenge blog Just Deserts has released its final post and it is the ending we were all waiting for

Posted on 13th August at 19:25 p.m.

Social media is buzzing over the video recently posted on Just Deserts. Judging from the angles, low quality, poor lighting, the video was filmed from a body cam in almost complete darkness. However, what is possible to learn from the video is that it captures a conversation and subsequent altercation between Rosalind Jenkins and Kimberley King. In the video, Rosalind explains exactly how she met her co-conspirators and where she got the inspiration for her plan.

With Rosalind Jenkins under arrest and her crew lying low, it's unclear how the post managed to get published. But boy are we glad that it did! The post, entitled 'The End', is short, containing very little except for a link to the video and an announcement that the website will soon be shut down. The website announced its final post on Twitter with the following...

@JustDeserts: This will be the website's final post. Head to www.justdeserts.co.uk/theend to see our final video #LoveWrecked #JustDeserts #TheEnd

Acknowledgements

Everyone says that writing is a lonely activity and I understand how that could be true but I've never felt lonely during this journey and that is testament to the brilliant people in these acknowledgements. These acknowledgements are long but as it's my debut I've decided against keeping it brief.

My first thank you must go to Siân Heap, my wonderful editor at Canelo, who saw something in an early draft of this book and has supported me to make it the best it can possibly be. Without her, none of you would be reading this book or these acknowledgements. Thank you Siân, for your faith in me, for your notes, and for always being there to offer advice if I wasn't sure how to do something. You will always have a special place in my heart.

A huge thank you to Emily Glenister, my superstar agent, who also took a chance on me and has been championing me and this book to everyone she speaks to and especially to me when I would give even a hint that I was worried about something. Emily, it has been such a pleasure to get to know you and, at risk of making this sound like a wedding speech, I cannot wait to continue my writing journey with you by my side. A big thank you to everyone else at DHH Literary Agency who do a lot to support aspiring writers, I was very privileged to be selected to pitch to you at DHH Pitch in Liverpool and it still boggles my mind to think I'm one of your writers.

Thank you to everyone at Canelo who have helped get this book into ship-shape: my copy editor, Becca Allen; proofreader, Abbie Headon; and, to Louise Cullen and Francesca Riccardi who were very kind giving up their time to answer all of my pre-publication questions.

Thank you to Lisa Brewster for the cover design, it is honestly everything I hoped it would be and much better than I could ever have thought up.

Massive thank you to all my friends both real life ones and the lovely writer friends I have met during this journey, I'm very grateful for you giving me your time to read multiple versions of this manuscript. A particular thank you to Imogen who has read all the works I've written and whose brilliant brain she always allowed me to pick. To Jenny, Barbara, Millie, and Frances who were always on hand for a quick read or to be my cheerleader if I needed it. To Alexa Donne whose videos on writing were (and continue to be) invaluable and to everyone at Author Mentor Match, especially Chelsea Ichaso, who provided feedback in those early stages to help this book shine.

Thank you to my parents who always told me I could do anything I set my mind to and raised me to never let fear get in the way, thank you for supporting me for these past 30 years but a particular thank you for keeping me well-fed and watered and providing a gorgeous place for me to write and edit even when it was during a lockdown; thank you to my Uncle Ian who gave me his advice whenever I was stuck on something and who once told me that if he didn't like a book he simply wouldn't finish it, it is therefore a huge compliment that he read everything of mine from cover to cover. Thank you to all of my family who have been incredibly supportive and excited about this journey, to know that I have a family who never once questioned my ability to do this and did nothing but give me positive encouragement shows what a lucky person I am. And finally, thank you to my wonderful boyfriend Krzysztof whose love of escape rooms and walking tours continue to provide a source of inspiration. Thank you for listening to me talking about writing over the last five years and for being patient during all the evenings and weekends I couldn't hang out with you because I was working on my book.

Do you love crime fiction and are always on the lookout
for brilliant authors?

Canelo Crime is home to some of the most exciting
novels around. Thousands of readers are already enjoying
our compulsive stories. Are you ready to find your new
favourite writer?

Find out more and sign up to our newsletter at
canelocrime.com